What the critics are saying...

ହର

4 ½ Stars "Second in the Supernatural Bonds series, this is a totally absorbing read with wonderfully fleshed out characters."~ *Romantic Times BookClub*

"The three protagonists keep the dialogue erotic, fun, emotionally intense, and a joy to read. Ms. Strong should most certainly be added to every paranormal reader's list of must buy authors. Her voices and characters grow stronger with every story she pens and it is always a treat to open up a new book by her. Don't pass this story up!" ~ *Fallen Angel Reviews*

"This is nothing short of a masterpiece. I thought this was *CSI, NYPD Blue, The X-Files,* and *Buffy the Vampire Slayer* rolled in one. Awesome writing. The sideline characters made just as much impact on the story as the main ones. Stories within stories. I cannot say enough praise for this book." ~ *Coffee Time Romance*

"Tristan and Pierce are compelling heroes who are a yin and yang match for spunky, yet vulnerable, Storm. The sensuality they share with their "forever wife" Storm is breathtaking. Their love story is truly a fairy tale that appeals to our senses and deepest wishes for happy ever afters!" ~ *The Romance Studio*

Jory Strong

Storm's Faeries

Supernatural Bonds

ELLORA'S CAVE
ROMANTICA PUBLISHING

An Ellora's Cave Romantica Publication

www.ellorascave.com

Storm's Faeries

ISBN #1419954245
ALL RIGHTS RESERVED.
Storm's Faeries Copyright © 2005 Jory Strong
Edited by Sue-Ellen Gower
Cover art by Syneca

Electronic book Publication September 2005
Trade paperback Publication May 2006

Excerpt from *Sarael's Reading* Copyright © Jory Strong, 2005

Excerpt from *Ellora's Cavemen: Dreams of the Oasis I* Copyright © 2006

Warning:

The following material contains graphic sexual content meant for mature readers. This story has been rated E–rotic by a minimum of three independent reviewers.

Ellora's Cave Publishing offers three levels of Romantica™ reading entertainment: S (S-ensuous), E (E-rotic), and X (X-treme).

S-*ensuous* love scenes are explicit and leave nothing to the imagination.

E-*rotic* love scenes are explicit, leave nothing to the imagination, and are high in volume per the overall word count. In addition, some E-rated titles might contain fantasy material that some readers find objectionable, such as bondage, submission, same sex encounters, forced seductions, and so forth. E-rated titles are the most graphic titles we carry; it is common, for instance, for an author to use words such as "fucking", "cock", "pussy", and such within their work of literature.

X-*treme* titles differ from E-rated titles only in plot premise and storyline execution. Unlike E-rated titles, stories designated with the letter X tend to contain controversial subject matter not for the faint of heart.

Also by Jory Strong

∞

Carnival Tarot 1: Sarael's Reading
Carnival Tarot 2: Kiziah's Reading
Carnival Tarot 3: Dakotah's Reading
Crime Tells 1: Lyric's Cop
Crime Tells 2: Cady's Cowboy
Crime Tells 3: Calista's Men
Ellora's Cavemen: Dreams of the Oasis I *(Anthology)*
Fallon Mates 1: Binding Krista
Fallon Mates 2: Zeraac's Miracle
Supernatural Bonds 1: Trace's Psychic
The Angelini 1: Skye's Trail
The Angelini 2: Syndelle's Possession

About the Author

∞

Jory has been writing since childhood and has never outgrown being a daydreamer. When she's not hunched over her computer, lost in the muse and conjuring up new heroes and heroines, she can usually be found reading, riding her horses, or hiking with her dogs.

Jory welcomes mail from readers. You can write to her c/o Ellora's Cave Publishing at 1056 Home Avenue, Akron, OH 44310-3502.

Storm's Faeries

Supernatural Bonds

&

Dedication

ဢ

Sue-Ellen Gower, editor extraordinaire
Raelene Gorlinsky, managing editor extraordinaire

This one's for you!

Trademarks Acknowledgement

~

The author acknowledges the trademarked status and trademark owners of the following wordmarks mentioned in this work of fiction:

Energizer: Eveready Battery Company, Inc.

Jockey: Jockey International, Inc.

Rolaids: American Chicle Company

Clue: Waddingtons Games Limited

Starbucks: Starbucks U.S. Brands

Luxor: Ramparts, Inc

Chapter One

The detective's shield felt heavy and uncomfortable in Storm O'Malley's pocket. Her stomach roiled and she wiped sweaty palms against her slacks. She hadn't been this nervous since she joined the force.

"You're not looking too good," Brady Sinclair, her new partner, said. "I puked my guts out on my first murder case. Crime scene guys and the coroner gave me hell for months—didn't let me forget it until another rookie came along and threw his breakfast up all over the carpet next to the corpse."

Storm looked at Brady and wondered what he thought about being teamed with a former beat cop who hadn't even aspired to the elite homicide squad. "I'm not going to puke."

Brady shrugged. "If you say so. All I'm saying is that you wouldn't be the first homicide detective to toss their cookies."

"I've been to my share of car crashes." She wasn't worried about reacting to a dead body. Her nervousness had everything to do with finding herself on the homicide squad and being afraid that she wasn't going to be any good at it.

Storm tensed as they rounded the corner and spotted the camera crews parked in front of an estate that screamed money. Brady grunted. "Damn. Used to be you could pull into a crime scene without having to wade through this shit."

"Not every day that one of the VanDenberghs gets killed."

"Yeah, that's sure a surprise, ain't it?"

His comment jerked a laugh out of Storm and calmed some of her nerves. She could do this. She was a damn fine cop.

A uniformed officer waved Brady through and he eased the unmarked police car in behind the coroner's van. "Looks like a damn party. You ready for the big time, Kid?"

Storm rolled her eyes. She hadn't been called a kid since she sprouted an uncomfortably large pair of breasts in the eighth grade. At least she'd grown into them, kind of, and for that she was profoundly grateful, though they didn't always lend themselves to police work. In fact, sometimes they were a damned nuisance—especially when she first joined the force and found herself almost permanently assigned the role of hooker in the various prostitute/john sting operations the police department ran. "Did you call your last partner 'Kid'?"

"Hell, my last partner called *me* Kid."

She shook her head, taking in Brady's appearance—the hound dog eyes that probably lulled perps into thinking he was a slow thinker, the brown suit that looked like he'd slept in it for a week and the tie that had so many stains on it that they were beginning to form their own pattern.

Brady opened his door. "I could call you 'Girl', but they just ran me through diversity training again—now I know that's not PC."

Storm laughed. "Again?"

Brady made a hand gesture. "Yeah, I know, old dogs and new tricks, yadda yadda yadda."

Storm grinned as she got ready to climb out of the unmarked unit. "Okay, let's go kick some butt, Pops."

Brady grunted and she could have sworn that his lips twitched upward a millimeter. "Got that right. Captain's probably already working up to a heart attack. He was praying it'd get quiet after those psychic killings. This is a lot of turnout for a simple case of murder—even for a VanDenbergh."

They were met at the door by a butler. A uniformed cop stood behind him and grinned when the formally attired servant said, "Detectives, the body is in the artifact room. Your associates have contained the other attendees of Mr.

VanDenbergh Senior's event in the recreation room." His nose twitched disdainfully. "Which would you prefer to visit first?"

Storm's first thought was, "You've got to be kidding." Her second was, "Sophie is going to love this." Her cousin was a mystery buff, and here was a crime scene that sported a genuine English-style butler.

Brady sighed. "Murder scene."

The butler nodded elegantly. "As you wish, Detective."

Death hadn't done much for Mr. VanDenbergh Senior's dignity. It also hadn't done much for the white carpet. He lay sprawled, the silk shades-of-Hugh-Hefner dressing gown parted to reveal pale-white scarecrow legs and age-spotted skin.

Cause of death looked pretty straightforward. A single shot to the forehead and, by the lack of collateral damage to the face, Storm guessed a small-bore weapon was used, and figured that they might get lucky and find the bullet still in his skull.

"Who found him?" Brady asked.

The butler's nostrils twitched with continued disapproval. "One of his guests. Apparently when he didn't return, she went looking for him."

"You hear a gun go off?" Brady asked.

"No. Today is the staff's day off. I was away from the estate. I'm back now at the request of the family."

Storm looked around the room, this time really taking in what she was seeing—the lack of windows, the glass cases, some containing single items, others containing small collections of seemingly related treasure, each case with a discrete keypad as though it was separately alarmed. Only one case stood empty.

Following the direction of her gaze, Brady said, "Bingo. Want to tell us what's missing?"

The butler stiffened. "You'll need to discuss that with Mr. VanDenbergh the Third and a representative from the insurance company. They're both waiting in the study, along with Mr. VanDenbergh Senior's lawyer."

Brady gave a soul-deep sigh that made Storm think of a decompressing hot-air balloon. "Let's see them."

"As you wish."

The butler led them out of the treasure vault, down a hallway and around a corner. When he would have walked past where a uniformed policewoman was standing, Storm said, "Hold on, what's in here?"

"That's the recreation room."

Brady grunted. "Might as well have a look."

The uniformed officer rolled her eyes before stepping aside so they could see into the room. Storm wondered about the reaction until she got a look at the six big-breasted women wearing thin little negligees and lounging on couches that were designed for a lot of things, but sitting around and having polite conversation wasn't one of them. If the elderly Mr. VanDenbergh Senior was playacting the part of Hugh Hefner, then these women were his buxom bunnies.

Brady turned away from the scene and Storm almost laughed at the sight of his slightly reddened face. But in true male form, he said, "And who says money can't buy happiness."

The uniformed officer choked back a snort. Storm couldn't quite suppress a smile. Brady's lips moved upward just the tiniest fraction and Storm wasn't able to resist saying, "You got one of those Hef gowns at home, Brady?"

This time Brady's lips did more than twitch. "That's for me to know, Kid, and for you to wonder about."

Storm shook her head and refrained from saying any one of a number of things that flashed through her mind. She'd worked with men long enough to know that once the conversation started going downhill, it could keep going…and going…and going…in a way that'd do the Energizer bunny proud.

They continued down the hallway until the butler stopped in front of a door with yet another policeman stationed outside. This time, in deference to the status of the occupants, he knocked before opening the door and announcing Brady and Storm.

Brady didn't bother heading for a chair, he moved into the room and got right to the point. "You want to go ahead and tell us what was stolen and how much it was worth?"

The men had been expecting the question, of course, but Storm still found it interesting to note their reactions. A short pudgy man who sat apart from the other two grimaced slightly. The man with the life-is-a-serious-matter expression stiffened his spine into an even straighter line, while the third man—a much-younger version of VanDenbergh Senior—managed to convey both a sense of boredom and an impatience to be done.

Stick-spine answered, "I am Miles Terry and I represent McKeller and Sons, Underwriters and Insurers. I believe that I'm most qualified to answer your question. The article stolen was priceless, of course, irreplaceable as only an item steeped in history can be. Mr. VanDenbergh Senior had it insured for five million dollars."

"And the article is?" Brady directed.

"A chalice."

A vague uneasiness washed over Storm. "A communion cup?"

The insurance representative squirmed in his chair, but it was VanDenbergh III who answered. "Let's cut to the chase here so we can all get on with our business. You saw the way the old goat was dressed? You saw the bimbos waiting in his fuck-room? Well, the chalice was supposed to belong to some famous Italian family—the Medici, maybe—or something like that. It was supposed to have been used by them in their orgies, kind of like Viagra for the Middle Ages. My grandfather's been after it for years." VanDenbergh III shot an unfriendly look at the short, pudgy man who had to be his grandfather's lawyer. "Apparently the old goat only just got his hands on it."

Brady grunted. "Where'd he get it from?"

Storm smiled slightly. *Follow the money.* But the instant Brady asked the question, Pudge firmed into a vision of lawyerly fortitude and she knew it wasn't going to be easy prying information out of him.

* * * * *

Storm grimaced as she looked down at the notes she'd taken during the interview with VanDenbergh's lady friends. Dumb, dumb-squared, dumb-cubed…all the way up to dumb-to-the-sixth-power. They gave generously endowed women a bad name.

Across the desk, her new partner was also paging through his notes. Grunting, he said, "Remind me to buy a lottery ticket, Kid."

Assuming that Brady was also thinking about the bunnies, Storm shook her head. What was it about men and breasts? Was bottle-feeding ruining them or was it just something in the genes?

Then again, maybe she was just a little sensitive. She'd be a millionaire several times over if she had a dollar for every time some guy's eyes never rose above her chest. Five stars for Brady on that one.

"A harem like that would kill you," Storm said.

Startled, Brady looked up. "What?" His face reddened. "Geez, Kid, what kind of a hound dog do you take me for? I was thinking about the boat. Baby like that was made for some great deep sea fishing."

It took some effort for Storm to bring the boat into focus. VanDenbergh Senior had several garages. The boat was in one of them, looking like it had never touched the salt of the ocean.

She shook her head. VanDenbergh Senior's house was a palace of material delights — from the artifacts in his vault, to the art throughout the house, to the vintage cars in their specially built garages, not to mention whatever jewelry he might have had locked away.

VanDenbergh Senior had so many valuables to choose from, why take only one thing. Hell, why kill him at all? While he was busy with his little orgy, the murderer could probably have made a dozen trips. Storm shook her head. "Let me see the picture of the chalice again."

Brady dug around in the disaster area of his desk until he found the picture they'd gotten from Miles Terry. He handed it to Storm.

"What do you think the chances are that the murderer left this behind and the bunny who found the body decided to stash it somewhere and come back for it later?" Storm asked.

Brady snorted. "That would require some thought and, from what I could tell, VanDenbergh Senior didn't pay a premium for smarts. Besides that, she wasn't gone long enough to get it very far. Only a minute before she was screaming the place down."

"According to the other women at VanDenbergh's private party."

"Now you're talking about six women agreeing to keep quiet about it, at least two of which seemed to actually care about the old guy?"

"Five million could buy a lot of silence."

Brady grunted. "Yeah. Okay. We can keep an eye on them. But I can't see the murderer leaving the chalice behind. Even if you figure this wasn't a burglary gone bad but a planned hit, who's going to walk away from something that valuable?"

Storm nodded. Brady was right. Compared to murder, walking away with something worth five million was a petty crime.

"Damn convenient that the thing managed to get insured before it was stolen," Brady said.

"Yeah, I thought so."

"Damn convenient that whoever killed VanDenbergh knew that today was the butler's day off."

"That, too."

"Also damned convenient that VanDenbergh's little orgy room is soundproofed. A few minutes later and whoever was in the old guy's house could have wiped the treasure room out while VanDenbergh was bouncing on the bunnies."

Storm choked back a laugh. "Which gets us back to a burglary gone bad scenario."

"I say we follow the money on this one. A couple of ways to go with that. Either the money motive is in the family—like maybe VanDenbergh III wanting his grandfather dead but being smart enough so he doesn't do himself out of five mil—or two, the money motive is tied up with this chalice…" Brady's mouth twisted as if the next words were too unpleasant to pass his lips, "of Eros. You got any sources that might know something about this thing?"

Storm's thoughts went instantly to Professor Tristan Lisalli and she swallowed against a suddenly dry throat. Would he know something…or was she just using it as an excuse to pay him another visit?

She'd consulted him about some elaborate script when she was assisting on the Dean murder case. Damn, if they'd made university professors like him when she was making career choices…well, sign her up. God!

Heat rushed to Storm's face as she remembered not only taking in his buns of steel and huge jeans-covered cock—but getting caught ogling him. It hadn't been her finest moment—but that didn't stop her from saying, "I know someone. I'll call him and ask for a consult."

"Okay, you run with the chalice angle. I'll run with the family money angle."

Storm nodded, her thoughts going back to the reactions of the three men in VanDenbergh's study when Brady had asked what was missing. The lawyer had grimaced. The insurance rep had gone official, and the grandson didn't seem to give a damn. "You know Brady, for a supposedly legendary item, one that was insured for five million bucks, nobody seemed very upset that it was stolen. Even the insurance rep didn't demand that we do something to get it back. That seems a little off-key to me."

"Hell, Kid, what'd you expect? They didn't even demand we solve the murder."

* * * * *

A laugh escaped Tristan Lisalli as he parked his Jaguar in front of Drake's Lair. He knew better than to enter a dragon's den—dragons and treasure went together like faeries and glamour—but given that the dragon was his cousin's friend and business partner, it was worth a shot. And besides, Tristan didn't have the luxury of waiting. There was so much more than just treasure at stake—and soon there would be dragons and other fey to contend with, along with the humans.

Anticipation rippled through Tristan at the thought of the delectable Storm O'Malley. His cock hardened as it always did when he summoned the image of the blonde-haired policewoman with the stormy gray eyes and the body designed for pleasure.

The single visit that she'd paid him had managed to stir quite a number of fantasies—and for a faerie who'd been alive as long as Tristan had, that was no small feat. Oh yes, she'd been armored in her police uniform at the time, but it hadn't hidden the fire of the woman. Nor had it dampened the flames of lust that had washed over his body when her focus had been trained on him. She'd sent his cock to full attention, but more telling, and far more revealing, she'd made his heart jump between hope and fear, a clash of summer breeze and winter wind.

Officer O'Malley had been off-limits that day because she'd been working on the Dean murder, and he couldn't afford to get mixed up in a high-profile case. No supernatural could. But after the Dean murder was solved, he'd fully intended to challenge Pierce with the seduction of a woman—the seduction of Storm. Of course, he'd intended that it would be so much more than just a seduction, but...

Tristan grimaced. The Fates did enjoy their little amusements, and while he didn't usually care to participate, this time it was impossible to resist. No doubt they were laughing at their looms.

Rather than being Officer O'Malley, Storm was now Detective O'Malley, and instead of returning to her job as a beat cop, she was involved in another high-profile case.

It was murder—again, but with a difference. Treasure.

What fey creature could resist the legendary Medici Chalice of Eros? Tristan smiled slightly at the human's name for the artifact. If only they knew its true name, its true purpose…

Regardless, having the chalice surface again, and get stolen, was enough of an excuse to draw Pierce in—to see if what Tristan suspected was true. That Storm would not only be his forever wife, but Pierce's as well.

"In the back room, sir," the maître d' informed Tristan before he could even ask where his cousin was.

"What is it this time?"

"Poker, with South African Krugerrands, American Eagles and Canadian Maple Leaves as chips, I believe." The maître d' kept a straight face, but his voice conveyed his amusement. "Pierce thinks the presence of the gold coins lends itself to the argument that a meeting of collectors is taking place. He's grown tired of the inconvenience of going to court and dealing with lawyers when the police raid the club."

"What does he expect? Last time he had twenty roulette tables set up. There's no such thing as legalized gambling in this city—unless you count the lottery."

The maître d' shrugged. "Apparently he can't help himself."

Tristan's hand went to the folded papers in his jacket pocket and he smiled. That's what he was counting on—that Pierce wouldn't be able to resist the temptation.

Chapter Two

ဆ

Storm had never felt less like eating dinner. She was so wound up that she wasn't sure she could even sit down, much less focus on the conversation around her. What she really wanted to do was hunker over her notes some more...or continue her research on the Internet...or get a phone call back from the professor and explore his brain...along with other things. She wasn't in the mood to sit around talking about...

She shook her head at the absurdity of her thoughts. She was more wound up than she realized. Sophie never got tired of hearing about crime and criminals. In fact, except for the small matter of getting physically ill at the sight of blood—an amazing contradiction considering some of the stuff Sophie wrote—her cousin would have been a great cop. And if Aislinn was here, hell, she was a great resource, too.

Storm knocked once before opening the door and moving into Sophie's apartment. Her cousin didn't disappoint her. The first words out of Sophie's mouth were, "This is going to be a great case! But don't tell me about it yet. Wait for Aislinn. She'll be over in a few minutes. She made something for you."

Storm's eyes went instantly to the necklace Sophie wore. It was a beautiful creation of finely wrought leaves cradling a dark blue crystal with hints of red. Sophie called it a heartmate necklace and, according to her, it would come to life in the presence of the man she was supposed to share her life with.

Normally Storm would scoff at the idea of a crystal "coming to life" much less predicting which man was the *right* man, but she'd seen enough of Aislinn Windbourne, now Aislinn Dilessio, to become a believer—at least when it came to

Aislinn's psychic ability. Hell, they'd *all* become believers by the end of the Dean case.

The homicide cops who'd worked on the case might not like to talk about it, might not want to acknowledge it, but they weren't so quick to go rabid at the mention of psychics anymore.

And of course, Trace Dilessio, the most vehemently rabid of them all had taken the biggest hit. Oh, how the mighty have fallen. It brought a smile to Storm's face. There was nothing better than seeing a macho man bite the big one and fall irrevocably in love.

Still, amusement over Trace's fate didn't quite offset the alarm radiating through Storm at the thought of Aislinn presenting her with a necklace like Sophie's. Not that Storm didn't want a man to share her life with but…crystals were fine for Sophie, Sophie believed in them. Storm preferred a little more rational approach, and besides, she needed to concentrate on the VanDenbergh murder.

There was another perfunctory knock at Sophie's door then Aislinn walked in with Trace right behind her as though he couldn't stand the thought of being away from her. The heat between the two of them blasted across the room, leaving a chill of loneliness in its wake.

Trace's face tightened with suspicion when he saw Storm. He pulled Aislinn up against his body, her back flush with his chest, his arms wrapped tightly around her waist in a gesture that screamed protectiveness and love. Storm's heart dipped and spiked. When she'd agreed to round up some men and meet Sophie and two of her friends for a few drinks at a beachfront bar, she'd never anticipated the dark, ultra-macho Trace would go for someone as delicate and gentle as Aislinn. But looking at the two of them now, it seemed so obvious. The dominant-submissive vibes they gave off were enough to have Storm wondering what it would be like to really give up control.

Aislinn shifted in Trace's arms and Storm shivered at the lust that shot through his face. What would it be like to have that kind of effect on a man? To only have to brush against his erection and have him fighting not to turn caveman then and there?

Not that Storm hadn't had her share of lovers—her breasts were magnets, sometimes unfortunately, that drew men whether she was trying to or not. But she'd never had one react to her the same way Trace reacted to Aislinn—like he wanted to own her completely. Storm wasn't even sure she'd survive that kind of encounter.

She shivered again and forced her mind away from those thoughts. One thing she'd learned while being a cop, mental toughness actually counted more than physical toughness.

"I heard you and Brady drew the VanDenbergh case," Trace said.

"Yeah, we did."

"VanDenbergh's name has come up a couple of times in connection with stuff that had..." Trace looked like he was going to choke on the word, "supernatural ties."

Excitement rippled through Storm. She'd wondered because of the chalice, but so far none of her research had given her a solid link. "What have you heard?"

Trace settled his body more tightly against Aislinn's. "The first time his name hit the radar screen was when I was still in uniform. A call came in for a break-in at a New Age church over on Santa Rita. Place is gone now, hell, there wasn't much to it even then. I was first officer on the scene and the guy running the show wouldn't let go of the idea that VanDenbergh was behind the theft. Some kind of bowl they used in their ceremonies. The old man kept going on and on about how VanDenbergh's lawyer had been to see him and tried to buy the thing and when that didn't work, he'd stolen it." Trace shrugged. "Trouble was everything that could be sold— including CDs and cheap candlesticks—had been taken."

"Did you question VanDenbergh?" Storm asked.

Trace snorted. "Right. That part of the case got kicked upstairs and the word came back down that it was a dead end.

Somebody higher up probably settled it during a golf game. Hell, there wasn't anything to make VanDenbergh a serious suspect. The church was in a bad area of town. Kind of a miracle it hadn't been hit before."

Storm frowned. "You said some kind of a bowl was taken. Can you remember more about it?"

"Shit, Storm, that was years ago. The only reason it's coming back now is because of VanDenbergh's murder. I think the old guy said they were using it to see into the future, some kind of bullsh—" He grimaced and brushed his face against Aislinn's hair as though he was offering an apology for his skepticism.

A small smile flickered briefly on Aislinn's face before sadness washed across it. "Patrick told me that he'd once attended a church with such a bowl. The bowl was known as The Vision of Ieliel."

The hair on Storm's neck rose at the mention of Patrick Dean—the murdered psychic whose death had inadvertently led to her ending up as a detective in Homicide. A creeping sense of déjà vu settled over her. "The Vision of Ieliel?"

Aislinn nodded. "Ieliel is one of the angels of the future."

"Did Dean say anything else about it? Was he there when it was stolen?"

Aislinn shook her head. "I don't know. He only mentioned it in passing."

Storm turned to Trace. "When you get to the station, could you dig up the case number or give me something so I could pull the file?"

Trace nuzzled the delicate butterfly earrings Aislinn wore at the top of her ears. "Sure. I'm going to stop by after I hit the gym."

"You said VanDenbergh's name had come up a couple of times in connection with supernatural items," Sophie reminded Trace.

He nodded. "The second time was in a burglary-murder a couple of years back. Far as I know, it's still open. Guy who specialized in *acquiring specific artifacts for select clients.*" Trace's lip curled. "That's what was on his card, but he was a fence — just too smooth an operator to get caught at it. Anyway, guy interrupted a burglary in progress and got whacked. Place was wiped out. VanDenbergh Senior was the only one with the balls to come screaming to the police, demanding that we locate an item he'd paid for but not yet taken possession of."

Storm pictured the old man in the Hugh Hefner dressing robe with six big-breasted women waiting for him in a room that screamed "made for an orgy" and didn't have any trouble at all believing VanDenbergh had the necessary balls to demand the police look for something he knew had been illegally acquired in the first place. But he wasn't stupid. "I assume VanDenbergh had some kind of phony paperwork that made it look like a legitimate purchase."

Trace shrugged. "Yeah, like I said, the fence was a smooth operator — there was plenty of paperwork to make everything look nice and legal — then again, it helped that most of what he acquired had a long history of being stolen and passed on to new owners."

"So what was stolen when the fence was murdered?" Sophie asked, and by the sparkling excitement in her eyes, Storm knew her cousin was irreversibly hooked on the VanDenbergh murder case.

"A scepter that supposedly belonged to an Egyptian high priest serving some god named Saa." Trace's lips quirked upward. "The only reason I remember it was because the guys on the case kept working *Saa* into their shop-talk."

Aislinn's eyebrows drew together. "Saa is the god of touching and feeling." Her face flushed with uncomfortable color. "In the afterlife, he also guards the genitals. For those who believe, Saa came into existence from the blood of the god Ra's penis."

All humor left Trace's face and for a split second Storm thought maybe the idea of bleeding cocks had killed his mood. Instead he turned Aislinn to face him and from his expression, the only person in Trace's world was his delicate wife. His next words confirmed Storm's suspicion.

"You remember what we agreed on, don't you, baby?" His dark voice carried a promise of punishment that had heat rushing to Storm's face. It was all she could do to tear her eyes away from Trace and Aislinn. But at least she wasn't the only one. Sophie was also caught in the same web of want, and seeing the loneliness and heartfelt longing on her cousin's face, Storm prayed that the necklace Aislinn had made for Sophie would work.

Aislinn's "I remember" came out butterfly-soft but didn't seem to temper the violence of the kiss that followed. When Trace pulled away, his lips firmed into a determined line as he focused on Storm. Even before he opened his mouth, she knew what his next words were going to be.

"You have questions about this supernatural stuff, fine. You can ask Aislinn. But she stays out of this case otherwise."

Storm only just barely managed to keep from rolling her eyes. He'd acted like this on the Dean case too. She wanted to point out that Aislinn had exactly zero connection with VanDenbergh's murder so there was no reason to involve her. Instead she settled for saying, "Sure, Trace."

* * * * *

The back room was full of dragons. True, they were in human form—they had to be—that was an inviolate law. No shifting while in the humans' world. Well, no shifting unless you were a Were, then all bets were off. Still, what was Pierce thinking to have so much gold in the same place as so many dragons? He might as well be holding a match in an armory full of explosives.

Looking up from his position at a round table, his cousin flashed a grin and waved Tristan over. As always, Tristan experienced a slight jolt at the sight of Pierce's face. Except for emerald green eyes, looking at his blond cousin was like looking in a mirror. Another amusement of The Fates, no doubt.

Pierce stood and clasped Tristan to him. "What brings you here, Cousin? Looking for a good game?"

Once again Tristan's hand brushed across the papers in his pocket. He grinned. "Not looking, I think I've already found one. Interested?"

Pierce grinned and made a wide sweeping gesture with his arm. "Better than this? The house gets a cut from every table."

"Much better."

"Tell me about it, Cousin."

Tristan laughed. To mention treasure anywhere near a dragon was to invite him to try and steal it for himself. And to mention the chalice, The Dragon's Cup, in such company was a death wish. "Not here."

"My office then." Pierce didn't wait for an answer but grabbed two glasses full of a deep, amber-colored drink and led the way.

As soon as they were seated, Tristan pulled a folded paper from his pocket and placed it on the desk between them.

"A challenge?" Pierce asked, the emerald of his eyes glowing with interest, though he didn't reach for the paper.

"Along with a woman."

"These human women are hardly a challenge, Cousin. A touch of glamour and they throw themselves at us." He shrugged. "Even with no glamour, they're drawn to the fey."

"This one is different." Tristan's voice hinted that the challenge was not just a game.

Pierce took a sip of the fiery brew that had been developed especially for the club's dragon clientele and studied his cousin. Surely not. Surely Tristan didn't still believe in the faerie tale of the forever mate. True, there were faeries who claimed to have found a lasting bond, but... Pierce shook his head in silent denial. He might be faerie, but he wasn't a believer in that particular tale.

Tristan reached over and unfolded the paper lying on the desk. For a second Pierce could only stare in disbelief at the picture of the cup. "You would wager this for a human woman? Our queen would grant you anything in her power to reclaim the chalice, Cousin. As would any of the dragon princes."

"That's why I offer it to you as part of the challenge. It was stolen today from a collector." Tristan reached into his pocket and pulled out a second piece of paper, this one a newspaper clipping hailing the police department for bringing an end to the psychic murders. "Storm has been assigned to the case," Tristan said, placing the clipping in front of Pierce.

The photograph showed four male detectives and one uniformed female officer. It was a grainy picture, but with a single glance, Pierce's cock rose in anticipation. "Why not simply enjoy her while we follow her to the chalice?"

Tristan suppressed a smile, knowing what his cousin's reaction was going to be, but also knowing that the trap had already closed. Now it was in the hands of The Fates, and may The Goddess help both Pierce and him. "I think she might be my forever wife – and perhaps yours."

Pierce laughed and took a deep, burning swallow of Dragon's Flame. True, he and Tristan had always been drawn to the same women and had enjoyed sharing them, but this... "If you're so sure she is yours, then take both her and the chalice. Or better yet, give the chalice to the queen in exchange for her rescinding the order that you are to couple with her current favorite should you return to our lands. Why draw me into this madness, Cousin?"

"Tell me this, Pierce, how long has it been since any woman, mortal or faerie, held your thoughts for more than the fleeting time it took to seduce her? How many stayed in your mind or wandered into your dreams after a brief meeting that had nothing to do with the easing of the flesh?"

The first stirrings of uneasiness rippled outward from Pierce's heart. "Have you heard me complain?"

"You hide your restlessness well by testing your fire against that of the dragons. But I know you as well as I know myself. There was a time when the quest for knowledge made me thirst for each new day, just as the hunt for treasure and adventure filled you with purpose. But I think those old pursuits are no longer enough for either of us. And I would be happy if you found that Storm was your wife as well as mine. It would please me to share her with you and to have your aid in keeping her safe. It is no small thing to take a mortal as a mate."

Pierce took another gut-burning sip of Dragon's Flame, contemplating Tristan's words. His gaze wandered over the picture of the woman, hesitating briefly before settling on the lost chalice of the dragons. Mortals! To have gotten their hands on something so powerful, something that never should have been created in this realm in the first place, and to turn it into the cup of orgies and debauchery…it was almost beyond understanding…and yet, thank The Fates and The Goddess that the Chalice of Enos had mistakenly come to be known as the Medici Chalice of Eros.

He knew there were many among the dragon lairs who would leave a swathe of destruction through this city to get their hands on the lost chalice. And though Pierce had no desire to tempt fate and find himself saddled with a mortal, he would play along with this madness of Tristan's, if only to guard his cousin's back. "What are the terms of the challenge?"

"Simple," Tristan said. "She is a law-keeper charged with the solving of a murder and the return of the chalice to its owners should she find it. You are known and respected by the dragons. If they think Storm is of interest to you then they will at least hesitate before harming her should they learn that she is hunting the chalice. I do not truly doubt that she is my forever wife, so I will give up my claim to the Dragon's Cup in exchange for your aid in keeping her safe. It will be yours to pursue if you are able to resist Storm. But if she is able to capture your essence and claim your fire, or if you admit that she is yours as well, then you must leave the cup for the dragons to chase among the mortals."

Pierce's eyebrows went up in question. "And if she is merely a human that we both enjoy, but soon forget?"

"I do not think that will happen. But if it does, then we will work together to locate the Chalice of Enos and later devise another challenge for which one of us claims it as our prize."

Chapter Three

ഏ

"I thought he'd never leave," Sophie teased as the three women moved to the kitchen.

Aislinn's eyes sparkled with suppressed laughter. "He can't help it."

Sophie opened the oven and pulled out a casserole. "And you wouldn't have it any other way."

Warmth flooded Aislinn's face. "No, we're right for each other—just as your heartmate will be right for you."

Storm's eyes went to the heartmate necklace Sophie wore and her gut did a little anxious twist. As if sensing the direction of her thoughts, Sophie said, "So do we have to wait or do we get to see whatever you made for Storm right now?"

Storm wanted to hold her hand up and say "No thanks" but something held her back—curiosity maybe.

Aislinn took a small silver box from her pocket and set it on the table in front of Storm. As soon as she saw the box, Storm knew she'd never be able to turn the gift away. "Did you make this?" she asked, awed by the faeries etched into the silver.

Aislinn nodded. Sophie said, "Open it!"

Storm picked up the box and settled it on her palm, surprised when it weighed more than she thought it would. Her heart thundered in her ears as she undid the tiny clasp and opened the box. Inside, resting on a bed of velvet, lay a clear crystal with shifting swirls of lavender and gold deep within it, held to the fragile links of a silver chain by two winged faeries.

"It's beautiful," Storm whispered as she traced a finger over the delicate faerie wings, her heart jolting slightly when she moved across the crystal and it felt hot to her touch.

Sophie leaned in closer and gave a small laugh. "And it's anatomically correct. Is it a heartmate necklace?"

Storm's eyes moved first to the tiny figures, noting that both fairies were male, and then to Aislinn's face. Aislinn shook her head and gently extricated the necklace from its box. The crystal flashed in the light, sending out pulses of color and…Storm gave herself a mental shake…just color. The necklace was *not* emitting anything but color.

"It's not a heartmate necklace," Aislinn said, cupping the necklace in her closed hands, her expression solemn as her eyes met Storm's. "Freely given, freely accepted, let the wearer see both the beauty and peril of the hidden realms." Aislinn opened her hands and the necklace swung like a pendulum between Storm and her — the crystal luminous and tempting. "And if The Fates so choose, let the wearer hold something of the fey with her heart."

Storm couldn't resist, she reached for the gift and in the instant her fingers touched it, she felt as though something shifted around her — but as soon as she blinked the feeling was gone and yet… Storm blinked again. Had Aislinn always looked like that?

Storm shook her head, trying to clear the soft hues of lavender and gold that she saw around Aislinn, but they didn't disappear. She shifted her attention to Sophie. Okay, her cousin looked the same…but the heartmate necklace…somehow it looked deeper, softer, brighter, more alive. Storm took a deep breath. *Calm down. It's just your imagination getting a little crazy here, right? Aislinn is different. You know she's different, kind of otherworldly, right? You've always said she reminded you of an elf or a faerie, so the thing she said about seeing hidden realms kind of made your imagination go wild. No biggie. You can deal with it.*

She closed her eyes for a minute. When she opened them, everything was back to normal, except…out of the corner of her eye she could still almost see the luminescence around Aislinn.

Storm sighed. Okay, she could live with that. She was just jacked up about the case. Overexcited with no way of doing anything until she got back to the station or could find a lead to pursue... Hell, maybe the reason she felt like she was going through her skin was because part of her was waiting to see if Professor Tristan Lisalli was going to call her back. She had to resist the urge to check her cell phone just in case she'd somehow missed his call — as if that was possible with the thing clipped to her pants.

* * * * *

Trace's pager buzzed just as he was walking into the Homicide bullpen. Damn, the place was dead except for his partner, Dylan Archer, and Storm's partner, Brady.

"Welcome to the party," Dylan said. "I'm glad you could peel yourself away from Aislinn and join us."

Trace pulled the pager from his belt and looked at the number. It belonged to his partner. "What gives?"

"Oh, how about a quaint little murder at a senator's house, a senator who just happens to collect swords, including one called the Medici Sword of Vengeance — now missing and presumed to be stolen during an interrupted burglary. Oh, and make the sword the possible murder weapon. According to the officer on the scene, the body and the head of the senator's aide were separated by a sharp instrument and several feet."

"Shit. Tell me the captain isn't — "

"Making dire predictions? Seeing another media nightmare? On the way to a heart attack?" Dylan rose from his chair and grabbed his jacket. "He's already screaming for us to get on it."

Brady pushed away from his desk. "I got a feeling the name Medici is going to give me a major case of indigestion. Mind if I tag along?"

"Suit yourself," Trace said.

Dylan winked at Brady before cutting a glance to Trace. "Between the VanDenbergh murder that Brady drew and this one, it might come in handy that you have an up-close and personal connection to a woo-woo practitioner. Medici Sword of Vengeance has a real ring to it. Maybe we're going to need a special consult to see if there are any kind of weird vibes at either crime scene."

Trace gritted his teeth. "You want to pursue that angle, then you better start looking for an information source, because you're sure as hell not going to involve Aislinn in this." He scowled at Brady. "I already warned Storm about that."

Brady's lips twitched upward. Dylan grinned.

* * * * *

Storm took a deep breath outside Lily's, the small beachfront bar where she'd brought Aislinn, Tiffany and Sophie the night she'd agreed to meet up with Dylan and a few of the guys from Homicide. It was a night that had changed all of their lives, but especially Aislinn's and Trace's.

So why had she mentioned this place when the delicious professor had called and suggested they meet over drinks and discuss the case she wanted to consult with him about?

She laughed at herself. Both the cop and the woman in her knew the reason…though both shied away from looking too closely at it. It was far easier to rationalize that since this was jazz night, played smooth and low so patrons could actually talk with one another, it made perfect sense to meet here.

Storm smoothed her hands over her khaki pants before checking to make sure the blouse was still tucked in. She should have opted for a baggier look, one that didn't so sharply contrast the size of her breasts against a trim, fit body.

She drew in another deep breath and forced herself to move toward the entrance, guarding herself against expectation and hope with the simple mantra—*think about the case*—looping continuously in her mind.

It worked until she got the first glimpse of Tristan. Then she knew she was in trouble.

Damn, even in a darkened bar, he glowed with sexual magnetism, his long blond hair drawing in what light there was and making it appear as though a golden haze of lust surrounded him. She couldn't take her eyes off him. Hell, her feet seemed to be on automatic pilot taking her right to him.

Apparently she wasn't the only one who wanted to eat him up. Storm frowned as a couple of women stopped in front of the booth, blocking her view of the delicious university professor and causing her aggravation meter to go up a notch—the way it did when she was in uniform and had to deal with a particularly obnoxious drunk.

She shook her head, trying to clear her mind and suppress the unexpected feeling of possessiveness. *Get a grip here!* She had never fought over a man in her life, and she was not going to start with this one—no matter how many erotic images flitted through her thoughts, and there were plenty of them.

She'd spent more time thinking about her brief encounter with Tristan than she'd ever admit to. She'd even gone so far as to pull up the university catalog to see what classes he taught.

She had *not* signed up for one of them. Her self-respect demanded that she draw the line somewhere.

Besides, she had a feeling that there were no audit spots available. Hell, there was probably a waiting list—a long, long waiting list of female students who wanted to be dazzled by his…knowledge.

He stood then, saying something to the women so that they turned and glowered at Storm before moving away from the booth. Storm's heart skipped a beat then raced when his smile reached out and stroked her from the inside out, reaching deep and brushing against every erogenous zone she possessed in the process.

"I took the liberty of ordering a glass of wine for you," he said when she got to the table. His hand enclosed hers, not shaking it as she'd intended, but bringing it to his mouth instead and brushing his lips against her knuckles.

For a shimmering instant Storm was dazzled, unable to look away as the golden haze of lust surrounded them both. And then his mouth quirked upward in the same smile that had caused her heart to race when she'd visited him in his office, only here, now, it eased them from staring into each other's eyes into taking their seats.

"Thanks again for being willing to help," Storm said, retreating behind the case before she did something out of character—like suggest they walk on the beach until they found a place where they could make love.

She took a deep breath and corrected herself. *Have sex. Let's not confuse fantasy with reality here.* Her cunt clenched, not caring what she called it, as long as the ache was soothed.

A waitress appeared next to the table, barely acknowledging Storm as she set their drinks down. Even after Tristan had placed several bills on her tray and told her to keep the change, she lingered, her presence like a crisp fall breeze that clears the air as it passes.

Storm blinked, grateful for the interruption. Of its own accord, her hand covered the necklace Aislinn had given her where it rested under her shirt.

It burned warm and comforting in her palm, but more importantly, the feel of the smooth male faeries holding the crystal somehow grounded her, somehow made her feel…back in control—even if she was still horny.

Tristan murmured something and the waitress finally moved away. The grin he directed at Storm shot right to her heart, and yet she had the presence of mind to joke, "I guess that happens to you all the time. At least she ignored me. I had to check my clothing for burn holes the day I came by your office. Your coeds didn't like seeing me there. Just walking down the hallway felt like running the gantlet."

His smile and husky laugh made her want to lean across the table and press her lips to his. "Not *my* coeds. Though I count myself lucky that you were courageous enough to contact me again. I've thought about your visit often and followed your success in the media."

Tristan lifted his glass and swallowed, the simple play of tanned skin over muscle enough to claim Storm's attention while his casual admission had her nipples going tight and hard as her panties grew wetter. She lifted her wineglass and followed suit, glad to have something to moisten her suddenly dry mouth with.

Was he being honest? Had he really thought about her? Or was he merely engaged in a verbal dance of seduction?

Did it matter? Would she really pass up a chance to be intimate with him?

No.

She tried to live each day to the fullest, to enjoy herself. It was her nature, and an acknowledgement of the danger inherent in her job, the gut-level understanding that the next car she pulled over or the next suspect she tried to bring in could be the one who ended her life.

So no. If spending time with him led to further intimacy, well…

As if sensing the direction of her thoughts, Tristan reached over and took her free hand in his. "Would you care to dance?"

Other couples were already moving to the dance floor as the band transitioned to a slow, moody melody. Storm set her wineglass down on the table and let him ease her from the booth and into his arms.

They were a perfect fit.

Storm closed her eyes and savored the brush of his chest against her tight nipples, the rub of his erection against her swollen, needy clit as he held her against his body, surrounding her with his masculine scent. Her breath caught when his lips touched her neck, pressing hungry kisses along sensitive skin, moving upward to her earlobe. She almost cried out when he teased it with his teeth before tracing the rim of her ear with his wet, sensuous tongue. And all the while, his hands stroked along her back, her shoulders, her sides, the top of her buttocks.

Her hands moved in tandem with his, discovering the contours of his body as he discovered hers, the firm muscles of his back, his sides, his shoulders. She luxuriated in the warmth radiating off his body, surrounding and caressing her like a perfect spring breeze, the pleasure of being held by him somehow making her heart feel light, her spirit carefree.

Tristan breathed in the scent of her, rejoiced in the feel of her soft skin. She was the one. His forever wife. She had to be for her to take over his thoughts so thoroughly. For her to command his body so easily.

His cock throbbed and yet he savored this closeness, this harmony of movement as the music surrounded them like a heavy fog, encasing them in a world that wasn't spoken, only felt. It was sweet agony and painful need.

He parted from her only when the music ended and the band moved into an upbeat, catchy tune meant for energetic steps and swirls. But rather than return to their table, he took her hand and led her outside. "Walk on the beach with me," he coaxed. *Dance with me underneath the stars as the fey have always done.*

Storm let him lead her away from the bar, past where manmade lights tried to conquer the darkness—and lost. When they finally stopped walking, she met his gaze and smiled as he took her back into his arms, pulling her body tightly to his, their gentle, swaying movements as old as time, the beat thundering in their veins as ancient as the roar of the ocean, the moon and stars allowing them privacy and yet providing them with enough light so that they could look into each other's faces.

She initiated the kiss this time. Nibbling along the full masculine lips, teasing and tasting him before coaxing him to let her tongue slip inside his mouth.

He groaned, opening for her so that their tongues could brush against each other, tangling and twining and stroking as their bodies grew heavy with need, his penis a hard, throbbing presence between them.

Storm shivered in reaction, trailing her hands down and around, finally hooking her thumbs in his back pockets so she could enjoy the flex of hard muscle as they moved to the music of mutual desire.

The need for air drew their mouths apart, but even then, their lips still hovered, nearly touching, as though they needed to be close enough to share the same breath. Storm laughed softly, enjoying the feel of his ass underneath her hands, enjoying the thought of it clenching and releasing as he drove his cock deep inside her.

Tristan smiled against her mouth, the sound of her laugh every bit as potent to him as faerie glamour was to mortals. "Share your amusement," he said, taking her bottom lip between his teeth and biting gently.

Her smile widened to a grin. Her answering laugh cupped his balls and curled around his cock, bathing him in an unfamiliar warmth. "I was just thinking about following you into your office and not being able to take my eyes off those gorgeous male buns."

His chuckle made her breasts ache for him to cup them, for him to run his thumbs over her nipples. "And then when you turned around, all I could think was, wow, the only thing better than the view from behind was the view from the front." Heat rushed to her face in remembered embarrassment. "Of course, that's when you caught me ogling you like one of the coeds. It was not my finest moment in uniform."

Tristan tugged at her bottom lip, sucking it into the wet heat of his mouth and sending an icy-hot jolt straight to her clit. She ground against his erection in reaction, pressing her own, much smaller, engorged knob against the heavy bulge of his blood-filled penis.

He released her lip and grabbed her hips with firm, strong hands, controlling the press and rub of their groins. "You've invaded my thoughts and my dreams since that visit," he admitted roughly. "I promised myself that I'd seek you out as soon as the fervor over the Dean case and the focus on the supernatural went away."

"And now I'm involved in another crazy case."

He shrugged. "The Fates love their little games. I would have called you and offered my services if you hadn't called me first."

Storm couldn't resist the temptation. She sucked his bottom lip into her mouth as he had done to hers, reveling in the way he gasped, in the way his cock pulsed against her equally needy body. "Exactly what kind of services were you going to offer?" she whispered against his lips.

His smile was purely male, arrogantly confident that he would be able to deliver whatever he promised. "My experience," he said, his fingers sliding into her waistband, burning her with their heat as he easily manipulated the top button of her khakis, freeing it before tugging her zipper down.

Storm's breath caught, her stomach muscles quivered and liquid arousal gushed from her spasming channel as her clit pressed rigid-hard against the silk of her panties. His fingers moved downward, stroking her lightly through the thin material and she arched, trying to hurry the instant when he reached her small, engorged organ.

He covered her clit, cupping it in his two fingers, alternating between stroking and pushing, driving her higher as her vagina continued to spasm, to feel desperately empty. "I can also share my knowledge of magic," he whispered against her neck, his breath and lips sending a shiver down her body.

She whimpered as his manipulation of her clit brought her close to the edge, his touch all the magic she wanted to know about in that moment. She wanted to rip her panties down, to feel first his hand and then his cock, but she could only manage a whispered plea for him to touch her, for him to finish what he'd started.

"Not finish it, Storm," he countered in a husky voice. "This is only the beginning."

She almost cried when his hand left her clit. But before the sob could escape, he eased her khakis and panties down so that the warm air blowing off the ocean was touching her fevered skin, and then his fingers were there, teasing, tormenting, stroking, exploring her swollen folds and flooded channel, commanding that she yield to the ancient and powerful needs inside her.

She came, shuddering hard against him, muscles clutching desperately at the stiff male fingers inside her sheath as her clit ground ruthlessly into his palm.

The orgasm was long and powerful, touching her on a level that she'd never been touched before, and leaving her feeling momentarily helpless, as though the ocean's roar was now inside her body.

"You bewitch me," Tristan said, his voice tight as his breath moved over her like a warm breeze. "You ensnare me and I have no desire to fight against the lure of you." His lips covered hers, his tongue stroking into her mouth, twining with her tongue, his lust moving through her—a hot, urgent gust of need.

She whimpered and he groaned in response, moving to kiss her neck, to nip, before going to his knees, his hands at her hips, holding her, not allowing her to escape his view. "Beautiful," he said, his eyelids lowered and his face flushed as he stared at the golden curls, the swollen lips of her sex.

"Tristan," she said, clamping her legs together against the intensity of his stare, both turned on and embarrassed by the hot wash of arousal trickling down her thighs.

He nuzzled into her, sucking her clit into his mouth and making her cry out. "Open for me," he ordered, his breath and heated words an intimate stroke along aroused flesh.

She had no will to resist. No desire to hide herself from him.

Storm shivered with anticipation when his hands trailed down from her hips, pushing her clothing lower, then returning so that his thumbs grazed her plump labia before parting the swollen folds of flesh, opening her just as the sun's bright rays called to the flowers to blossom and yield their secrets.

"Beautiful," he whispered again, before nuzzling the golden down of her pubic hair and tracing along her slit with the tip of his tongue, rubbing back and forth, then pressing his lips to her lower ones, licking and sipping as though drawing the sweetness from a honeysuckle.

Storm tunneled her fingers through his hair, holding him to her, unable to look away from the sight of him kneeling in front of her, unable to hold back the husky moans of pleasure and the whispered pleas for him to continue, the hoarse demands when his tongue and mouth became more aggressive, more demanding, until finally her back arched and her face lifted toward the star-filled sky, the sultry ocean air whipping through her hair and over her sweat-moistened skin as she cried out in release.

Tristan stood, guiding her face into the hollow of his shoulder, then stroking her naked buttocks with one hand while the fingers of the other moved to her cunt, silently petting her, praising her for giving him the gift of her pleasure.

She found her sense of humor when the ocean's primal beat eased from her body as though retreating into the surf. "Good thing you hung on to me. If you hadn't, I would have collapsed in front of you like one of your coeds."

"Not *my* coeds," he corrected, nipping her neck in mock punishment as he withdrew his fingers and restored her clothing, surprising himself by how much pleasure he took in tending to her needs, in bringing her to orgasm and then easing her panties up and refastening her pants, covering her so that her beautiful pussy was hidden from any eyes but his own…and those of his cousin, though Tristan didn't expand his senses to determine exactly where Pierce was.

Here, so close to the warm ocean breeze, Tristan was in his element. He had known the moment Pierce arrived, his cousin's curiosity getting the better of him so that he'd yielded to the temptation to come and see for himself this human woman who was both challenge and prize.

Storm stood in Tristan's arms, aware of the heavy bulge pressed against his pants. She wanted his cock inside her. Wanted to both to be ridden and to ride him. But more than that, she wanted to give him the same incredible gift that he'd just given to her.

Butterflies danced in her stomach, but she didn't let them stop her hands from trailing down his sides as her lips hovered over his in a smile. "Thanks for that demonstration of your expertise — and your offer to share your knowledge of magic," she whispered, taking his moan into her mouth as her fingers made quick work of his fly and moved to caress his straining erection.

She teased him as he'd teased her, cupping him through the soft fabric of his Jockeys, one hand massaging tight, heavy balls while the other moved up and down his shaft, only briefly pausing to brush over its leaking head.

Tristan watched what her hands were doing to him until the sensation became too intense, and then he buried his face in her soft hair, breathing in the scent of her, of them. His heart roared and flames as hot as a dragon's breath rushed through his blood, through his cock.

He ground out a curse when her hands left him, his own twitching, prepared to grip his cock in order to find relief, but then she sank down and he felt her hot breath, the nibble of her teeth along his still-covered erection.

"Storm," he pleaded, begging as no faerie male should beg a mortal female.

She laughed against him, a heated, sultry sound that wrapped around his cock. And then her hands settled on his hips, tugging at the waistband of his clothing, peeling them down, freeing his penis.

All thoughts of his watching cousin vanished as Tristan cried out at the feel of her wet mouth, the caress of her tongue as she explored his shaft, as she licked over every inch of him except the part that needed her the most. "Storm," he panted, burying his fingers in her hair and trying to hold her so that he could plunge the head of his penis into her mouth.

She laughed again, this time a sound of pure feminine power as she gripped his cock in a tight fist, driving him higher by letting him feel only the stroke of her tongue over its sensitive head.

He jerked in reaction and a wave of icy-hot sensation shot up his spine. Her fist tightened in response and he cried out, arching, wanting to pump madly into her mouth.

She took him them, welcoming everything above her hand, lashing him with her tongue, sucking him mercilessly until all control rested with her. He was helpless against her, his fey glamour useless against the need she generated. He cried out then, fisting her hair in his fingers as his essence escaped, torn from him by the one who was his forever wife.

This time it was Tristan who would have fallen to the sand if not for the support of his companion. This time it was Tristan who shivered as she licked him clean, caressing him with soft strokes, praising him with the satisfied sounds she made before rising and tucking him back into this clothing.

By The Fates and The Goddess alike, this human woman had managed to ensnare him! But the satisfaction that warmed him made it impossible for him to be afraid of the consequences.

"Come back to my home," he said, his cock readying itself as he saw the answer on her face.

"Lead the way."

He took her hand, feeling a flicker of Pierce's anticipation as it moved past him on the breeze before disappearing into the night. They retraced their steps, moving at a steady pace away from the magic-filled darkness and primordial ocean. When they reached the manmade light, Storm frowned, pulling her hand from his and removing a thin cell phone from her pocket. "I had it set to vibrate," she said, her frown deepening as she opened the phone and read the message. "There's been another murder. The captain wants me at the scene."

"Where?" Tristan asked, wondering if other supernatural beings were already trying to recover the chalice.

Storm shook her head. "I can't tell you." Then to ease any sting the refusal may have caused, she pressed a kiss to his wonderfully male lips. "But I don't doubt that the media is already on it. By tomorrow, I might be able to talk to you about it as my," she smiled against his mouth, "expert consultant."

Tristan laughed and curled his fingers around her upper arm, returning her teasing kisses with just enough bite to let her know how sorry he was for the evening to end. "I'll be at the university all day tomorrow. Call ahead and I'll clear my schedule for you."

Storm pressed against him and groaned with frustration at the feel of his thick, waiting cock. "I've got to go," she sighed, reluctant to leave, yet needing to.

Chapter Four

ഇ

The sight of blood and the crime scene unit hovering over a headless body pushed thoughts of Tristan behind a door marked *later* in Storm's mind. "Who was she?" she asked Brady.

Her partner glanced down at the tattered, stained notebook in his hand. "Anita Vorhaus, age twenty-four, political science graduate working as an aide to Senator James K. Harper. Trace and Dylan have him in a room down the hall. What we know so far is that the senator called together an impromptu meeting at his office, but says he forgot an important set of papers. His aide came to his house to get them. When she didn't call or come back to the office, the senator called a neighbor, one Malcolm Berk, and asked the neighbor to come over. It was the neighbor who discovered the body and called the police, then the senator. The best guess right now is that Vorhaus interrupted a burglary in progress or someone was watching the house and used her to gain access to it, then killed her."

A heaviness settled in Storm's chest. She'd seen plenty of fatalities, most of them in wrecks, but some of them hookers or drug users. It was always worse when they were young. Her eyes took in the scene, frowning at the distance between the fallen torso and where additional crime scene technicians— along with Skinner, the head of the lab—were hovering, blocking her view, their cameras flashing in rapid bursts. "The head's all the way over there?" she asked, grateful that the perp hadn't taken it as a souvenir.

Brady grunted. "Yeah. Severed by an eighteen-inch sword with a ruby in the hilt. Called the Medici Sword of Vengeance. Supposedly forged to inspire soldiers in the battle against evil."

A shiver moved along Storm's spine. "I guess that explains why the captain called us in."

Brady shrugged. "I was already here. Tagged along with Dylan and Trace. Soon as I heard the word Medici, I figured there was no use going home and getting comfortable in front of the TV."

"You talk to the captain?"

"Yeah. He stopped by, probably trying to head off political heat. Did the dance with the senator, let him know that this case was a priority, and that we hadn't missed the fact that there might be some connection between this and the VanDenbergh murder. The captain wants us all in a meeting tomorrow, his office, time-to-be-determined. My read is that we'll stay lead on the VanDenbergh case, Trace and Dylan'll get this one, but we'll coordinate and work 'em close."

"Makes sense." She looked from the torso to the location of the head again. "It'd take a lot of strength to sever a neck like that. Not just a strong sword. It'd also take lots of practice to be able to do it with one stroke."

Brady removed a peppermint candy from a wrinkled jacket pocket, unwrapped it and popped it into his mouth, then crunched on it loudly, demolishing it within seconds. "Yeah, writing's on the wall with this one. Lots of man-hours. Lots of pounding the pavement. Makes the VanDenbergh case look like a walk in the park." He pulled another peppermint out.

Storm shook her head. "What's with the candy?"

"Better than chewing the enamel off my teeth. Anything having to do with politicians makes me break out in a cold sweat. I'm going to have to send my suit out to the cleaners just from being here tonight."

Storm eyed the wrinkled suit, limp shirt, and stain-patterned tie that made up Brady's usual look and held back a laugh. "Yeah, I can see that."

Skinner stood and motioned to Storm and Brady. They moved forward, detouring smaller display cases containing knives and daggers.

Anita Vorhaus' head had been moved, readied for transport, but not yet completely bagged. Storm crouched down and forced herself to look, to see the young woman's face before turning her attention to the area where the head had been.

"Shit," Brady said on a sigh. "The captain's going to love this."

The perp had used the victim's blood to draw a small symbol-bound pentacle.

Storm's stomach tightened. Some of the symbols seemed vaguely familiar. But she wasn't sure where she had seen them. VanDenbergh's place? Sophie's apartment? Aislinn? "I'd better get Trace," she said.

Brady grunted. "Yeah, have fun, Kid. He's going to go apeshit, especially after drawing the Dean case last time."

Storm stood, leaving the room and heading down the hallway toward where a uniformed officer stood in front of a closed door. Yeah, Trace was going to go apeshit all right, but in a different way than he had in the past, and not for the same reasons.

Being with Aislinn had changed him. Exactly how much, Storm could only guess at. She hadn't known him except by sight before the Dean case. She still didn't know him well. But she was pretty sure that Trace accepted the possibility of the supernatural—then again, he'd be hard pressed to deny it after using the link he had with Aislinn in order to save Aislinn's life. Though of course, when asked, he claimed it was cop gut-instinct that had led him to guess where the killer was taking Aislinn. Storm thought she knew the truth.

Still, she grimaced. Just because Trace didn't go rabid at the mention of "supernatural shit" anymore didn't mean he was going to be calm about it showing up now—in a high-profile case where all the stops were going to be pulled out, where every move the police made was going to be scrutinized and reported. Where Aislinn's name was sure to surface as reporters rehashed the Dean murder, expanding on a supernatural theme as they vied for new angles and tried to tell the police how to do their job.

Oh yeah. Trace was going to go apeshit—with his testosterone in overdrive as he tried to guard and hoard his wife, his heartmate.

Storm stopped in front of the uniformed officer. "Trace in there?"

"Yeah, both of them are, along with the senator."

"One of them needs to come back out to the scene."

The cop stepped aside. Storm gave a sharp rap on the door, then stepped inside.

For a brief second her vision dimmed, almost going completely black. She swayed, only vaguely aware of reaching out for the doorframe with one hand while clasping the necklace hidden under her shirt with the other. As quickly as the disorientation arose, it disappeared, though not completely. Her vision was still dark around the edges, framing the senator as he sat behind a heavy desk, his face stern, an elegant, old-fashioned letter opener in his hands.

Storm shook her head and the frame containing the senator faded. She grimaced inwardly, reading a glimmer of condescension in his eyes, a flash of his true nature before his political persona took over and buried it behind a seemingly pleasant face.

Both Trace and Dylan were on their feet and she could tell she was in for some razzing when she got back to the station. At least she hadn't fainted, though it must have been close for them both to be shooting her worried looks, their bodies tense, as if they expected to have to leap forward in order to keep her from hitting the ground.

Blood rushed to her face and they only barely suppressed their grins. Shit, she was in for it. From them. From the rest of the guys in Homicide. Nobody made a better target than a rookie, and even though she wasn't a green kid right out of the academy, she was new to them, new to their department.

"One of you needs to come out to the scene," she said, resisting the urge to apologize, to come up with an excuse.

Trace nodded and stepped forward. "We're done here."

Storm escaped back into the hallway, half-expecting Trace to start in on her. Instead he said, "What've you got?

"The crime scene guys lifted the head. There's a pentacle underneath. Victim's blood most likely, some strange symbols around the pentacle and in its center."

"Goddammit! The fucking sword was bad enough. Now this! This shit drives me crazy!"

Storm almost smiled at the sight of Trace unconsciously touching his wedding band, the gesture reminding her of how he'd brushed his face against Aislinn's hair in a silent offer of apology for his skepticism when they'd been at Sophie's apartment.

Damn. That seemed like a lifetime ago, not just a few hours. She checked her watch out of habit. More than a few. It was still dark outside, but they'd moved relentlessly into a new day.

"Weren't the senator and his aide working a little late?" Storm asked. Attractive young woman. Self-righteous, self-important politician. Put the two together at night and…

Trace grunted. "Yeah. Already followed up on that. Five other people in the office working with them. Had a uniform get the security disks. They all show up in the parking garage, leaving at the same time as the senator did, right after he got the call from his neighbor."

"Too bad. An affair gone sour, blackmail, a jealous wife setting up a hit, any of those would be better than an innocent woman getting killed because she was in the wrong place at the wrong time."

Trace rubbed the back of his neck. "Tell me about it."

They stopped next to the pentacle with its cryptic symbols and Trace knelt down, a scowl forming as he studied the killer's message. "Any of it look familiar?" he asked Storm.

"I think I've seen some of the symbols before. But nothing's so clear that it's jumping out at me." She motioned toward the crime scene tech with a camera. "If you give me one of the prints, I can ask around."

Trace nodded and stood. "Sure, no problem." There was a short pause. "But not Aislinn, Storm. She doesn't need to see this kind of shit."

Dylan moved into the room then, his face hard and tight. "I just got finished talking to the captain. We've got another hot one." He came to a stop and looked down at the pentacle. "The media's already having a field day. They're running with a story about blood sacrifices and power objects."

A muscle ticced in Trace's cheek. "Meaning?"

"Bullshit on bullshit."

"That's not exactly enlightening," Brady said, unwrapping a peppermint candy and popping it into his mouth.

Dylan felt like he had a second pulse beating in his temple. Christ, he hated this kind of shit. He liked understandable crimes done by the usual subset of crazies, losers and criminals.

He pulled back his sleeve and checked his watch. "Well, in a couple of hours the papers will be out and you'll get to read all about it." He couldn't keep the frustration out of his voice. Christ, it was going to be a fucking circus with the investigation taking center ring.

"Stop dicking around and just spit it out," Trace growled, the set of his shoulders indicating that he was braced to hear something he'd hate.

Dylan sighed. "Some crackpot called the media and told them that certain powerful artifacts—like the senator's sword and VanDenbergh's chalice, for instance—have to be *recharged*, especially when they change hands. Hence the reason we now have two murders, and a possibility of more to come."

"Ah shit," Brady said, this time patting his shirt pocket and pulling out a roll of Rolaids.

"Yeah," Dylan said, "and guess who's gonna get covered in it."

There was a moment of silence as they all inwardly agreed. Trace ended it by saying, "Let's check with Skinner. If we're done, I'm outta here." His features were hard, his body rigid with tension and Storm would have bet her paycheck that he was thinking about Aislinn and keeping her clear of this stuff.

One side of Dylan's mouth quirked upward. "How low will The Pro go? Used to be Trace had the ladies running to him, but now he's always in a hurry to get back to the little woman. Next thing you know, he's going to be taking Lamaze classes and telling us about potty-training."

Brady snorted while Storm managed to hide her smile. Some of the tension left Trace. He grinned. "What goes around comes around. You'll get yours one day, and I'm going to enjoy seeing it happen."

"That day will never come. I'll be the last bachelor standing." Dylan made a show of looking at his watch. "And if I hustle, I can still meet, mingle and be the answer to some woman's sexual prayers. Let's hit it before she settles on second best."

Storm choked back a laugh and left the crime scene, wishing it weren't so late, wishing that she was heading back to Tristan instead of heading home. The door marked *later* opened, flooding her mind with thoughts of what had happened on the beach, flooding her body with anticipation and heated need.

Chapter Five

❧

Morning came before Storm was ready for it. She reached over and slapped the alarm clock, needing a few more minutes before crawling out from under the covers and heading to the station.

Warm sunshine flowed through her window, and for a minute she couldn't understand why the walls of her bedroom sparkled with color. Then she remembered the necklace Aislinn had given her.

She'd hated to take it off last night, but the thought of the delicate chain tangling in her hair had finally made her remove it. Even then, she hadn't wanted to put it in the ornately carved box. So she'd hung it from a small lamp on one of her bedside nightstands.

And now the sun was dancing through it, bringing it to life. Storm smiled and rolled to her side, her eyes instantly going to the delicate, anatomically correct male faeries holding the crystal between them, as though it was their world and they were offering it to someone, to her.

"Get a grip," she muttered, blushing at her own flight of fantasy. Still, she couldn't stop herself from reaching over and grasping the necklace, pulling it off the lampshade and bringing it closer so she could study it.

It felt warm in her hand and she shivered as the heat traveled up her arm and through the rest of her body like the rays of the sun stretching across the sky. Her breasts flushed and grew heavy, the nipples tightening to hard points and aching so that she used her free hand to cup and tweak the areolas as fire spiked through her clit.

Rolling to her back, she dropped the necklace onto her stomach so that she could free both of her hands. Memories of what she'd done on the beach with Tristan flooded through her and made her cry out with need.

Her fingers tightened on her nipples, squeezing, tugging, wishing desperately that he was there, wishing desperately that he'd touched her like this on the beach so she'd know exactly how his hands would feel on her breasts, how his mouth would feel. But he'd ignored that part of her, as though he knew how often other men had centered their attention there, acting as if she had nothing else to offer.

Sweat broke out on her skin at the intensity of her need to have him tease and soothe, touch and suck and bite, to give her breasts the same attention he'd given her clit and cunt.

With a small sob of frustration, she released one nipple and moved the freed hand between her thighs. Her clit throbbed at attention, the hood pulled back so that each stroke of her arousal-wettened fingers made it jerk in painful pleasure. Her channel clenched and leaked with each burst of sensation, and her touches grew harder, firmer, as she tried desperately to mimic what Tristan's lips and fingers and tongue had done.

Frustration rode at the edge of her need, making her writhe and struggle for relief, as the fear that she wasn't going to be able to come trickled into her consciousness. God, what had he done to her?

Her other hand moved from her breast to the necklace resting on her abdomen, unconsciously seeking its heat. She clutched it in her hand, and at the feel of the smooth, heated faerie bodies with their erect penises, the resistance inside her melted, tumbling her into an orgasm just large enough to take the edge off.

For a minute she lay on the bed, wondering how soon she could see Tristan. Praying that last night hadn't been a case of starlight-induced lust, and that he was still interested.

Her thumb grazed over the naked faeries, rubbing the still warm cocks, and she shook her head, laughing at herself. Obviously, it'd been way too long since she'd had real sex.

* * * * *

Pierce lounged in the doorway of Tristan's den, not bothering to hide his amusement as his cousin hunched over his desk in a mortal-induced orgasm. When Tristan's panting finally subsided and he straightened in his chair, Pierce casually sauntered in and took the seat opposite to his cousin's.

"Amazing that you should allow a human so much power over you, Tristan," he drawled. "To let one call on your essence in order to give themselves pleasure…" his eyebrows rose and his lips curled at his own impending humor, "or perhaps she is enjoying the…taste…of faerie glamour and is trying it out on another human."

Tristan grimaced but didn't rise to his cousin's baiting remarks, or to the unspoken confirmation that Pierce had witnessed Tristan's ecstasy when Storm had taken his cock into her mouth and brought him to release.

That she could draw on him from a distance, that she needed to call on him in order to orgasm only proved to him that he was right about her importance in his life. But he knew it was pointless to use such logic on Pierce, a non-believer, when it came to anything but transitory pleasure.

With the wave of his hand, Tristan used his elemental tie to the air and water to send a swirling, cleansing, drying mix of moisture and breeze over his seed-covered abdomen and cock. Pierce watched, amusement present from both his expression and the loose-limbed way he sprawled in the antique chair he sat on. But he didn't speak again until Tristan had closed his fly and buttoned his shirt. "What do you know of the Medici Sword of Vengeance? I have never heard of such a treasure, and yet I assume it's the reason our human quarry raced away before you could introduce me to her last night."

Tristan frowned, unexpectedly annoyed with his cousin. "She has a name, Pierce."

"A rather appropriate name if I remember correctly." A small fire formed at the end of Pierce's fingertips. He bundled it up before tossing it from one hand to the other like a baseball. "Storm. Yes, I can see why one who boasts a tie to both air and water would be drawn to this particular woman." The amused grin surfaced again. "Already she has you unsettled."

"And you have yet to meet her. Perhaps when you do, you'll find yourself trapped in the heat of a firestorm." With a slight flick of his fingers, Tristan sent a cold, damp, current of air over Pierce and extinguished his fiery toy. "But as amusing as I find that image to be, I'll have to put it aside for later. This so-called Medici Sword of Vengeance concerns me."

Pierce leaned forward. His demeanor changing from amused regard to serious intent. "Tell me what worries you."

"The media is already screaming that the murder and theft at the senator's house is connected with the VanDenbergh case that Storm is working on."

Pierce shrugged. "Let them speculate, at least no one has mentioned the loss of the chalice by name yet, and by all accounts VanDenbergh had a wealth of artifacts, any number of which could be viewed as an important object of power. It would be a small matter to spread a story and misdirect the news media."

Tristan shook his head. "It is not just the media coverage that troubles me. I have learned that Severn Damek is making inquiries about the Sword of Vengeance."

"You are sure of your sources?"

"Very."

Pierce's worry suddenly mirrored Tristan's. "It is not Severn's usual fare."

"No."

"You think he has learned of the missing Dragon's Cup?"

"Yes."

"I said nothing…"

Tristan held up his hand to halt Pierce's words. "I trust you as I trust myself. That is why I share my worry with you. You know Severn better than I…"

"And not well at all," Pierce said, rising from his chair and pacing restlessly, his words not entirely true. One had only to know that Severn Damek was a dragon prince to know that he was deadly, possessive, dangerous—and would stop at nothing to get his hands on the Chalice of Enos.

* * * * *

"Captain's office in about five," Dylan told Storm as she walked into the Homicide bullpen.

"Thanks." She moved toward her desk, feeling the attention of the men around her.

Shit. Had she lost a button? Was her blouse gaping? Or worse, had thoughts of visiting Tristan's office and the inevitable moist panties that came with it translated into a visible wet spot?

She gritted her teeth against the need to check herself out. *Hang tough.*

She got to her desk and found the reason for their attention. Someone had put smelling salts in the center of her workspace.

Cops. They just couldn't help themselves.

The tension in her body eased. This she could handle. This she'd expected.

Without saying a word, she picked up the smelling salts and threw them in her trash can.

Someone snickered. Brady leaned back in his chair, sending her a wink before saying, "Told 'em they needed glasses. Told 'em that The Kid wasn't the type to faint over something like strange symbols and a headless body."

Any weakness and they'd react like sharks with blood in the water. She shuffled through some papers, a show that she was moving on to business as usual. "Damn straight. Anything new surface since last night?"

Brady grunted. "Not on my end. Old Man VanDenbergh's lawyer's got everything locked up as tight as a virgin's..."

When he didn't continue, Storm said, "Political correctness training kicking in, Brady?"

Male snickers sounded around the room. Dylan strolled over and leaned against her desk. "One of the lovely ladies in personnel told me that they wrote up a money-back guarantee clause after they sent Brady through diversity training the last time. Figured if they didn't, the consultants were going to milk the department dry."

Brady shook his head. "You know what my problem is?" He stood and put on his wrinkled, stained jacket.

"Besides no taste in clothes?" Dylan asked.

Brady frowned and looked down. "What's wrong with this? Brown's a good color. Earth tones, that's what the guy who sold it to me said. Said it'd give me a grounded look, which would come in handy in my line of work."

Storm buried her face in her hands to keep from laughing and possibly hurting her partner's feelings. Maybe when she knew him better, she could steer him in a different direction...maybe to something black, so the stains wouldn't show up.

Dylan snorted. "Grounded, huh? Were you pulling this guy in for assault with a deadly fashion sense?"

This time Storm couldn't contain her laugh. Brady shook his head. "I'm just misunderstood, that's my problem."

Trace joined them, a file and a notepad in hand. "Hell Brady, you need a wife, that's your problem."

Dylan groaned. "Oh man. Married only a short time and it's already a case of misery loves company."

Trace laughed. "Well, the captain's going to lay out a different type of misery if we don't get to his office."

Storm grabbed her notepad with a sense of déjà vu as she remembered making this same walk with Trace, Dylan, and two other detectives at the start of the Dean murder case.

The captain's secretary waved them into his office and they took seats. "Well," Captain Ellis said without preamble, "I've already talked to the mayor, the senator, VanDenbergh's lawyer and about half a dozen other people with the last name VanDenbergh, along with five other rich collectors and one church leader who thinks this might be the start of the Apocalypse."

He reached over and patted a collection of message slips. "These are calls from reporters, most local, but some from as far away as Australia. On the heels of the Dean case, the media is feasting. Miguel is still dealing with a family emergency, so he's not available. Say the word and I'll pull Conner back from vacation. Otherwise, it's you four. Officially working hard to solve your respective cases, unofficially working together if they look like they're connected. First off — do you need Conner? Second, tell me what you've got so far. Brady and Storm, you start first."

Brady shrugged. "I don't have squat yet, Captain." He exchanged a look with Storm. "Right now, I think we're okay with Conner on standby, ready to come in if we get some solid leads."

Storm nodded. "I'm meeting with a professor over at the university. He might be able to shed some light on VanDenbergh's stolen chalice and where it might end up."

The attention in the room shifted to Dylan. He grimaced and said, "Lab came back with the results on the symbols left by the perp. The blood used to make them, and the pentacle, wasn't the victim's. Lab guys think it was animal blood, most likely goat blood."

Captain Ellis settled heavily and wearily in his seat. "So do we assume that the murder was premeditated? And if so, who was the intended victim?"

Dylan shrugged. "Don't know. Skinner had a couple of his guys take a shot at interpreting the symbols, but they came up empty-handed. Said they just don't know enough to even make an educated guess."

"You need Conner?"

"He still playing mountain man at his family's cabin?"

The captain nodded and Dylan looked at Trace. "On standby is okay with me. He could be here inside a day, day and a half if we needed him."

Trace nodded. "Yeah, leave him on vacation for now."

Captain Ellis leaned forward, his attention on Trace, and everyone in the room knew what he was getting ready to say. "I'm sure by now you've all heard the media twist on this thing, objects of power needing to be recharged with blood sacrifices, yadda yadda yadda. Probably bullshit, even if the killer or killers believe it. Panic setting in among the wealthy collectors in this city...of which there are more than we'd guess, according to the mayor and the senator and the five collectors who called me this morning. So we're on this like flies on shit. We're lifting every stone no matter what scum is underneath. We're..." Someone groaned and the captain came up for air.

"You get the picture. We don't hesitate to ask the questions that need to be asked." Once again his focus sharpened on Trace. "We ask the questions even if we don't want to ask them, and we use whatever resources we have access to. Period. Any questions? Comments?" When no one said anything, the captain nodded. "Get to it then. Same as last time. You're all good detectives. I'm not going to micromanage you. But keep me posted."

They rose and left the office. In the hallway, Storm asked if she could have a copy of the photo showing the pentacle and symbols. Dylan opened the file he was carrying and passed one to her. "You showing it to your professor?"

She wished Tristan was *her* professor. "Yeah. It's probably a long shot. I'll ask him about the missing sword, too."

"Appreciate it."

Storm stopped in the Homicide bullpen to call Tristan's university phone number and leave him a message letting him know that she was on the way. Brady was also making a call, when he was done she said, "Touch base later?"

"Yeah, I've got a meet scheduled with the insurance guy, and another haggling session with the lawyer."

"Sounds fun."

"Yeah, Kid. Like an ulcer and a bad case of gas."

* * * * *

Dylan grimaced as he slid into the unmarked police car. It was like being in the same enclosure as a rabid panther. Make no sudden moves. Make no sound. And maybe, just maybe, he'd get through this with his skin still on his body. Because partner or not, there was so much anger rolling off Trace right now, that he wasn't sure anyone was safe—except for Aislinn.

Man, he couldn't begin to understand the thing between Trace and his wife. Yeah, he could understand the physical attraction. He could even understand a man and his wife loving each other. And he could sure understand dominant, possessive feelings—even though he hadn't ever felt the possessive part of that equation himself.

But the bond between Trace and Aislinn was...he didn't even have words to describe it...it was beyond anything that he'd ever encountered. Hell, he wasn't sure he even wanted to understand it, because he had a horrible feeling that if he ever did understand it, it would mean that he'd fallen for some woman as hard as Trace had fallen for Aislinn.

No thanks. Life was great just the way it was—even if he sometimes missed the days of hanging out with Trace after hours, hitting the bars and scoring the women.

But it wasn't as though he lacked drinking buddies. Conner was usually game, so was Miguel, and then there were a couple of his old buddies in Vice. They were always fun to mix it up with—and their scruffy bad-dude look always drew a few more choice babes to the table.

Yeah. Life was great. Couldn't get any better—well, outside of solving this case.

Dylan risked a glance at Trace and saw the muscle jumping and twitching in his partner's cheek. Not a good sign. Of course, the fact that they were turning onto the street where Inner Magick was located probably accounted for the spasms.

Oh boy. He'd be willing to bet Trace never willingly stepped foot in the shop Aislinn had practically inherited—a shop that specialized in tarot cards, runes, crystals and an assortment of other stuff that Dylan didn't know anything about and didn't want to.

"Son of a bitch," Trace growled, slamming into a parking place and getting out of the car a second before Dylan spotted a van with a local newspaper logo on the side.

Shit. So much for lying low and waiting in the car. Dylan scrambled out after his partner. Maybe the captain would put him up for some kind of medal if he prevented Trace from sending the reporter through the plate glass window and causing *an incident.*

He found Trace glowering at Aislinn's assistant—Marika, if the name elegantly fashioned on her necklace was to be believed. All five foot nothing of the girl was trembling as she bravely stood in front of a curtained doorway with her arms outspread. "She's with someone right now and can't be disturbed."

"You've got three seconds to move or I'll…"

Behind Marika, the curtain pulled open and Aislinn's gaze met Trace's. Almost instantaneously, the anger seemed to drain out of Trace and if Dylan didn't know better, for a split second, he would have sworn that his partner looked downright sheepish.

Jesus, sometimes when Trace and Aislinn were together, it was spooky. Like they were having a conversation that only the two of them could hear.

When the two of them finally stopped staring into each other's eyes, Aislinn squeezed Marika's arm. "Go ahead and take a break. You wanted to pick up a book, I'll watch the shop while you're gone."

"You sure you're going to be all right with this guy…" Her eyes widened and her lips formed a small o. "Ohmygod, this is Trace isn't it? Sophie's told me all about him, but I didn't recognize him right away."

A blush colored Aislinn's face a delicate shade of rose. "Yes. This is my husband, and his partner, Dylan."

Marika ogled the men for a minute before looking back at Aislinn. "What about your client, do you need me to stay long enough for you to finish up?"

Aislinn shook her head. "No. We were just about finished when Trace arrived. I let my visitor out through the back entrance."

"Oh, okay. Cool. I'll run down to the bookstore, then maybe swing by Starbucks on the way back. You want the usual?"

"That'd be great, thanks, Marika."

Aislinn's assistant took one last look in Trace's direction and Dylan could have sworn he heard her mutter "Wow, wow, wow!" before leaving Inner Magick.

"Who was here with you?" Trace growled.

Aislinn moved over, standing on her tiptoes so that she could brush a kiss against his mouth. "Someone here on personal business, and before you ask, we didn't talk about the murders or anything related to them." She slipped her arms around him, burying her face in his chest and hugging him tightly. Trace sighed, wrapping his arms around her and rubbing his cheek against her pale blonde hair.

Dylan couldn't look away, the sight of them holding each other like that—as though they needed the contact—had something twisting deep in his heart, carving out an empty spot that suddenly had him thinking of finding someone to fill it.

Christ! He jerked his attention away from Trace and Aislinn, focusing on the display of crystals in the glass case that served as a counter. "I can wait in the car if you guys…"

Aislinn laughed softly. Trace grunted. "I forgot the folder. Hang tight while I get it."

As Trace moved toward the door, Dylan's eyes were drawn to a clear green crystal. Surprised, he pulled a ring out of his pocket and laid it on the counter so that he could compare the crystal in the ring to the one in the glass case.

Aislinn joined him. He cut her a look and grinned, deciding to risk being ripped apart by Trace. "Make my day, baby, tell me this piece-of-junk ring is worth something."

She smiled, a Mona Lisa smile that immediately unnerved him. "It's worth quite a bit in the right hands. Where did you get the ring?"

Dylan snorted. "An old bum named Commander Joe. He's a homeless guy that Trace looks after."

"Yes, I've heard of him."

Her expression was so puzzled that Dylan felt compelled to add, "He said he found this ring with a bunch of other junk in a dumpster. I believe him. The Commander's not a thief. He has his route and checks it every day. Hell, if the ring is really worth something, I'll pass the money on to him."

"It's only worth something in the right hands," Aislinn repeated, the Mona Lisa smile returning. "Pick it up and hold it between your palms."

"Ah, Aislinn…"

She laughed quietly. "If you don't, then I'll tell Trace what you said. 'Make my day, baby'." Her soft inflection put a completely different slant on his words.

Dylan chuckled and picked up the ring, pressing it between his hands. Damn the thing seemed to absorb his body heat and then some. It almost felt like any minute it was actually going to burn his palms.

He jumped back involuntarily and ended up against the wall when Aislinn covered his hands with her own. Oh Christ, if Trace walked in now…

Yeah, that was the sound of the door chime. He risked looking up and meeting Trace's gaze.

Ah shit…he'd almost rather see jealousy than the amused, this-is-going-to-be-great-fun look on Trace's face. It didn't help that it felt like some unspoken conversation was going on between Aislinn and Trace again, and this time he was the main topic.

Crap. He should have thrown the ring away. He didn't really know why he hadn't, except that it just ended up living in his pocket, kind of like his loose change and the twenty-five-dollar chip from the Luxor that he kept to remind himself of his last vacation in Vegas.

Dylan tried to bluff his way through the moment. "So would you take the thing on consignment? Maybe sell it if the right person comes along?"

Aislinn removed her hands from his. "It already belongs to the right person." Her nose wrinkled. "But it won't do any good in your pocket. You need to wear it."

"Oh yeah, that'd go over well, me sporting a lady's ring."

Trace surprised the hell out of him by saying, "Hey, we've got some time. Aislinn could reset it for you. Right, baby? We wouldn't want Dylan to miss out on some incredible good fortune just because he can't wear the ring."

Dylan didn't like the laughter he heard in Trace's voice, and the Mona Lisa smile that Aislinn was still wearing was enough to have his heart jumping around in his chest like he was sitting in the front seat of a roller coaster and looking at the first big drop.

He opened his mouth, fully intending to say, *Hell no, I'm going to toss the ring into the first trash can I see*, but before he could do it, his mind circled back to the words *incredible good fortune* and he said instead, "So this might be a lucky charm for me?" Not that he believed wholeheartedly in that kind of shit. A man made his own luck. But hey, there had been that lucky bat when he played ball in college, and the Luxor chip had brought him a little luck when he played in Atlantic City, and...

Aislinn held out her hand and he dropped the ring into it without a peep of protest. She ducked her head, blushing slightly. "I'll be right back. I've already got a ring made for you, I was just waiting for the right stone."

Dylan was startled by her comment, and oddly touched. "You made me a ring?"

"For your birthday, but this is better."

Aislinn disappeared behind the curtain. Trace set the folder on the counter then moved around the small, comfortable shop, examining the items on display.

True to her words, a short time later Aislinn emerged from the back room. Dylan expected her to simply hand him the ring, but instead she handed him a small velvet pouch with cryptic golden symbols on the outside.

Oh Christ, he did not like the look of this. But he didn't want to hurt Aislinn's feelings and have Trace either pissed at him or thinking he was a guy with no balls because suddenly he was scared of a little ring.

"Thanks." It was little bit unnerving having them both stare at him like he was a five-year-old sitting at a birthday table and surrounded by relatives. He took a deep breath and resolved just to get it over with.

The bag opened easily enough and the ring dropped right onto his palm and straight to his heart. He didn't know a lot about jewelry, but he could tell that she'd spent a lot of time on this. Dylan slipped it on the ring finger of his right hand, feeling oddly like it belonged on the other hand. "Thanks," he repeated, at a loss for additional words.

Trace hugged Aislinn to him, burying his face in her hair, and Dylan could have sworn that his partner was laughing. But when Trace looked up, he was straight-faced and somber. "Okay, now that we've taken care of that, we better get back to police business." He reached over and flipped the folder open. The photograph of the symbol-inscribed pentacle was on top.

Aislinn shivered, pushing backward against Trace rather than moving forward to examine the photograph more closely. "I can't help you with those symbols."

Trace's arms tightened around her. "Close the file, Dylan." Once Dylan had flipped the cover back in place, Trace said, "Can you tell us anything about them, baby?"

"They're symbols of dark magic." She shivered again. "For calling demons and demon lords."

"Fuck," Trace growled.

Dylan grimaced. Yeah, the captain was going to love hearing this one. He risked a quick glance at Trace and saw the struggle taking place on his partner's face. The need to know more and question Aislinn further in direct opposition to the need to protect her against everything, including being afraid.

Shit. "Can you point us toward someone who'd know what the symbols mean?" Dylan asked.

Aislinn shivered one final time, then nodded before moving out of Trace's arms and going around the counter. Neither man said anything as she began writing an odd, foreign script on stationery with an Inner Magick header. When she was done she folded the letter and sealed it in an envelope, writing a phone number and an address on its cover, then finally a name. Seraphine Jordain. Handing it to Dylan, she said, "I don't know her well, but Seraphine can help you." Aislinn hesitated, then added, "Please be careful. Both of you."

Chapter Six

ဆ

Storm's heart jumped at the sight of Tristan casually leaning against the hallway wall, his blond hair unbound and flowing over a soft green shirt as the sunlight ricocheted off school-related posters and surrounded him in a soft barely there red haze. His attention was focused on something in his hand and she couldn't believe she'd found him like this, alone in the hallway — not a coed in sight. Smiling, she started to call out, then thought of a more satisfying way to let him know she had arrived.

Anticipation rose as she moved forward, glad that whatever he was studying seemed to command his entire attention. Damn, he was gorgeous. A god among humans. Her eyes traveled over his body, resting on the bulge in his pants, remembering what it was like to free his cock and take it in her mouth, to make him beg.

Unbidden, she wondered what it would be like to handcuff a man to her bed and tease him until he was helpless with lust. Then trust him enough to do the same to her.

She took a shaky breath and tried to force her mind back to the case. But it wasn't ready to go there. Murder had interrupted what they'd started last night and now her body argued for a time-out from work, a chance to finish what they'd begun — or at least get a little relief.

"Hi," she whispered, suddenly, unexpectedly nervous as she moved into his personal space, pressing her body to his, one hand caressing over his wonderful butt, the other brushing over his abdomen then settling on his cock before she lifted her face for a kiss.

There was only a fleeting impression of green eyes and a sensuous mouth as he dropped the paper he'd been holding and pulled her tightly to his body, covering her lips with his as he turned and pressed her against the smooth surface of the wall.

In the space of a heartbeat, Storm felt overwhelmed by lust, as though the heat of it was being thrust through her body with the aggressive stroking of his tongue into her mouth. Last night he'd been smooth and gentle, but today he was rough and hard, ravenous—seemingly as hungry to continue what had been interrupted as she was.

As if he knew her early morning thoughts, one of his hands freed her shirt from her pants and pushed underneath, moving upward and forcing her bra out of the way so he could cover an aching, tight nipple with his palm.

Storm sobbed in reaction, her body arching and pressing against his hand. God, she had never been so desperate for a man to touch her breasts.

Fire. It consumed Pierce. Starting at his core and racing outward, engulfing him in lust. By The Fates, Tristan's taunt had turned to truth.

And you have yet to meet her, Cousin. Perhaps when you do, you'll find yourself trapped in the heat of a firestorm.

His other hand joined the first, pushing underneath her clothing. He cupped and molded her breasts, relishing the feel of her nipples against his palms, their stiffness a demand for him to claim them with his mouth as well. The heat of her skin scorched him, the smell of her arousal made his nostrils flare and quiver, his lungs expand as he tried to breathe her in.

Pierce deepened the kiss, wanting to swallow her, consume her, make her a part of him. Her moans and the way she pressed her body to his, rubbing against his erection as though she craved him as desperately as he craved her only fanned the flames.

He growled as thoughts of Tristan intruded, as the unwanted knowledge that she thought he was his cousin dampened his pleasure but not his desire. By The Goddess, Storm was worth the price of the Dragon's Cup. He would have her underneath him, he would hear her cry *his* name as he shared his fire with her, as she writhed against him, opening herself fully to him, begging for his cock, his taste, his touch, his very essence.

He still thought Tristan crazy for believing in the faerie tale of a forever wife, but it had been centuries since a woman—either mortal or fey—had called to him as this one did. And he was no longer an adolescent just coming into his power as he had been the last time.

Storm clawed at his fabric-protected back. God. He was burning her alive. Making her want to rip off her clothes and his, then wrap her legs around him as he fucked her against the wall. She pressed harder against him, aware of where they were, of the possibility that a student or faculty member could show up at any time, but she couldn't seem to make herself care, not with his fingers tormenting her nipples and his mouth breathing fire into her.

She cried out when his hands left her breasts and traveled down to her hips. Her skin was covered with a fine sheen of sweat and she felt like she was burning up. But before she could pull her mouth from his and beg him to take her nipples between his fingers again, he lifted her, his hands silently urging her to do the very thing she was thinking about, to wrap her legs around him so that his cock would be cradled between her thighs.

She complied, hating that clothes separated them. But then he began moving and she sobbed into his mouth at the exquisite feel of him rubbing against her—repeatedly striking her clit through the layers of their clothing. She locked her arms around his neck and he rewarded her by moving both hands upward until they cupped her breasts again, pushing the plump mounds together, trapping her necklace between them, so that it burned hot against her skin as his fingers tortured her nipples.

He met her moans with his own. His movements between her legs intensifying, driving her higher and higher until her world became her nipples and her clit, until they were both shaking and shuddering as orgasm washed over them, cooling the need but not sating it completely.

Slowly she unwound her legs from around his waist and let her feet touch the floor, though she didn't lift her head from where it rested against his collarbone. She felt shaky, dazed — almost mortified.

A small laugh escaped. Almost. Hard to be embarrassed when they'd both lost control and come.

God, she hadn't done anything like that since she had first discovered how good boys could make her feel but was still too embarrassed by the size of her breasts to take her clothes off.

She nuzzled into him, enjoying the heat of his body and the soft feel of his hair as her fingers toyed with it. "I can't believe I caught you without a single one of your coeds around."

He laughed softly and ran his fingers down her spine. "Only time will tell whether or not we're lucky that you caught me."

Uneasiness slid through her at his response, brushing over her spine as a door opened down the hallway and a warm breeze passed over her. She leaned away from him so that she could view his expression. Green eyes stared down at her where last night they'd been blue — but the face was the same, the body was the same, her reaction to him was the same.

She vaguely remembered noticing that the eyes matched the green of his shirt before they'd started kissing…but now that she was really looking at him…she had the horrible feeling that the eye color was real and not a case of wearing contact lenses for the sake of fashion.

Hang tough, she ordered for the second time in one day, humiliation threatening to make her queasy, to make her lose her breakfast where the sight of a corpse wouldn't. "You're not Tristan."

The man holding her smiled slightly, but didn't answer as another masculine hand curled around her waist and pulled her into his arms. "My cousin, Pierce," Tristan murmured, enfolding her in a hug and momentarily chasing her thoughts away, "who finds pleasure in tempting The Fates and drawing trouble to himself."

There was only a second to process the information as she met Tristan's warm, familiar gaze. Then his lips were covering hers, his tongue was stroking hers, his kiss fanning the firestorm that had started with his cousin but hadn't been completely extinguished.

Storm moaned, unable to pull away, to end the kiss, even though she was acutely aware of Pierce's presence, of his body heat pressing into her as if he were also part of the embrace.

She felt a moment's loss when the kiss ended and both Tristan and Pierce retreated. But warmth and heated need rushed to fill the emptiness when Tristan took her hand and said, "Perhaps we should move into my office."

Alone, either man was a fantasy, but together…for a brief moment she allowed her mind to envision what it would be like to lie between them, enjoying their attention while at the same time being free to explore their bodies — learning how they were alike and how they were different.

Guilt intruded, and she pushed those thoughts from her mind. That Tristan hadn't been upset finding her in his cousin's arms probably meant that it was a prank Pierce had played before, but that didn't mean…

Pain seared through her heart, chasing the heat from her body and slowing her steps, making her reach for the necklace as her cop-mind took over. She'd left a message, so Tristan knew she was on her way. He knew about what time she would arrive…and Pierce had been waiting in the hall — head bent, eyes hidden — where she was sure to come upon him and mistake him for Tristan.

Storm was surprised at how much it hurt to think she'd misjudged the situation. Last night had seemed so... Tristan had been so...

Big boobs. Small brains. Nonexistent morals.

Yeah, she'd been hurt by guys with those kind of thoughts before. She just hadn't seen it coming. Not with Tristan.

Storm pulled her hand from Tristan's grasp and took a deep breath, fighting the urge to excuse herself and escape back to her car. Okay, they'd had their fun, maybe even placed a bet on what would happen — they were guys, and she'd been around enough men to know that betting and keeping score seemed to be hardwired into some of them. But she still had an important case to work, two if she included the one Trace and Dylan had pulled, so she'd just suck it up and hang tough until she got the information she'd come for.

God. She was getting sick of telling herself to hang tough. Three times in one day — and it was still pretty early. Maybe when this was over, she'd go back to being a patrol cop. Yeah, it wasn't glamorous. And there were plenty of tough moments. But a patrol cop kept moving, so the bad times didn't seem to stick as long or hit as hard.

When they got to Tristan's office, she pulled a folded piece of paper out of her back pocket before sitting down, not wanting to distort the photocopied picture of the pentacle and symbols from Trace's crime scene any more than she had to. Now she was sorry she'd taken the extra step, maybe if she'd been holding an eight-by-eleven glossy she wouldn't have been so quick to wrap her arms and legs around Pierce — or maybe it would have caused her to hesitate long enough to note the eye color.

Okay. Deep breath here. Forget about it. You're better off knowing now — not later. Let's just get this done and get out of here.

"Can you tell me anything about the Medici Chalice of Eros?" she asked, her attention on Tristan who'd taken a seat behind his desk, though it was hard to ignore Pierce who'd chosen to pull his chair so close to hers that she could see him in her peripheral vision, and feel the heat of his body radiating across hers.

Tristan's face looked troubled but she braced herself against feeling anything but impatience to get her questions answered and move on. His eyes flickered to Pierce, then back to her. A silent message that had Pierce backing off, shifting in his chair so he wasn't in Storm's personal space.

"The name is a misnomer," Tristan finally said. "The true name of the artifact is the Chalice of Enos."

"The Wizard?" Storm said, her surprise mirrored on both Tristan's and Pierce's faces, though for a different reason.

Pierce was the first to speak. "You've heard of the Wizard Enos?"

Damn. Only Sophie, and now Aislinn, knew of Storm's passion for collecting books on faeries. Not that she was ashamed of her long-standing hobby, it just didn't go well with a kick-ass cop persona, and there was no way she wanted to be the focus of cop-humor on the subject of faeries. They'd have a field day with that one.

But the imaginary world that included faeries had been an addiction of hers since the first book she'd gotten as a birthday present when she was a child. Now she had everything from newly released books to old tomes that were just about to fall apart. Her favorites were the old, hand-illustrated children's books featuring the fey creatures, but some of the books in her collection were text only—including the book where she'd read about the wizard named Enos. Well, what she'd actually read was the translation of what the book was supposed to say—and she hadn't known what it actually said until recently, when she found out that Aislinn knew the ancient language.

Storm's hand went unerringly to where the necklace rested under her shirt as she struggled to appear casual, smooth and in control. She wasn't up to sharing personal information with Tristan, not anymore. But she didn't see any harm in telling him what she knew about Enos. It was a small price to pay in order to get what information she could and then leave.

"I've got some old books," she said. "One of them has a story about Enos. From what I remember, he was envious of the dragons because they had so much treasure and wouldn't share any of it. So he cursed them and made them barren. But a dragon could get around the curse by giving Enos some of his or her treasure. In return the wizard would let the dragon drink from a chalice which would restore fertility, at least for a little while." She frowned. "Eventually Enos either died or the chalice, which was also called The Dragon's Cup, was stolen, or possibly he gave it away. Anyway, for a while it supposedly belonged to a faerie queen who used it in orgies, and then it disappeared."

Storm took in both Tristan's and Pierce's startled expressions. "So is that the story you know?"

Tristan nodded slowly. "It is a little known story among..."

Big-boobed, small-brained women with nonexistent morals, the part of her that was still hurting supplied.

Storm gritted her teeth. *Enough already. Hold a pity-party when you get home if you have to, but not while you're on the job!* Geez, obviously, there were still some pockets of pain left over from the days when her breast size was a ten on a scale of zero-to-ten and her confidence level was a minus one.

She stiffened in her seat and forced the conversation forward. "So what makes you think that the Chalice of Eros and the Chalice of Enos are the same? Granted, I could buy that an 'n' could get converted to an 'r' over time—especially when records were handwritten—and Eros isn't any more real than dragons, wizards and faeries, but the Medici were, and I'm sure if McKeller and Sons was willing to insure VanDenbergh's artifact for five mil, it had to come with a pretty impressive provenance." She shrugged. "And besides, does it really matter what the true historical name of the thing is?"

"Very much so," Tristan said, his expression serious. "It widens the number of people who *will* be trying to locate the object if the family is foolish enough to leak that it was stolen to the media."

She didn't like the way he emphasized *will*. "You're saying there's going to be a mad scramble among collectors to recover this thing?"

"Yes," Pierce said, his lips twisting into a grimace. "There are others who will move to take possession of the chalice — others who are far more deadly and determined to possess it than those who think it is only a legendary cup that once belonged to the Medici Family and is famed for bringing about lust-inspired orgies."

Storm frowned. She did not like the sound of any of this. "So whoever killed VanDenbergh and took the chalice had better be looking over their shoulder?"

Pierce and Tristan exchanged a look, before Tristan said, "I'm afraid so."

"Shit."

That brought a chuckle from both men and for a second Storm smiled, forgetting her hurt. But only for a second.

"If you were the thief, what would you do with the chalice? Sit on it until the heat died down?"

"The thief will want to," Pierce said. "He or she will know it's the smart thing to do. But rumors will already be surfacing about the incredible riches that some will offer for it. It will be too tempting. So the thief will surface and will most likely die."

A chill ran through Storm and she turned her attention to Pierce. "You sound pretty sure of that, like you know what you're talking about."

His smile was like Tristan's, except there was a certain recklessness in Pierce's expression, a wildness that had unwelcome and unwanted heat coursing through Storm's body. "I've hunted treasure for...ages...and I've seen what some are capable of doing in order to obtain what they want."

"Do you know anyone I can talk to, someone who'd know what offers are out there and if the thief is shopping the chalice around?"

"Yes."

She gritted her teeth, hating to ask him for a favor—trying to keep her thoughts off what had happened in the hallway. "You'll give me the name and number?"

"No. He is not a man who would respond to your inquiry under normal circumstances. But if I take you, you might be successful in gaining information from him."

"When?"

"I will make the arrangements for later today."

Storm nodded stiffly. "Tristan has my numbers." She turned her attention to Tristan. "Can you add anything else?"

"No. Unlike Pierce, I have always pursued information as opposed to more concrete treasures."

Storm unfolded the photocopy from Trace's crime scene and laid it on Tristan's desk, noting his immediate dismay and the way he retreated, moving his chair backward slightly. "Can you tell me anything about this?"

"I'm afraid this is not something from our realm...of knowledge. This was found at the senator's house?"

Storm hesitated only briefly before nodding, finding it interesting that some of the tension left Tristan's body with her answer. "Do you know anyone I could talk to about the pentacle and symbols?"

Almost immediately his body tightened again. "No one that I trust."

She frowned and looked at Pierce, noting how his expression was almost identical to Tristan's. "What about you?"

"No."

Tristan reached over and refolded the picture, as though the very sight of it continued to disturb him. "Despite what the newspapers are saying this morning, it is unlikely that the two murders are connected. One interested in the Chalice of Enos would have no interest in the Sword of Vengeance. And there is no truth in the stories of recharging the chalice's power with the shedding of blood. That has never been part of the cup's history." He frowned slightly, as though he were going to add more, but thought better of it.

"What do you know about the sword?"

Tristan shrugged. "Not much more than what was in the newspaper."

Storm looked at Pierce. He shook his head. "When Tristan called to tell me you were coming here, I had time only to make a few phone calls, but I learned nothing from them. Perhaps if I had a picture of this sword, I could learn more."

"I'll try and get you one." She picked up the folded picture and slipped it back into her pocket as she mentally ran through her questions and their answers, trying to ensure she'd covered everything and wouldn't need to call on Tristan again. "I think that covers it." She stood and offered a handshake, bracing herself against his puzzled look, his questioning eyes when she didn't let him carry her hand to his lips as she had the previous evening, nor did she let him hold it beyond the time required for a polite gesture.

To Pierce she nodded and said, "I'll wait for your call."

He rose from his chair, exchanging looks with his cousin before saying, "Until later then," and leaving.

When Storm turned to follow him, Tristan moved around his desk, catching up with her at the door, trapping her against it, his hand holding it closed while the front of his body pressed to her back. "You're upset."

Storm took a shuddering breath. Wishing she could say she was immune to him. But even angry and hurt, having his warm body pressed to hers and feeling his erection against her buttocks made her ache for him.

She'd hoped to escape without a confrontation, without shining a great whopping spotlight on how hurt and humiliated she felt, at how embarrassed she was about reading more into last night than was really there. Moonlight madness was what her grandmother would probably have called it. But then Granny K had been a believer in werewolves and vampires and other creatures of the night.

"I need to get back to work," she said.

Tristan's cheek rubbed against her hair. "You're upset about what happened in the hallway. I'm sorry I didn't warn you about Pierce. I invited him here because I knew he would be a help to you on your case. And he was curious about you after I told him about you."

Her heart jumped, her body weakening traitorously, her words escaping before she could stop them. "Told him what?" *That I was easy?*

"That you'd been in my thoughts since the day you visited my office—that even though you were involved in another high-profile case, I wouldn't stay away this time. I didn't think you would be taken in by him, though I knew he might be tempted to try and steal a kiss. I never meant for you to be upset. I'm sorry, Storm."

She closed her eyes and leaned her forehead against the door. She wanted to believe him—desperately. And that scared her.

"It went a lot further than a stolen kiss."

"Is that the reason you're upset?" He rubbed his cheek against her hair again, sighing softly. "Please don't be. Neither of us meant to hurt you. Pierce is my friend, my cousin, the brother of my heart. If it went further than a kiss, then it happened because he was genuinely attracted to you, not because he was amusing himself at your expense."

Tristan's hands moved to her sides, sliding down and around to pull her tightly against his body. "Say you forgive me," he whispered. "Say you forgive us both. Let us make it up to you by helping you with your case."

She rubbed her forehead against the smooth surface of the door, some of her innate humor choosing that moment to return. Maybe this was her punishment for letting herself fantasize about being in bed with both of them. God, could it get any worse? Being trapped in the company of two gorgeous, orgasm-inspiring men?

"Tristan…"

"Forgive us. Spend time with us," he whispered, perhaps already sensing her capitulation, because even as his plea succeeded in pushing the last of her hurt away, his hand was moving around to cup her mound through her pants. "I hated leaving you last night, and afterward I cursed myself for not convincing you to call me when you were done." She moaned as his fingers traced over her erect clit. He grew bolder, opening her pants with his other hand, then slipping inside, going right to her warmth and wetness.

She gasped, unable to stop herself from arching into his touch, from reaching back and circling his neck with her arms. He groaned into her hair as one hand pushed up underneath her shirt until he could palm her breast, taking the nipple, already made tender by Pierce, between his fingers.

Storm cried out in response and he shifted to the other breast, squeezing and toying with the nipple, asking, "Did he touch you here? Is that why you're so sensitive?"

It should have made her mad, or embarrassed, but the way he said it had heat uncoiling in Storm's belly and moisture rushing from her channel. The hunger for him building as she felt his cock surge against her buttocks in reaction to the arousal bathing his fingers.

"Your body is beautiful, Storm. But your mind and your dedication to finding justice outshine your physical attributes. Is it such a surprise that Pierce would be drawn to you? That he would forget himself and want you to respond to him?"

His hand left her cunt, moving to join his other one underneath her shirt, coating her nipple with her own arousal and making her shiver as his fingers alternated between gentle presses and firm tugs that had her vagina clenching and her womb fluttering.

"Let's finish what we started last night," he whispered, taking her earlobe between his lips, sucking and teasing the ultrasensitive flesh.

"Your coeds…"

He gave her earlobe a small painful nip. "Not *my* coeds. They are children who think they're adults. Only a woman can meet my needs. Only you, Storm. Ease me. Forgive me. Let me bury myself in your warmth."

"Someone will…"

"Pierce is in the hallway. He will not let anyone interrupt us."

She should say no. She knew she should. But when he drew her away from the door, she didn't protest. He bent her over, placing her hands on the edge of his desk, opening her shirt and bra so that her breasts hung free and the crystal in the necklace bathed the area around them in color. He laughed as his hand covered the delicate pair of faeries for a brief second, and then he was pulling her pants and shoes off, leaving her in nothing but the open shirt and bra, the black thong.

Storm thrilled at the way his breath changed, at the way his hands lingered on her bare flesh, conveying without words just how desirable he found her. It was like something out of a naughty schoolgirl fantasy, to be positioned like this over the teacher's desk, and Storm decided to embrace it, to enjoy every second with this man who made her feel so incredibly desirable.

She looked backward over her shoulder, her heart racing at the raw hunger she saw on his face, at the way he had his cock in hand, at how its deep purple head was already glistening with precum. She spread her legs then, arching to give him a good view of how wet the insides of her thighs were, provocatively showing off her firm buttocks and the way the thong hugged her body.

He moved in then, cupping her hips and slowly sliding her underwear down before he positioned his erection between her thighs and rubbed back and forth over her swollen lower lips, coating himself in her wetness until she couldn't stand it any longer, until she moaned, changing the angle so that the head of him lodged at her entrance.

He groaned and his hands tightened on her hips, holding her still when she would have impaled herself on him. "Tristan," she pleaded and he slid home, filling her as no other man had ever done.

She cried out, unable to hold the sound inside as he started thrusting, his balls slapping against her swollen flesh and sending ice-hot bursts of pleasure through her clit. She widened her stance and lowered her chest, changing the angle so he could forge deeper. His strokes became harder, fiercer as his hands moved to her breasts, his touch sure, possessive, a man who knew how to give and receive pleasure.

Storm tightened around his cock, milking it as his fingers squeezed and released her nipples, driving them both higher until they were shaking, panting, straining, and then crying out in release.

Tristan rubbed his cheek against the back of her shirt, whispering her name as his body continued to tremble. She wanted to close her legs and trap his cock inside her forever, and as if wanting the same thing, his arms moved around, holding her against him, his penis still filling her channel.

"Come to my house for dinner tonight," he said. "Don't make me sleep alone again tonight, only able to touch you in my dreams."

"I'll try," she said. "If I can get away from the case."

His grip tightened. "Even if it's only for a few hours, see me tonight. Let me love you where I can take my time, where I can show you how beautiful I find you, how much pleasure we can share."

Storm closed her eyes and rocked back and forth on his cock. "I think I have an idea about the pleasure."

He laughed softly. "I can do better."

She couldn't help but smile. "If I make it to your place, I'll expect you to keep that promise."

His hands slid to her breasts, cupping them gently, almost reverently as his palms smoothed over suddenly tight nipples. "I'll keep any promise I give you, Storm."

She shivered, suddenly wishing desperately that it was the end of the day. "I'd better get going if I have any hope of meeting you for dinner."

His hands left her breasts and trailed down to her abdomen. "I don't want to leave your body," he whispered.

"I don't want you to leave."

They stood for another moment, savoring the closeness, the intimate connection, and then he reluctantly pulled out of her, leaving her feeling empty and needy.

Chapter Seven

✠

Dylan shoved his hands into his jacket pockets and maneuvered the garment in an effort to cover the front of his pants. Fuck. He should have let Trace go into Inner Magick alone. Seeing Aislinn and Trace together had only primed the pump. *Big time.* That was the only reason he'd accept for the state of his cock. A witch! He didn't care how often he'd gone for red hair and green eyes, the supernatural shit was guaranteed to make his dick go limp. The problem was that seeing Aislinn and Trace together had left him thinking about sex on a subconscious level so that when they got to Seraphine Jordain's place…

Christ, he couldn't remember the last time he'd gotten this hard, this fast. And the damn ring…it felt like it was going to melt down on his finger. But when he'd slipped it off momentarily, he'd actually felt worse—like something important was missing and taking his luck with it.

Son of a bitch. A witch, for god's sake. Aislinn must be laughing her head off.

Dylan frowned, thinking about Aislinn's reaction to the symbols in the crime scene photograph, about her concern and the underlying fear that had radiated off her when she asked them to be careful. No. Aislinn wasn't laughing. But Trace sure as hell was enjoying himself. Yeah, his partner knew he was sporting a woody big enough to hit a home run with. Goddamn. What'd he ever do to deserve this?

Dylan watched Seraphine's expression as Trace set the folder containing the photo from the Harper crime scene down on the coffee table and yammered on about confidentiality. He told himself that it was standard procedure for one cop to concentrate on reading the subject while the other did the talking, but son of a bitch, the truth was that he couldn't seem to take his eyes off the witch—not that he really believed in that bullshit.

Christ, she had a mouth made for exploring a man's dick. And that knowing little smile she'd sent his way when he eased into the chair… A night in his bed would…

His cock jerked in anticipation while his thoughts screeched to a halt. Fuck that. No way. He'd jerk off in the shower before he'd get involved with someone like her. There were plenty of women out there, plenty of redheads. Hell, he'd spent the night in a redhead's bed last night. Candy? No, Stephanie. Shit. That didn't sound right either. Hell, it didn't matter. The point was. He didn't need *this* redhead.

He leaned in, catching a trace of her elusive scent and feeling a moment of uneasiness when his eyes settled on the bracelet she was wearing, on the green stone that almost seemed alive, the one that looked identical to the stone in his ring.

Trace opened the folder and Dylan's thoughts snapped back to being a cop and getting this case handled before it turned into something even worse. "This is the drawing we found at the scene," Trace said. "What are we dealing with here?"

There was a long moment of silence between the question and Seraphine's answer. And then Dylan wished like hell he hadn't heard her say it.

"A demon."

"A demon?" Trace asked, and Dylan had to give his partner credit for sounding like he believed it was possible.

Seraphine smiled, a small hint of movement that somehow managed to convey amusement along with an understanding that she knew the cops across the table from her didn't believe the answer she'd given them any more than they were going to accept what she was about to tell them.

She turned the photograph, reorienting it so that the symbol at the tip of her fingernail was at the top. "This is the demon's name. The rest of the invocation commands him to appear as a man, binds him to a particular area, and orders him to use a sword to slay the next person who enters—as long as it is not the one who summoned him—and then to place the head of the victim on the pentacle before hiding the sword in a certain place and returning to the realm you would think of as Hell."

"All of that is in these symbols?" Trace said, not managing this time to hide his skepticism.

Seraphine laughed, a soft trill of sound that shot straight to Dylan's cock, wrapping around it and stroking, making his teeth and ass clench as he felt drops of precum escape the engorged head. "Yes, all that is contained in the symbols."

She eased back in her chair and her amusement faded. "I know you don't want to believe me." Elegant fingers toyed with the envelope in her lap. "But Aislinn has asked that I share my information with you." Her eyes dipped for a moment, straying to Dylan's hand and making it seem as though the ring on his finger heated up another couple of degrees. A hint of a smile returned to Seraphine's face. "And now I find myself compelled to assist you for other reasons."

Her fingernails tapped the envelope gently, drawing Dylan's attention to them and sending a shiver up his spine as he envisioned them clawing at his back and buttocks while he took her, his cock ramming in and out of her as her loud, throaty screams of pleasure and hoarse demands for more filled the room.

Christ. What was wrong with him—beside the obvious hard-on and the lust he couldn't seem to suppress? Yeah, he'd been attracted to his share of women, never had a problem getting it up, getting it in, and getting it off, all while making sure the woman involved enjoyed it, too. But this was way beyond anything he'd had to deal with before.

Fuck, it almost reminded him of how it was when Trace first hooked up with Aislinn, hell, how it still was between them. Dylan gritted his teeth and focused on the picture, figuring maybe asking questions would keep his mind off his dick. "So if

I'm reading you right, our perp has actually studied this kind of stuff—what is it called, black magic—and is using bona fide symbols in a way that would be understandable to other practitioners. Am I correct?"

"It's called by many names, some more accurate than others. But in answer to your question, yes, the person you are looking for is knowledgeable about calling and commanding demons. And in answer to the next question, someone interested in this kind of magic would be extremely careful to keep his or her interest hidden—not because the interest is evil or wrong—but because society has already judged anyone who would summon a demon as evil. There are people I can talk to on your behalf, but I'll need to tread carefully, and it's possible that it will lead nowhere. It would help if you could leave the photograph. There are distinctions between practitioners, variances in the size of their pentacles and the way they draw their symbols."

Trace frowned. "You won't give us names?"

"No. I'm sorry, I can't. A great deal of trust is involved when one person shares this type of knowledge with another person."

"We're trying to solve a murder here," Dylan growled. "A kid just out of college who had her life snuffed out."

"And I will assist you by asking those who might know of a connection between the murder and a practitioner who is well versed in demonology." She met his gaze without flinching. "You'll have to trust me. Or not. It is the only way I can aid you beyond sharing what I can about the incantation in the photograph."

Trace sighed. "Let's get back to the incantation then." This time he pulled a notebook out of his pocket and had her repeat her interpretation of the symbols.

Dylan tried to force his thoughts along the same lines as the perp's thoughts, which was a stretch since he didn't believe in this bullshit—even though he did believe that Seraphine knew what she was talking about and so her interpretation was the one the perp would be acting on.

"First point," Dylan said, writing in his own notebook. "The way you read the symbols, this entire scenario was staged to commit murder. And it didn't need to be a particular victim, just whoever walked into the room. Right?"

"Yes. The victim could have been anyone other than the summoner." Seraphine smiled slightly and ran a glossy fingernail along the photographed pentacle. "This would have been done beforehand, most likely in goat's blood, though possibly using chicken's blood."

Trace grunted, surprising Dylan by admitting, "Goat."

"Next point," Dylan said, checking his notes and once again trying to put himself in the same frame of mind as someone who actually believed a demon was going to show up. "What do you mean by 'bound' to a particular area?"

This time her smile reminded him of a teacher with a lackluster pupil who was suddenly starting to shine. "There would be limits as to how far the demon could travel. Depending on the summoner's confidence level, there might even be a double circle. For instance, a salt circle anchored with symbols inside the room where the murder was committed, and a second, larger circle around the home—all to ensure that the demon didn't escape and perhaps prey on the one who summoned it." She leaned forward and extended her hand toward Dylan's notebook. "May I?"

"Sure." He handed it to her and almost cried out as fire raced through his body and straight to his cock when her fingers brushed his skin.

She made a small gasp, quickly retreating with the notebook, though nothing could hide the telltale peaks of her nipples or the faint rush of color across her face. In that instant, all Dylan could think about was moving into her personal space and peeling her shirt open so that he could feast on her breasts first with his eyes and then with his mouth. Christ, he had to have her. He would have her. He shifted, ready to stand and drag her into his arms but Trace's choked-off laugh caused Dylan's attention to waver long enough for him to come to his senses.

Fuck. What the hell was wrong with him? He stood abruptly. Knowing he was never going to hear the end of it, but he couldn't take much more of this. "I'm going to step outside for a minute. I need some fresh air."

Neither Trace nor Seraphine said anything until she placed Dylan's notebook on the table in front of Trace. A line split the page into two portions. On the top half, she'd drawn several different symbols. On the bottom half only one. "These are the marks I'd expect to find along the binding circle," she said as she tapped above the line.

"All of them?"

"One or a combination of them."

Trace thought about the layout of the senator's house. The room where his swords were was like a converted den. No windows and only the one door. "The circle is probably close to the walls." He made a note to check with the crime scene guys and see if they'd found traces of salt when they processed the room.

Seraphine nodded. "The symbols would probably have been placed near the windows and doors. Once a demon is summoned it must remain in the shape the summoner commanded. It is constrained within the limits of that form."

"That's why the incantation said the demon was to appear as a man. It would need hands to hold a sword, arms to swing it." Trace's frown deepened. "It would also take a lot of strength to cut through vertebra and sever a head from a body with one stroke."

"Yes. A demon would have more strength than an ordinary human." She grimaced. "I misspoke earlier. The translation literally says that the demon is to take the shape of a human."

Almost immediately something that had been bothering Trace cleared up. There'd been no sign of a struggle, nothing to indicate that Anita Vorhaus had felt threatened or worried. And yet she'd gone into the weapon room instead of going directly to the senator's kitchen and retrieving the papers he'd left on the counter. "Could the demon have taken the form of someone the victim knew and lured her into the room where she was killed?"

"Possibly, but unless the demon knew the person it was imitating well, there would be subtle differences that would make someone instinctively wary. Did the victim die afraid? Was there a lingering sense of terror when you entered the room where she was killed?"

"I don't know if she died afraid. She didn't have time to defend herself, and there was no evidence of rape or other trauma." Her second question struck a chord that Trace's subconscious had heard, but he hadn't tuned into, and probably wouldn't have admitted to even if he had. Some crime scenes resonated with horror or brutality. This one hadn't. It had seemed professional, despite the gruesome nature of the murder and the fact that most crimes involving blades were more personal, as though the perp needed to feel the damage and death through the steel.

Seraphine's smile was sad. "Then the demon probably presented itself as a non-threatening female."

Trace didn't want to ask. Hell, his gut was already twisting and burning. "Did Vorhaus have a chance of winning against the demon once she knew it wanted to kill her?"

"If she'd gotten out of the circle she could have escaped. If she'd been able to give it what would be a mortal wound to a human, then it would have *died* and returned to its own realm, though it would be obligated to return later to do the summoner's bidding."

Trace tapped the single symbol on the bottom half of the page and noted that it also appeared in the photograph. "And this one? You said the demon was supposed to place the sword in a certain spot when it was done. X marks the spot, right?"

"Yes."

"So if our perp is a true believer, then we should find the sword where this mark is?"

"If it hasn't been removed by the summoner."

Trace grimaced, knowing he didn't want to go where this was heading, but he was too good a cop to ignore it just because he didn't really want to know. For Christ-sake, he was heartbonded to a half-elf, though there were still plenty of days when he tried his best to pretend they were just your average married couple. He saw too much weird shit from regular humans to want to venture into even stranger worlds.

His eyes settled on the bracelet and he actually managed a laugh. "Aislinn's work?"

"Yes." Seraphine's eyebrows arched as she made a point of looking at his wedding band, a heartmate joining ring that had once belonged to Aislinn's father. "I see you know what it means."

"You and Dylan?" Trace couldn't resist asking.

Her smile said she was up to the challenge. "Yes."

He shook his head, not sure who to feel sorry for. "Okay, lay it out for me while Dylan is taking a breather. You believe a demon killed the girl?"

"Yes."

"So we're talking Satan worshipper?"

"Perhaps. But not necessarily. In this case, think of the demon as a weapon—one most often used as a destructive instrument, though they don't necessarily have to be used in such a way."

"Why bother, why not just hire someone to do it?" Trace said, thinking out loud.

"Maybe the killer wanted to prove something to the senator."

"Extortion?"

Seraphine laughed, a warm sound that made Trace smile. "You're the detective. I'll leave that to you."

"I guess we can't conjure up the demon and ask who had him kill the girl?"

She shook her head. "There's always a price to pay when summoning a demon. It's not a bargain to be entered into lightly."

"So our perp is going to get away with murder? I can't take this stuff into court."

"You won't need to."

Trace frowned, not liking the sureness in her voice, or the underlying message that justice would be served—just under another system. "Even if the perp deserves it, I can't close my eyes to a murder," he warned.

She smiled, a quick flash of amusement before she shook her head and repeated, "You won't need to. There are occult laws in place, many of them centering on keeping a barrier between the normal world and the supernatural world. To summon a demon for a crime like this opens the door of possibility that the same demon might one day be sent to punish the summoner. Whoever called the demon would know this. They'd also know that most demons, by their very nature, don't like being used by ones they consider inferior. Torment is often a demon's appetizer, the main dish being death by whatever means the demon chooses. Human prisons, by contrast, look like a safe haven."

"So find the perp and he'll most likely confess in order to avoid a demon with a cause?"

Seraphine laughed. "I'm sure it won't be quite that easy. Don't underestimate the murderer's cunning. Demons almost always bargain, and even then, they look for loopholes that allow them to play with the one stupid enough—or brave enough, depending on your point of view—to call on them. Whoever called this demon will be both confident and intelligent."

She unclasped her necklace and removed two charms from it, touching them both briefly to her lips before handing them to Trace. "These will help protect you from the things you can't see while you search for the killer. As long as it's on you somewhere, it'll act as a ward." Her lips curved into a slight smile. "If you could ensure that Dylan keeps one of them with him…"

Trace grinned. His partner didn't stand a chance against this particular redhead.

Chapter Eight

** හ**

Lust roared through Pierce at the sight of Storm, a hot flame that flared deep in his center and threatened to burn away his control. He tightened his grip on the steering wheel in response, knowing that he didn't dare touch her as she slid into the Jaguar, filling the small space with her mortal essence and feminine scent.

By The Fates, he'd almost managed to convince himself that his reaction to her at the university was to be expected, a result of her having been with Tristan, of having taken some of his cousin's essence within herself—the tie to air, coupled with a body made for pleasure, fueling Pierce's own desire.

He shifted in his seat, already knowing that it was pointless. His cock was hot and hard, as anxious as he was to feel her soft female flesh, to explore and caress and consume, to tunnel into her wet core made slick with welcome for him.

Let the dragons chase their chalice. Let them have the priceless treasure. His hunt for it had ended in the instant he'd looked into her storm-gray eyes and felt her hands on his body, firm and electric, her touch sending a wild jolt of desire throughout him, making his breathing rough and fast.

A wave of heated need pulsed from his cock to his heart as his gaze met hers. He wanted to pull her into his arms and kiss her, taste her, to rip open her shirt and watch her breasts flush with desire as the nipples tightened into hard pebbles, demanding that he lean forward and feast on them.

As if sensing the direction of his thoughts, she looked away, color rising in her face. Her body stiffened and she tried to escape by bringing up the case, asking, "Who are we going to see?"

Pleasure and an unexpected tenderness moved through Pierce. Despite the desire raging through his body, he didn't give in to the temptation to dazzle Storm with fey glamour so that she would come to him, yield to him, beg him to take her now in any manner that suited him. There would be time enough later for her to burn underneath him, and then between his body and Tristan's — by her own choice.

"We're going to see a cousin of Tielo's, my business partner. Tielo will be there as well, interceding on our behalf if necessary."

Storm's body remembered Pierce's touch and reacted to his presence despite her mind's insistence that she was not going to lust after Tristan's cousin. She shifted in her seat, fiddling with the seat belt as she forced her mind to concentrate on the case and nothing but the case. When she thought she could look at him again without fantasizing, she glanced his way and said, "Maybe you should just lay it out for me so there's no misunderstanding. Who are we going to see and why do we need your partner there? This *is* a murder investigation, I'd expect your contact to cooperate willingly, but if he won't…"

Pierce's lips curled upward in a sultry smile and his eyelids lowered, unwillingly making heat pool in Storm's labia. "Do you always fight fire with fire?" he asked, somehow making her think of hungry flames licking greedily at kindling.

"I do what I need to do in order to get the job done and I don't put up with a bunch of bullshit. Does that answer your question?"

The smile went from sultry to amused. "You were well named. I can see why you captured Tristan so easily." *Why you captured me.*

Storm's pulse jumped at the words she imagined in the air between them. She looked away, not wanting Pierce to see the hope in her face, the confusion. Had she really captured Tristan? And if she had, how come it now didn't feel like it was enough? How come she was having to fight to suppress the memory of Pierce's hands on her breasts, his cock between her legs as they dry-humped like a couple of desperate teenagers in a corner at recess? How come the fantasy of having both men together invaded her thoughts every time she dropped her guard?

Against her will her nipples ached, and she could feel more blood rushing to fill her cunt lips as she remembered Tristan's whispered words. *Did he touch you here? Is that why you're so sensitive? Your body is beautiful, Storm. But your mind and your dedication to finding justice outshine your physical attributes. Is it such a surprise that Pierce would be drawn to you? That he would forget himself and want you to respond to him?*

Pierce laughed softly, almost as if he could read her thoughts, and her nipples tightened further in response, becoming hard, visible points underneath the bra and shirt she'd changed into so that Pierce could drop her off at Tristan's house for dinner after this mysterious meeting was finished.

She turned back toward him, his quick glance at her chest sending a burst of flame straight to her clit. "Stop playing games, Pierce. Who are we going to see and why all the cloak-and-dagger stuff?"

His eyes flashed in concert with his smile. "Severn Damek. And by your expression, the other part of your question has also been answered."

Severn Damek. Shit.

Storm resisted the urge to pull out her cell phone and call Brady to tell him where she was going. The elusive billionaire had been a major source of speculation for not only the press, but for the police. There were rumors that he was the head of an organized crime family, there was speculation that he'd fled from another country with untold treasure and that even now there was a price on his head. But the truth of the matter was that very few people knew anything about Severn Damek other than the fact that he owned a huge, walled estate outside town, and didn't welcome visitors into his home.

"When we were in Tristan's office, you said there are others who are far more deadly and determined to possess the Chalice of Enos than those who think it once belonged to the Medici Family. I assume you were talking about Damek."

"Yes. Though he's not the only one who wants the chalice."

"So the fact that he's willing to meet with me must mean he already knows it's been stolen."

"Yes. When it comes to valuable items, especially ones of great history, he is an extremely serious collector. I imagine he spends a small fortune paying informants — among others."

"Others, being thieves?"

"Perhaps." Pierce cut a look over at Storm. "A word of warning, admire any of the treasures you might see in his home, but don't touch them unless he invites you to do so. He's very possessive of the things he owns."

"Sounds like a prince of a guy."

Pierce surprised her with an amused laugh. "Yes. He is that. Though to his credit, he doesn't insist on formality."

Storm's eyes narrowed, but before she could pursue the idea that Severn was somehow royalty, they arrived at the heavy gates leading into his estate. Her breath caught at the sight of the beautiful dark blue dragons that were carved in bold relief on either side of the entrance, the threads of red woven through them glowing hot like embers among coal.

Pierce rolled down his window and touched the button on the intercom. As soon as he announced himself, the gates swung open to a view of amazing flower gardens and an elegant house that caught the red-gold rays of the setting sun in its windows and made Storm think of a phoenix rising from the flames.

"Incredible," she breathed, trying to capture the image in her mind so that she could share it with Sophie. Her cousin, with her wild imagination, would soak this up and somehow work it into one of her novels, turning it into a fantasyscape...or something darker, depending on what she was writing.

A long-haired blond opened the front door for them just as they reached it. He nodded to Pierce and said, "Severn waits in his study for you." He turned without a word and moved down a hallway rich with tapestries, stopping only when he got to an open door, motioning them to continue inside, though he didn't follow.

Study was a misnomer. The room would have been a welcomed addition to any museum. It sparkled with a collection of dragons that left Storm stunned by their beauty, unable to do anything but shift her focus from one statue to another in amazement — until her eyes finally encountered the man leaning casually against a bookcase, the lighting casting him in a powerful wash of red and deep blue.

Shit. She'd never bothered trying to picture Severn, but she'd always assumed he'd probably be an old man.

Wrong! The man studying her was mouthwateringly gorgeous with his deep auburn hair and the dragon raging across his bared chest.

"Where's Tielo?" Pierce asked and Severn's lips quirked upward.

"I told him that there was no need to attend this meeting. It suited my purposes to meet the detective who is looking for the chalice. So I assured him that you would leave in the same condition in which you arrived."

Storm frowned, not liking the arrogance or the implication that others had left in far worse condition than the one they'd arrived in. Severn laughed and moved forward with lethal grace, stopping so close to her that she felt scorched by the heat radiating off his skin.

His eyes met hers before moving to her chest and she stiffened involuntarily as his nostrils flared and his eyes glittered. Pierce moved in so that his body was touching hers and she could feel tension rushing through him, but before she could tell Severn to get the hell out of her personal space, an odd thought came to her, making her pause just long enough for their host's next words to confirm what she'd been thinking. "Let me see your necklace."

The request was a purring growl that coming from Pierce or Tristan would have made Storm's cunt and nipples tighten with anticipation, but coming from the man in front of her, it only made her frown deepen, though a small part of her wanted to roll her eyes and say, *Don't you think you're taking the dragon thing too seriously? Get over yourself.*

Instead her hand moved to cover the hidden faeries and their crystal. "No. You've got plenty of your own treasure to admire. Can we move on to the purpose of this visit and talk about the Chalice of Enos?"

Dark blue eyes narrowed as though Severn wasn't used to being defied and didn't like it now. Pierce's hand moved to circle Storm's upper arm in a gesture that was both protective and possessive, sending a bolt of fire through Storm.

The moment lingered, long and tense, before finally Severn nodded curtly and stepped back, moving around to take a seat behind an antique desk that also sported a variety of jewel-encrusted dragons. "Tell me the name of the person who created the necklace for you," he surprised Storm by saying.

How did he know that the necklace had been made for her? Or was he just guessing it was special because she wouldn't share it with him? Or was he testing her somehow—though she didn't know why he'd bother. "Tell me whether or not you've heard anything about the chalice surfacing."

Severn laughed. "That assumes the information I requested of you is of equal value to what you ask of me."

"Or maybe it means that we should get down to business. You're not known for inviting people to your home, especially policemen. So obviously there's a reason for me being here."

He steepled his fingers in front of him. "Very well then. When you begin to look into the history of the chalice, you will find that my family has been trying to acquire it for years. There have been a number of occasions when we were close to achieving our goal, but it slipped from our grasp and disappeared from sight—just as it has done once again. Several weeks ago I was in negotiations with a man who called himself Richard Stewart. Just as we were nearing an agreement, he claimed that the chalice had once again been stolen. At the time, I thought it was a ploy to get me to offer more money, or perhaps he was using me to lure another bidder into buying the cup. I don't generally deal pleasantly with those who think to cheat or play with me...but for the chalice, I was willing to be more flexible. Unfortunately, I don't know whether Mr. Stewart was telling the truth or not about the chalice. I heard nothing more of its whereabouts until the police were called to the VanDenbergh estate."

Storm gritted her teeth at the implication that someone, perhaps someone on the force, must have leaked the information to Damek. But at least the media hadn't found out about it. Yet.

"Where can I find Stewart?"

"A good question."

Storm frowned. "He disappeared?"

"Yes." Severn's expression darkened. "Or a man by that name never existed at all."

"You never met him?"

"No. He operated through intermediaries who also claim that they never met him. I've spent a large amount of time and money verifying the truth of their statements."

Storm shivered at the hint of menace in his voice. He was not a man it would be wise to thwart, or to lie to. "So what makes you think Stewart was legitimate? For all you know, he was trying to pull a con on you."

A small smile played over Severn's lips. "There are any number of little-known identifying features on the chalice, tiny images woven into the larger tapestry of the story engraved on its surface. Given specific questions, Stewart could correctly describe those images."

Storm's mind raced. Was this why VanDenbergh's lawyer was stonewalling about where the chalice had come from? Did he know it was stolen property? Or was there something more sinister going on? Had the mysterious Stewart always intended to sell the artifact, then steal it back, perhaps planning to do it over and over again if it was successful? Definitely a risky proposition.

Even though she hadn't seen armed guards patrolling Severn's home, she didn't doubt it was well protected, just as she didn't doubt that the elaborate collection of dragons were only the tip of the iceberg when it came to Severn's treasures. And given how thoroughly he seemed to embrace the dragon as his personal symbol, only a fool would try to steal from him. Mythological dragons were notorious for both collecting treasure, and guarding it well.

"How did Stewart first make contact with you?" Storm asked.

"A picture of the chalice was delivered to one of my family members while he was," his gaze moved to encompass Pierce, "enjoying a friendly game of chance at Drake's Lair."

Storm's glance followed Severn's and found Pierce frowning. "We've got surveillance at the club. Tielo…"

Severn smiled slightly. "Has already explored that lead. The messenger delivering the photograph was paid in cash by a woman he'd never seen before, or since."

Storm's mind circled through facts and suppositions, coming inevitably to the conclusion that she wouldn't be here if Severn hadn't already explored every possible path that might lead from the mysterious Stewart to the chalice. So the fact that she *was* here, and that he was *so generously* sharing information with her meant he had somehow concluded she was his best bet at locating the chalice once again, and acquiring it.

"I assume you've spoken with the VanDenbergh family or their lawyer about purchasing the chalice should it resurface?" Storm asked.

"Along with giving them my condolences for their loss, of course." His expression was so bland that Storm almost laughed. His next words confirmed her initial impression of the family's interest in the chalice. "But I doubt seriously that the family will pursue its return. They seemed quite content with the prospect of a large insurance settlement."

"So the police are your best bet for locating it at this point?"

"Unfortunately, yes."

She frowned, irritated by his answer even though she'd asked the question. "Don't expect us to contact you."

He laughed, a flash of white teeth that made her think of a dragon getting ready to breath fire. "That won't be necessary."

"Who had the chalice before Stewart?"

"A hundred years ago, when my family last located it, the chalice belonged to an English lord. It was stolen from his estate days before it was to go to auction. We don't know where it's been since that time."

Storm's eyebrows lifted slightly. So he'd been serious about his family's long quest to take possession of the chalice. She looked again at all the dragons in the room, including the red and dark blue one on Severn's chest. A small smile formed. If his ancestors were like him, was it any surprise that they were obsessed with finding the Dragon's Cup?

"Anything else you can tell me about Stewart, VanDenbergh or the chalice?"

"No."

"What about the Medici Sword of Vengeance?"

He shook his head. "It's not the kind of treasure that interests me. But I anticipated that you would ask and made some calls as a show of good faith. There have been no murmurs about it being available." His fingers steepled again. "In fact, there is some question as to how authentic the senator's treasure really is."

Storm's heart gave a jerk of excitement. "You're saying it's a fake?" She wondered how much it was insured for.

"I'm suggesting that its value is questionable, though I'm sure its worth is well documented." He smiled slightly and

Storm knew then that any further information he had would be used later, as a bargaining chip.

"You said that you were sent a photo of the chalice. I'd like to take it with me. Maybe our lab guys can pull something from it."

"I'm afraid it's not possible to give you the original, though I can provide you with a copy of the picture." He retrieved a photograph from his top drawer and handed it to Storm.

She studied it for a moment. The picture they'd gotten from Miles Terry, the insurance representative, was better than this one, though the one she held in her hand appeared to focus less on the jewels around the rim of the cup and more on the intricate scenes depicted on the body of the chalice. And unlike the other picture, which presented the chalice as if it was on display, the photo sent to Severn showed the Dragon's Cup in a velvet-lined traveling case.

Clever presentation? Or had Stewart not wanted to risk capturing any piece of a background that might somehow identify where the chalice was?

Storm looked up to find Severn studying her intently. "Is there a number I can reach you at if I have additional questions?" she asked.

He tilted his head slightly and retrieved a card from a dragon-shaped holder, holding it out to her, but not releasing it immediately when her fingers touched the opposite edge. "Satisfy my curiosity. Let me see your necklace."

Storm hesitated, strangely reluctant to show it to him. His eyes flashed with amusement. He gave a small laugh and surprised her by touching his chest and saying, "Despite the influence of the dragon, I can promise that your treasure is safe from me."

She nodded and he released the card. She tucked it into her pocket and pulled the necklace from beneath her blouse. The light in Severn's study brought out myriad shifting colors—the gold and lavender Storm had noticed when Aislinn first gave the necklace to her, the blue and green she'd seen first thing in the morning, and now there was a touch of red swirling inside the crystal.

"Priceless," Severn said. "A gift that few are lucky enough to receive. It was designed for you?"

"Yes."

"A name please. I might be interested in having some work done."

Storm wasn't prepared to give him Aislinn's name, but she could compromise. "If you're really in the market for something unique, you should visit Inner Magick."

Recognition flickered in Severn's eyes. "Of course. Your necklace would have to be from there."

Chapter Nine

ॐ

A swirl of conflicting emotion surged through Storm when they stopped in front of Tristan's beautiful Victorian house and Pierce got out of the car, moving around to open her door and take her arm, his touch remaining, his fingers continuing to burn through the fabric of her shirt even after she was standing. "Are you eating dinner with us?" she found herself asking.

His eyes darkened, locking onto hers. "Would you like me to join you and Tristan?"

In a heartbeat the fantasies she'd experienced on and off all day returned full force, and she didn't hide from the truth she could see in his eyes, that he was thinking about joining them for more than dinner. A rush of moisture dampened her panties and she licked her lips, wondering how she'd gone from being enthralled with Tristan to wanting Pierce as well.

"Is Tristan expecting you for dinner?" she countered.

"I'm sure he's leaving it up to you as to whether or not to invite me in," Pierce said, moving closer, surrounding her with the heat of his body and subtly reminding her of how wonderfully they'd fit together when she'd mistaken him for Tristan in the university hallway, when she'd wrapped her legs around him as they brought each other to orgasm.

"Come in for dinner then," she said, unable to stop herself from issuing the invitation.

Tristan met them at the door, pulling Storm into his embrace and melding his lips to hers, his tongue stroking into her mouth in a way that promised he'd do more later. "Your meeting with Severn went well?" he asked several minutes later when he lifted his mouth from hers.

"Well enough," Storm said. "No concrete leads, but some very useful information."

"Good." He rubbed his cheek against hers. "I had reservations about Pierce taking you there. It's always risky parading treasure in front of Damek."

Storm laughed. "I can see why he's got the reputation he does. He takes the dragon thing to an extreme. He zeroed in on my necklace almost immediately." Color washed over her cheeks. "I have to admit, it's the first time that a guy has stared at my chest like that and not been interested in anything under my shirt except my jewelry."

Tristan laughed, eyes sparkling as a quick flash of a smile appeared on his face. "Severn was probably only momentarily distracted by your necklace. You're the treasure I was worried about him trying to acquire. He hasn't yet found a mate." Tristan brushed his mouth across hers. "It's a good thing Severn's interest in you was limited to the cup. Otherwise Pierce would have found it necessary to challenge him to a fight."

Warmth flowed straight to Storm's heart at his words, along with an awareness of Pierce standing close enough that she could feel his body heat against her back, making it seem as though he was connected to the two of them—just like it had felt when Tristan kissed her in the university hallway.

Storm leaned in and captured Tristan's lips, teasing along the seam of his mouth with her tongue. He responded, deepening the kiss, his hands going to her hips and pulling them tightly against his so that she could feel his arousal.

A small warm wind kicked up, caressing Storm's skin, surrounding her with the scent of both Tristan and Pierce. Together they made her think of camping out under the moon and stars on a summer night, a fire built for companionship and not necessity.

When the kiss ended, Tristan said, "Would you care for a tour?"

"I'd like that. I think I've already fallen in love with your house. It feels like it's got a personality."

Both men laughed and she shivered when Pierce stroked a hand down her spine, saying, "Believe me, it does."

Tristan moved and ushered Storm inside, but not before she saw the glance he exchanged with his cousin, a silent communication that had her nipples tightening and her womb fluttering.

She forced her mind away from speculation, instead looking down the hallway and taking in the blues and greens, the polished glow of wooden floors. The old furniture, with most surfaces holding at least one book. It was a professor's house, and yet it fit the modern man standing next to her.

An unfamiliar longing filled her. She could see her collection of fey creatures and books fitting in here, an integrated part of their surroundings, much as Severn's dragons had fit his home.

Tristan's house felt alive, as though it shared itself with those fortunate enough to live within it, and with each room, Storm fell just a little bit more in love with the old Victorian, with the man at her side, whose hand felt so right in hers.

The house was filled with the colors found in nature, with antiques still in use and not simply displayed as showpieces, and in every room, there were books. Moving through the house felt like she was moving through Tristan's soul.

Tristan's heart swelled with each step, with each appreciative comment Storm made, with each stroke of her fingers along a polished wood surface or book spine. Despite his sureness that she was his forever wife, he'd been nervous that his home wouldn't agree, that it would make her feel unwelcome, turning the air frigid around them and making him fight even to keep her physically comfortable. But the house had warmed to her instantly, had felt the honor in her, the lack of artifice. She'd said that she was already in love with his house, and his home had found her words true, welcoming her with muted light and warm air, with the sweet scent of the flowers in his yard, their flavor carried in through the open windows and blended into a smell Storm would find pleasing.

He'd never brought a woman here before, hadn't been completely sure the house wouldn't be jealous. That thought brought a smile to his face and he had to fight against laughing. The house hadn't always been so alive, certainly not to the point where he had to worry about its reaction to people and things. When he'd purchased the Victorian, it'd had character and charm in abundance, but it wasn't as it was now. The years had changed it. As he'd filled it with ancient tomes and various power-touched artifacts and antiques, the original "character" had grown and developed into a personality, fully capable of making itself felt, and of using some of Tristan's own connection to the elements to express itself.

This time a small laugh did escape and Storm asked, "What's so funny?"

"I'm just thinking that I'm glad the breeze is bringing in the smell of flowers and not the smell of fertilizer."

She laughed and wrinkled her nose. "Does that happen very often? Having your beautiful house smell like a pig farm?"

"No. But I was worried it would tonight, when I wanted everything to be perfect for you." He leaned down and brushed his lips against hers.

Surprise showed in her face, then uncertainty, and a flash of guilt. "I don't expect perfection, Tristan. I'm not perfect."

He wondered at the guilt, then smiled inwardly, his cock hardening when she inadvertently told him the direction her thoughts had veered by asking, "Where does Pierce live?"

So his cousin was on her mind. Good. He'd suspected as much by her inviting Pierce in for dinner. And she was certainly in Pierce's thoughts. There was no disguising the hard-on his cousin was sporting when he came into the house.

"There's an apartment connected to Drake's Lair," Tristan said. "He stays there, though he is often here."

Storm grimaced at the mention of Drake's Lair. She'd let the reference to the infamous club pass when she was at Severn's. Thank god it was just across the county line, so not in her jurisdiction. It was a running joke in the department at how often the place had been raided, each time with the same outcome, no charges being pressed, no one going to jail, despite the presence of gambling machines and large amounts of money.

"He co-owns it?" she asked and Tristan laughed, pulling her into his arms.

"Said with all the disdain of a law officer."

Storm smiled despite herself…and because he was nibbling along her neck. "I am an officer of the law. And if you're that hungry, you can show me the kitchen and we can eat dinner."

He sucked her earlobe, then probed her ear canal with his tongue. "I'd rather eat you."

She shivered, remembering the feel of his mouth on her as he'd knelt in front of her on the sand.

His tongue moved to trace the shell of her ear. "You liked being my main course and my dessert combined, didn't you?"

She gave a shaky laugh. "You know I did."

"I'll do that for you again. I promised you a night of pleasure."

She turned her head, forcing his mouth away from her ear so that his lips hovered over hers. "And I'm definitely going to hold you to your promise."

He gave a husky laugh, then closed the distance between them, trapping her body against the wall as his lips covered hers, as his tongue sought hers, twining and sliding against it until she was moaning, desperately rubbing herself against the bulge in his jeans.

"I'm not sure I can wait until after dinner to feast on you," he said, his breath coming in short pants as he pulled back far enough to allow them to drag much-needed air into their bodies.

She opened her mouth to say "then don't", but before the words were out, Pierce was in the doorway, his gaze hooded, though he couldn't hide the erection pressing against the front of his pants as he eyed them. "The oven buzzer went off. I assume you didn't intend to let dinner burn while you took your…tour."

Tristan levered himself away from Storm and she had to fight back a moan at the loss of his touch. Pierce's gaze moved over her body, taking in the hard outline of her nipples, making her flush with both arousal and guilt before Tristan's hand found hers and he led her to the kitchen, where the table was already set for three.

Had Pierce done it? Or had Tristan intended to invite his cousin if she didn't?

Storm let herself be seated in a cozy kitchen nook, sliding along the bench seat and immediately becoming entranced by the magical forests and fields, complete with fey inhabitants, that had been carved and painted on the walls around her. "This is amazing," she said.

Tristan and Pierce set the food on the table and joined her, Tristan at her side, while Pierce sat on the bench opposite Storm. "I'm glad you like it," Tristan said.

"Like? How about love and covet." Storm surprised herself by laughing and admitting, "Until this minute, I didn't truly understand how a collector like VanDenbergh, who has so many other beautiful things, could become obsessed with obtaining a certain artifact—even to the point of having it stolen or buying it when he knew it was stolen." She looked at the walls that made up the nook. "Now I do."

Tristan reached for her hand and brought it to his lips, pressing a kiss against the smooth skin on its back. "You're always welcome here, even when I'm not home. Come and enjoy the house."

A lump formed in Storm's throat. She wondered if he knew how much his offer meant to her, how much it touched her heart.

"That's a dangerous thing to say," she teased, afraid that if she didn't, she'd end up embarrassing herself with tears. "You might never get rid of me."

He pressed another kiss against her hand before releasing it. "Eat. My feelings will be hurt if this meal I've slaved over cools and isn't appreciated."

They ate a meal of salad, lasagna, and bread so delicious Storm could have eaten nothing else but that. They drank wine, talking and laughing. Sometimes about the antics of Tristan's students. Sometimes about Pierce's adventures both at Drake's Lair and on his various hunts for lost or stolen artifacts. Sometimes about the arrests Storm had made, the situations she'd encountered. And through it all, Storm couldn't shake the feeling she was on a date, not just with Tristan, but with Pierce.

"That was wonderful," she said much later, when she'd polished off a piece of chocolate pie and finished a cup of coffee. "Did you really cook all of this? Or would I find take-out containers if I checked the trash can?"

Tristan laughed, throwing his arm around her shoulders and leaning into her. Pierce grinned. "Is that your naturally suspicious nature asserting itself, or are your detective skills rising to the occasion?"

Storm grinned. "Maybe both."

"Then I suggest a game while we let Tristan's delicious meal settle before he shows you the backyard." Storm's eyebrows lifted in silent query and Pierce shook his head. "I won't ruin my cousin's surprise by telling you what's out back."

"I have ways of making you talk," Storm said, heat rushing through her nipples when Pierce's eyelids dropped momentarily, his face tightening in a way that flooded her mind with erotic images of handcuffing him and teasing him with her mouth and hands, tormenting him until he burned out of control.

She forced the images out of her mind, hastily asking, "What game are you suggesting then?"

Pierce's smile widened and the amusement she read on his face made her wonder if he was getting ready to propose a game of strip poker. It wouldn't be the first time a date had asked her to play that particular game.

Her body stiffened in realization. There it was again, the thought that she was on a date—with both men.

"I'll get the game," Pierce said as he and Tristan slipped off the bench seats, gathering the dishes and moving them to the counter before Pierce left the kitchen, only to return a minute later with a boxed game.

Storm laughed. "*Clue?*"

"Of course, what better game to play with a detective in the house?" Pierce joked.

Storm shook her head. He continued to surprise her. He and Tristan looked so much alike, and yet they were such different men. Tristan, serious and romantic, making her think of a multilayered cloud mass. Pierce, daring and raw, teasing one moment, then dangerous, like a flame that might easily jump its boundaries and burn out of control.

"Let me guess," Storm said, looking at Pierce. "You'll be Colonel Mustard and Tristan will be Professor Plum."

Pierce grinned. "I see we have our work cut out for us, Cousin. And what about you, Storm?" His hand darted over to cover hers, to squeeze it. "Will you be the rule-enforcing Mrs. Peacock? Or will you let yourself go tonight and be Miss Scarlet?"

Was there really any choice with these two men? Storm picked up the scarlet red game piece and settled it on the game board—eventually claiming victory, made all the sweeter because it had been a hard-fought, honest win.

"Ready to show me the backyard?" Storm said as they rose from the table and stretched.

Tristan took her hand in answer and led her from the room, giving her a moment's pause as she wondered if Pierce was going to follow, or leave.

She'd expected the flowers, their scent permeated the house, but she never would have envisioned how elaborate Tristan's gardens were, how private. But it was the hot tub that caught her attention.

"My idea of heaven," Storm said, looking up at the star-filled night sky as she imagined them making love on the firm, padded cover of the hot tub, before pulling it off and sinking into the welcoming water.

Tristan encircled her with his arms, pulling her back to his front. "Winner's choice what we do next."

Storm leaned into him, enjoying the feel of his erection trapped between their bodies, enjoying the memory of how his cock had felt inside her. Her nipples were aching points—had been since Pierce had picked her up after work—and her cunt was swollen, slippery, an empty place that needed to be filled.

Tristan's promise to give her even more pleasure than he'd given her in his office whispered through Storm's mind just as one of his hands moved to the waistband of her pants, undoing the top button and easing the zipper down before sliding his fingers inside her panties. She cried out in reaction, quivering as his fingers glided over her erect clit and dipped into her sopping wet channel.

His lips brushed against her neck before settling on the sensitive flesh, sucking and biting until she felt like tearing her shirt and bra off and turning so that she could guide his mouth to her nipples. As if sensing where she needed to be touched, Tristan's other hand moved to cup her breast, to tease her nipple through the layers of her clothing, and she knew that she was almost too far gone to call a halt. "Pierce is here," she whispered, the reminder doing nothing to cool things down.

Tristan's mouth and tongue shifted their focus to the outer shell of her ear. "Does it matter that he's here? Would it shock you to learn that there have been times when I've enjoyed watching him pleasure and be pleasured by a woman, when I've enjoyed having him watch me, when we've both taken a woman together?" He made quick work of the buttons on her blouse and the front clasp of her bra, pulling them both off her before taking her nipple between his fingers. "I wouldn't force it on you, Storm, but I won't lie and tell you that the thought of him touching you upsets me. If you wanted to share yourself with him, I'd call him to us. We could make love, then play in the hot tub together."

The hand in her panties retreated from her slit so that his fingers could concentrate on her engorged clitoris. "Or I could tell him to go find another woman and I could keep you to myself. What do want?"

There was a movement in the doorway and Storm's heart jumped when she saw Pierce. His eyes had darkened and his nostrils were flared, but he made no effort to look away from where she stood in his cousin's arms—or to leave.

Storm's gaze moved to where the large outline of his cock was pressed against the front of his pants. "Join us," she said, wanting to regret the words, but unable to.

Chapter Ten

🙠

Pierce shed his shirt as he moved toward them and Storm's breath caught in her throat at the sight of his bare flesh. The moonlight caressed his skin, making her think of pale flames leaping and dancing as they flared hot and intense. He stopped in front her, his eyes traveling over her body, lingering where Tristan's hand disappeared into her panties, then moving to her breasts where his cousin's other hand rested, and finally settling on the necklace.

"You've caught us both," Pierce said, his voice rough, raw. "Now what do you intend to do with us?" He closed his hand around the necklace and Storm's nipples and clit burned.

Pierce used the chain to pull her forward so that their faces were just inches apart. His eyes were full of lust and challenge and Storm couldn't resist the lure of him. Her lips covered his, her tongue teased against the seam of his lips as her hands trailed down his sides.

He growled, low and deep, fighting her for control of the kiss as his hand covered one of her breasts and his fingers grasped the nipple, tugging and tweaking, his grip painfully erotic. Storm moaned, almost unable to think under the twin assault of Tristan's and Pierce's hands.

One of her hands moved from his hip to the front of his pants, rubbing along the thick cloth-covered erection. Her touch driving him higher, making him more aggressive.

Tristan's hand left her breast and moved to the chain, sliding down it until Pierce yielded the faerie-held crystal and stepped back. The loss of his heat making Storm shiver.

Tristan whispered kisses along her neck and said, "You've caught us both. What can we do to serve you?"

Storm said the first thing that came to her mind. "What about taking your clothes off for a start?"

"As you wish," Tristan said against her neck, and Storm's heart jumped at the sultry expression on Pierce's face as he immediately toed off his shoes and began unbuckling his belt. But when Tristan started to take his hands off her body she dared to expand their sudden game, to see how far they were willing to go. "No, not you. Only Pierce."

Tristan's hands stilled and he laughed, a husky sound that poured through her and found its way to the swollen folds of her labia. His erection pressed tight against her buttocks and Storm couldn't stop herself from rubbing against his thick arousal as Pierce's pants and underwear dropped to the ground, as he stood in front of her, naked and aroused, his cock full and ready.

She watched Pierce's eyes as she took his penis in her hand, exploring the tip with her thumb before moving down the shaft, and then underneath to cup his heavy balls. It was like stroking fire, and the flames in his eyes promised a lust hot enough to consume them both. Storm returned to Pierce's shaft, stroking up and down, tightening her grip when she saw him struggling not to react to her touch, and then she released him. "Let me see you do it," she challenged. "Let me see how you like your cock to be touched."

"You're playing with fire," Tristan warned.

She laughed and raised her arms, arching and spearing her fingers through the long strands of hair on either side of Tristan's face. "But you're here to help put it out."

"I think I'm much more likely to fan the flames," he said as his fingers slid over the small head of her clit, circling and pressing, working her in the same rhythm as Pierce worked his own cock until she was frantic to feel skin against skin, to feel at least one of them inside her.

She released her grip on Tristan's hair, grabbing his hand and stilling it as she did the same to Pierce's. Tristan pulled his hand from her panties, going instead to her waistband and pushing her pants and underwear down, kneeling so that he could remove her shoes and free her of her clothing.

He pressed kisses along her buttocks and spine as he rose, and then she heard the sounds of him undressing. She brushed her thumb across the head of Pierce's penis, spreading his leaking arousal across the silken skin. His cock jumped underneath both of their hands and he closed the distance, trapping their hands between them before covering her lips with his and pouring lava-hot lust into her mouth with his kiss.

She moaned and pressed closer, suddenly desperate to take one man's cock in her mouth while the other man's cock tunneled in and out of her cunt. When Pierce lifted his mouth from hers she said, "Sit on the edge of the hot tub, let me put my mouth on you. Let me have you the same way I had Tristan the first time."

Pierce's eyes flared as he did what she told him to do, but when she lowered her head, licking over his feverish skin, teasing him, making his cock pulse and jump under the lashes she gave him with her tongue, his hands fisted in her hair, holding her against his hot flesh as he pushed into her mouth, controlling the thrusts, controlling the pleasure, reasserting how dangerous it was to play with fire.

Storm moaned and spread her legs, needing Tristan to be a part of this, to be a part of her. He gave her a stinging bite on one buttock and then he was there, hands on her hips to hold her steady as he pushed his cock into her channel.

For a moment they all stilled and Storm was stunned by the pleasure, by the desire she felt for both men, by the lust radiating off them. She'd never felt so powerful, so sure of herself sexually, so captivated. They'd joked that she'd captured them, but they'd done the same to her.

A shiver raced through her and the movement set both men into action again. She moaned at the dual sensation of having Tristan pump in and out of her cunt as she laved and sucked, driving Pierce higher and higher with the dangerous press of her teeth against his cock as he fucked her mouth.

Fire raged through Pierce, roaring and out of control. He'd suspected it was too late when she made him come in the hallway. But now he knew.

Her mouth was a sweet torture. A treasure he'd find nowhere else.

He'd fought the knowledge since yesterday. Railed against The Fates even though he knew it would do no good other than to serve as a great jest for them.

He, who could command fire, had been trapped by a mortal! Unable to fight her touch, her order to strip and yield his body to her.

And now he couldn't keep himself from moaning in pleasure as she sucked him, making his back arch and his testicles pull tight against his body until there was no holding back, no resisting the fiery need to give her his essence, to shoot his seed into her.

His fingers tightened on her hair in reaction and he forced his eyes open, looking first at Storm and then at Tristan, mesmerized by the pleasure on his cousin's face, by the sight of Tristan's cock tunneling in and out of their woman.

A hot fury of lust washed over Pierce, forcing the air from his body so that he started panting, struggling against the need to come, but his frenzied movements were like fuel to an already explosive fire.

Storm's mouth became more aggressive, milking away the last of his resistance, the last of his control until he shouted in release, his seed spewing in a lava-hot eruption that jetted from his cock, the flames of his pleasure burning hotter with the sounds of Tristan's cries and Storm's moans as they orgasmed with him.

And still it wasn't enough.

Pierce fell back on the padded cover of the hot tub, pulling Storm with him and urging her to straddle his body, to sheathe his cock in her wet slit. Later he would take her in a way that demonstrated that he had no intention of letting her control him, but this time he needed to be inside her, and he wouldn't deny his cousin the pleasure of sharing the joining with them.

Satisfaction whipped through Tristan at the sight of Storm taking Pierce into her body and he hastened to join them, straddling Pierce's legs as his hands cupped Storm's breasts and his own cock slid along the crevice between her buttocks as she pleasured herself on Pierce's cock.

He buried his face in her shoulder, pressing kisses against her skin as she arched, thrusting her hard nipples against his palms. "Take us both at the same time, Storm," he whispered, his fingers tightening on her areolas, "love us both at the same time."

She answered his plea by lowering her upper body so that she lay on Pierce, by moaning and panting as Tristan gathered their combined juices and prepared her back entrance, by holding steady as he slowly worked himself in.

Tristan had thought to offer her words, to offer her promises, but once he was inside her, his cock separated from Pierce's by only a thin barrier, there was nothing he could offer but the thrust of his body, the wild uncontrollable, ravaging power of fire and air together.

Storm thrashed between them, so hot that she felt like she might go up in flames. They were everywhere, everything, pleasure and pain, ravenous need and incredible satisfaction.

She ate at Pierce's mouth, wanting to swallow him whole. She ground her breasts into Tristan's hands and savored the feel of his lips on her neck, her ear.

Words couldn't begin to describe the incredible sensation of having two men inside her at the same time, their hot flesh pressed against hers, touching hers in so many places that it was almost as though they were one skin, one being, bound together by pleasure so extreme that there was no holding it in, no containing it, no limiting it.

It was like a raging forest fire that creates its own weather, a burning howling wind that decimates everything in its path. And yet she didn't feel destroyed, she felt more alive than she'd ever felt.

She wanted it to never end. And at the same time, she wanted the exquisite release that was just out of reach.

And then the men shifted, changing the angle so that each thrust sent shards of exquisite agony through her clit. So that tears ran down her cheeks and she tightened on their cocks, making them work harder, pump harder, fight to get what they wanted until there was no escaping orgasm, no holding back the cries as Storm welcomed their scalding seed deep in her body.

She didn't want to move afterward, didn't want them to leave her body. It was only the promise of the hot tub and a glass of wine that gave her the strength to even contemplate the idea of releasing them. She wanted more. Needed more.

"I'll be back in a few minutes," Tristan whispered against her neck as he eased out of her. "A quick shower and I'll bring the wine." He laughed when he gained his feet. "I trust the two of you can manage to uncover the hot tub." Mumbles met his comment and he smoothed his hand over Storm's buttocks before giving her a light slap. "The night of pleasure I promised has only just begun. I would continue our play in the hot tub," he said, then moved into the house.

Pierce clasped Storm to him and she could feel his heart pounding furiously against her chest. It should have felt awkward, embarrassing. Instead it felt right.

"You'll have to get up first," Pierce said, his hands stroking the sides of her breasts. "I don't have the strength to push you away."

She rose up on her elbows so she could look down on his face. He immediately cupped her breasts, sending fire through the nipples as his thumbs rubbed over them.

Storm closed her eyes, savoring the sensation. God, his touch was so incredible. So wonderful. There was no doubt, no self-consciousness. There was only pleasure.

His fingers tightened on her nipples and she arched her back in response, the movement bringing them closer to his face. He took advantage, flicking a taut peak with his tongue and making her cry out as heat filled her belly and her cunt clamped down on his penis.

"Suck me," she said, the demand escaping before she could stop it.

He groaned, his cock stiffening inside her. And when he latched on to a nipple, biting and sucking, Storm couldn't keep herself from grinding her clit against him, from moving up and down, fucking herself on his cock as she watched him feast on her breast as though he was starving for the taste and feel of her.

Pierce let her ride him for long moments, and then the burning desire to claim her overwhelmed him, the need to hear her screaming his name gave him the strength to stop suckling at her breasts and move, rolling her underneath him and grabbing her hands, pinning them to the hot tub cover as he held his cock motionless inside her. She cried out, wrapping her legs around his hips in response and writhing against him. Her mouth went to his, her words adding fuel to the flame. "Don't stop, Pierce. Oh God, please don't stop. Fuck me."

It was a command he readily obeyed, slamming in and out of her, rejoicing in the sound of his own name coming from her lips as he pleasured her, as she gave to him something he'd longed for without being aware of it—a belonging that would forever change his life.

The night filled with the sounds of flesh striking flesh, with whispered pleas and fevered moans, with the sharp cry of release. And even then, it was hard for them to separate from one other.

From the shadows Tristan watched as they rose and pulled the cover off the hot tub, then scrambled into the heated water and moved once again into each other's arms, murmuring and kissing — the breeze moving over all three of them — warm, laden with the heady scent of flowers, and underneath, passion.

Satisfaction moved through Tristan, and lust. It pleased him to see Storm take his cousin, share herself with him with no thought of what it might gain her. It pleased him to know that she accepted and welcomed Pierce.

It had not always been so for Pierce. Despite the fact that his mother, Tristan's aunt, was the queen's own sister, a lady of the court, his father was an untitled lesser fey from another's court — an ill-fated coupling done when the Court of Koterja had visited the Court of Otthilde while the queen still had the Chalice of Enos in her possession.

Tristan's heart had long ago hardened toward the queen and her two younger sisters — his aunt and his mother. Even for the freedom to come and go from Faerie without the threat of having to bed Morgana hanging over his head, he wouldn't give the Dragon's Cup back to Queen Otthilde. She'd treated it like a trophy, pulling it out to dazzle the nobles of other courts, but then hastening to dispose of any embarrassing results from the use of it.

Pierce's father had been disposed of in such a way, though none could prove it — and none dared to speak of it out loud while at court. Only one faerie with a tie to fire had been among those traveling with King Koterja and that untitled fey had disappeared.

Tristan had been a baby at the time, unaware of the drama taking place around him. The heady excitement when the queen's sister was found to be pregnant. The loud crowing of the lord who served as her consort. And then the birth of Pierce. Followed by the discovery of his fire and the tittering whispers that the queen's sister must have lain with the servant traveling with King Koterja.

In the old days, especially among the lesser nobility who had a better chance of hiding such an indiscretion, Pierce would simply have been swapped for a human baby, whose new fey family would then go to the queen and claim that their own faerie child had died and they'd taken a mortal's to ease their loss. They would offer the queen a beautiful gift, and in exchange she would allow the child to be made faerie.

But such was not an option for Pierce. In a world where all were beautiful, rank and privilege and shallow regard came not from merit but from the ancient bloodlines. Queen Otthilde was of the water and air, as was Tristan, as was most of her court. Pierce's fire was viewed as primitive, coarse, a raw force without refinement or depth. That alone was bad enough in the eyes of the court, but worse was to follow. The fire drew him to the dragons, and he readily made friends among them.

Tristan's lips twisted into a grimace. Once the fey were pure elements, but as the stronger ones had taken form, evolving as the humans did, into a body that walked upright, that used intellect and developed a language so that fire could speak to air and water and earth, so too had the fey developed the other emotions—losing the fine balance that, while often harsh and violent, had sustained them. Like the humans who had walked among them, at first only vaguely aware, and then both frightened and worshipful, the fey had erupted into war, not only among themselves but with the other supernaturals, weakening themselves in the process.

Had the form that the fey chose led them astray? Or had they been changed by the humans' beliefs, the humans' worship and fear of them? Tristan shook his head. It was a question he'd long studied and pondered—but a question without an answer all the same.

Storm moved and the moonlight was captured for a moment in the crystal of her necklace. Some of the lesser fey still had gossamer wings, but the ones that had chosen the same shape as the mortals had long ago given up wings—though the myth persisted, or perhaps it was the glamour that artists captured and shaped into something they could understand.

Her soft laughter distracted him from his thoughts and Tristan's cock pulsed, urging him to rejoin them, to slide into her channel this time and let Pierce experience the tightness of her other entrance. By The Goddess and The Fates, Storm filled his heart with the sky, with the ocean.

Tristan set the tray with the wine on the edge of the hot tub before sliding into the water, a smile forming when Storm gave Pierce a lingering kiss, then moved to welcome him, her smile caressing him as surely as the water did. He took her lips, her heat, his cock pleading to sink into her, and in a heartbeat he knew that he couldn't wait, even for the pleasure of sharing her.

"I've got to have you again," Tristan murmured. "Trust me. Give yourself to me. Wrap yourself around me."

Her eyes widened slightly but she did as he asked, gasping softly when his cock filled her, then giving him the words he desperately needed to hear, "I trust you."

He sealed his mouth to hers, his breath becoming hers as he rolled with her in the water, his connection to the element allowing him to fuck her in a hot wet cocoon—to thrust in and out of her as violently as the mermen had once done to the humans they lured into the sea when they inhabited this realm. She tensed for only an instant, and then yielded, her body clinging to his, her hands and arms tightening on him not with fear, but with pleasure.

He wanted to stay underneath for hours, but had to limit himself to minutes—until the day when she knew what he was, when perhaps she carried enough of his essence inside her to survive such a coupling. He kept her under as long as he dared, then surfaced, rising so that he could put her on the edge of the hot tub and thrust into her as his mouth released hers and captured her nipple instead, sucking and biting until she screamed in release, her slick, tight sheath fisting on his cock and triggering his own orgasm.

With a groan he sank backward, pulling her with him into the water, luxuriating in the feel of it, the feel of her, the presence of his cousin. When he and Storm had finally regained their breath and settled on the seat-ledge, Pierce handed them each a glass of wine before his hand moved to caress Storm's breasts, his smile wicked as he held up his wineglass and said, "Here's to keeping your earlier promise, Cousin, to doing better when it comes to showing Storm pleasure."

She laughed, brushing a kiss across Pierce's mouth. "Any better and you two might just kill me."

Chapter Eleven

🔊

As Storm walked into the Homicide bullpen, she prayed that she wasn't glowing from all the sex. God! She'd never felt this good, this happy—and the promise of being with both men at the end of the day… Fuck! Oh yeah, now she could see why it tended to be a man's favorite word. She was having a hard time getting it off her mind…getting Tristan and Pierce and what they'd done together off her mind. But somehow she had to keep it contained, one little hint of a love life and she'd be in for some amazingly juvenile—though admittedly sometimes funny—teasing from the other detectives.

"Anything new?" she asked Brady as she plopped down in her chair and looked over their combined desks.

His gaze lingered a few minutes at chest level before lifting to meet hers, but in his case she didn't suspect him of lechery. She knew he'd been staring at the Starbucks cup in her hand.

She shook her head and sighed. "Pass your cup and I'll split the mocha with you." He grinned and passed a coffee-stained mug. Storm frowned when she looked inside it. "When's the last time you washed this thing?"

"I'm letting previous flavors enhance the current contents, kind of like chefs do with their cast iron skillets."

Storm poured half of her Starbucks into the mug and handed it back to him. "Remind me never to eat at your place, Brady."

Brady took a swallow of the coffee. "Anything good come out of your mystery meeting yesterday?"

The word *come* lingered in her mind and she felt like doing a little dance. She resisted the urge, but allowed herself a huge smile, knowing that Brady wouldn't connect it with sex when she said, "Severn Damek."

"Shit." Brady straightened in his chair. "He's after the chalice?"

"Has been for years. But I don't think he's behind this. In fact he reluctantly confessed that the police seem to be his best bet for locating it now."

Brady's eyes goggled. "Severn Damek—as in, that's who you met last night?"

"Yeah." She filled Brady in on the meeting, ending by passing him the photograph Severn had given her and saying, "Looks like we need to put more of a squeeze on the lawyer, or the insurer, and find out where VanDenbergh got the chalice. Could be as simple as whoever sold it to him, also stole it back. And we need to find out how VanDenbergh got it insured if it was known to be stolen." She grinned. "Better pull out a peppermint. I'm getting ready to talk about politicians."

Brady reached for a candy. "The senator?"

"Severn implied that there was something off about the value of the sword. His exact words were, *I'm suggesting that its value is questionable, though I'm sure its worth is well documented.*"

Brady crunched his candy with a thoughtful expression on his face. "Insurance fraud? Don't need a body for that, though it does draw attention away from an insurance motive."

"Yeah. I'll pass the info on to Trace and Dylan."

Brady shook his head. "Two cases and they're both fucking nightmares—pardon my French and send me back to diversity training."

Storm laughed. "What'd you come up with following the VanDenbergh money around?"

"Well, for starters, most of the VanDenbergh money is stashed in trusts. So far I've found out that VanDenbergh III enjoys his poker—in the casino and online. Lots of money going out but not a lot of winnings coming back in." Brady shook his head in disgust. "Guy lives rent-free on a beautiful cabin cruiser his grandfather owns. The thing's in a slip over at Sundance Yacht Club, and he wastes his time gambling, pissing his *allowance* away."

"So you thinking maybe he offed Gramps in order to speed up his inheritance?"

"Maybe. No way to check VanDenbergh III's story about spending the day at the dog tracks."

"Anyone else look like a possibility?"

"Do you find sharks in bloody water?"

"That bad."

"Let's just say Old Man VanDenbergh's tendencies to collect whatever he wanted passed on to his descendants. A couple of sons in real estate, a couple of ex-wives and plenty of fancy mistresses, rumors of illegitimate children all the way around—including one who's pretty much got a team of federal agents circling her all the time for animal rights extremist activities—grandkids with 'entitlement attitudes', plenty of money motive everywhere you look. But I still like VanDenbergh III for this."

"What about the will?"

"Lawyer's dragging his feet about letting me see it. Says he's got to wait for the other partners to get back plus get the okay from all of the family members involved before he feels 'comfortable' about sharing privileged and confidential information with us. And I already tried to put the squeeze on him about where the chalice came from, he wouldn't budge."

"Anything from Trace or Dylan?"

"No." Brady swallowed the last of the shared mocha and set his mug down with a heavy thump. "Might as well hit the crime scene again. The captain comes in here and sees us sitting, he's going to start chewing on our asses."

"There's a picture. At least he's got a bottle of Rolaids for afterward. Going to need it with an old, tough hide like yours."

"Ha, ha. Funny, Kid. Keep that up and you're going to be heading straight for diversity and sensitivity training."

"What? For disrespecting my elders?"

Brady's lips twitched upward a millimeter. "Let's hit it."

The same butler ushered them into VanDenbergh's treasure room. Storm took in the scene again, squinting as her eyes moved over some of the artifacts, noticing that the lighting on some of them was different, more intense, almost a halo effect. She frowned, thinking it was strange that she hadn't seen that when she was here before. It was the same odd lighting she'd noticed around Sophie's heartmate stone the other night.

Storm shook her head and forced her thoughts back to the case. "So was the theft of the chalice intentional?" she asked. "Or was it convenient, something to cover up a motive of murder?"

Brady stopped next to her and put his hands in his pockets, jingling his loose change as he looked around. "Our guy just got the chalice and it's got a rep for being the answer to an old geezer's orgy prayers. Anyone who knew he had it would figure that VanDenbergh Senior was going to call the party girls and bring out the party bowl ASAP. Say VanDenbergh III knew it, five mil isn't too bad a payoff if that's the party favor the killer gets to keep—assuming he didn't off Gramps himself."

Storm nodded slowly. "Could be. Or maybe VanDenbergh III and the killer made a deal to split the take from the chalice, with VanDenbergh III getting some of it back in a poker game down the road. Declared income that will offset his losses, nice and legal, so no one will think too much about it."

Brady grunted. "Damn. He takes it back that way and we'll never be able to pin it on him."

Storm began moving around the room, studying the locks on the cases and the items they contained. Whoever had designed the lighting was a genius. She couldn't see a difference, but the closer she got to some of the items, the more noticeable the halo effect. She was betting the more famous or more valuable ones were the ones that were highlighted, surrounded by a warmer, softer glow.

None of the displays looked as though they'd been disturbed, and nothing seemed to be missing—and yet—Storm could almost swear that something was missing from a case containing a collection of ceremonial knives and daggers, *athames*. She frowned at the unfamiliar word, wondering why it had come to her, then remembered hearing Sophie say it before. "Do we know what's supposed to be in these cases?" she said, half turning to look at Brady.

He grunted and leaned closer to look at some figurines. "Lawyer's supposed to be getting us that information."

Storm was momentarily distracted when she realized the figurines were actually combinations of various figures positioned in amazing sexual positions. "Don't use those for guidance," she said, "not without spending some serious time in the gym first. You'd never hear the end of it when the guys showed up at the hospital to visit you."

Brady shook his head. "I told you, Kid, I'm no hound dog. You think this position is really possible?"

Storm snickered and couldn't stop herself from moving closer to the display he was studying. She wasn't sure which combination he was looking at, but her attention was immediately drawn to one at the edge of the display. Unlike some of the other items she'd been drawn to, the three figures didn't have special lighting, and yet she couldn't take her eyes off the two blond faerie men—one with delicate blue-green wings, the other with red-blue wings—who were making love to an equally blonde human woman, trapping her body between theirs in a way that left no doubt about the pleasure they were all experiencing.

Shit. She could feel the blood rushing to her face just looking at them—thinking how it had been with Tristan and Pierce. What it felt like to be the center of their attention, giving and receiving like the big-breasted figurine between the two fey men. Her throat went dry, and in that moment—for the second time in two days, she knew what it was like to want something so badly that she'd almost be willing to steal it! She wouldn't of course, but if the figurines were auctioned off, she'd somehow find a way to buy them.

Storm forced herself to move back to the display of knives, once again getting a vague impression of something missing. "A guy like VanDenbergh Senior would have information here at the house about his treasures. He'd want to be able to check his facts in order to brag when he was pulling out stuff and showing it off."

"Yeah. And you'd think the family would want to cooperate. But they've got everything going through the lawyer and he's doing just enough to look like he's cooperating, while still running around and covering his ass."

"I keep thinking something's missing from this case," Storm finally admitted, figuring if someone was going to tell her she was imagining things, she'd rather it be her partner and not the department shrink.

Brady left the display of figurines and moved to the case, pulling out a peppermint candy and popping it into his mouth like he'd done at the senator's house.

Storm grinned. "You sure it's not knives that make you break out in a cold sweat and chew the enamel off your teeth?"

Brady dug into his pocket and pulled out another candy. "Suck on this, Kid, it'll keep you from smarting off to your betters."

"Elders, not necessarily betters." She took the candy and unwrapped it while he leaned closer, studying the display.

For several minutes there was only the sound of candy meeting its demise. When Brady straightened, he was frowning. "Wouldn't it be real interesting if a sword was missing over at the senator's place and a knife was missing here? Only that begs the question, does anyone else know it's missing? 'Cause I think you're on to something here, Kid. Can't put my finger on it exactly," he looked around the room, "except this display feels different somehow, like the same person didn't arrange it." He exhaled a loud gust of peppermint-scented breath. "But that doesn't mean shit without facts to back it up. And if we start asking a bunch of questions, we might tip someone off and end up screwing ourselves."

Brady's gaze wandered to the adventurous figurines as he concluded his sentence, and Storm joked, "I don't think that position you were asking about is really possible — not without a lot of yoga lessons." Brady's lips twitched upward and she added, "So we wait for the list, compare what's on it to what's actually in the cases?"

"Unless you can come up with a source who can tell us for sure something is missing."

"Over the years, VanDenbergh probably paraded a lot of people through this room. Wonder if he has a guest book," Storm said.

"If he does, it probably reads like a cross between the society pages and a list of call girls."

Storm shoved her hands into the front pockets of her slacks. *In for a penny, in for a dollar*, her grandmother used to say. "Aislinn might be able to help us find out if something's missing."

Brady's eyes shifted back and forth between Storm and the case with the daggers like a typewriter carriage in the hands of a manic secretary. "Trace's Aislinn? You want to involve Trace's wife in this?"

"That'd be the one. And maybe just a phone call." She grimaced and removed her hands from her pockets. "Got another one of those peppermint candies?"

He handed her two, reaching for his shirt pocket and pulling out a roll of antacids for himself. "You're talking about calling in a psychic, right?"

"I'm talking about calling in someone who might *conceivably* have been here as a guest of VanDenbergh's at some time in the past," Storm said cautiously. "A *helpful citizen* who might comment that she's fairly certain something is missing, and therefore give us some fuel to make the fire underneath the lawyer and the family hot enough so we can get some answers. That's what I'm talking about."

Brady grinned before schooling his features into a serious cop face. "Good thinking, why don't we step outside and see if there are any helpful citizens willing to come forward."

They returned to the car, Brady using his cell to check for messages and news, Storm using hers to contact Aislinn.

Part of her couldn't believe she was actually "calling in a psychic", and yet she'd seen too much lately not to be willing to at least ask Aislinn if she could help—especially after she'd personally seen Aislinn react when she'd returned to the site of Patrick Dean's murder. Storm grimaced, remembering Trace's words. *You have questions about this supernatural stuff, fine. You can ask Aislinn. She stays out of this case otherwise.*

Aislinn answered the phone and for a split second Storm hesitated, but then she pushed forward, explaining the reason for the call. There was only a heartbeat of silence between when she finished speaking and when Aislinn gave an answer that both surprised and pleased Storm. "Ilsa Fontaine can tell you what you want to know. Call her. She'll help you."

It was a name from the Dean case, a psychic with both a connection to Aislinn and to Sophie, which made Storm feel confident as she took down the number then placed the call, picturing the gypsy-like older woman who lived on the beach and read runes for her private clientele.

"I'd be happy to assist you," Ilsa said, "Should I take a taxi? I don't drive and my neighbor isn't here to offer me a ride."

"We'll come get you," Storm said. "Are you available now?"

Madame Fontaine laughed. "Of course. Come on over."

"It's a go," Storm said as she folded her cell phone and slipped it back into its holder.

Brady shook his head and started the engine. "I can't believe I'm doing this."

"Think of it as an extension of your diversity training."

Brady actually smiled. "I like your thinking, Kid. Next time they try to send me back to school, I'll mention this little trip to see the psychic. That should be good for a get-out-of-class-free pass."

* * * * *

The senator's wife opened the door for Trace and Dylan. "I hope this won't take long, detectives, I'm on my way out to an important meeting."

"Shouldn't take more than a few minutes," Trace said, disliking the woman almost immediately, and somehow getting the feeling that it was mutual.

She stepped back and let them in, then followed them to the room where the murder had taken place.

"Have you or the senator received any threats or had anyone try to extort money from you?" Trace asked, thinking back to the conversation with Seraphine.

The senator's wife laughed. "No, Detective. The motive for this murder doesn't appear to lend itself to such drama. The sword was the most valuable item in my husband's collection. As horrible and senseless as Anita's death was, I'm afraid she was just in the wrong place at the wrong time."

Trace's eyes narrowed. The wife's expression was carefully remorseful and her body language backed it up, but he couldn't shake the feeling that she was somehow...gleeful.

He frowned. Maybe they needed to look closer at the relationship between the senator and his aide. They'd almost ruled out jealousy as a motive for the killing, but...there was something about the wife that didn't feel right to him.

Trace knelt just inside the door. They'd gotten a lucky break when the senator had called the mayor, who'd called the chief, who'd then called the captain directly, wanting the crime scene cleared ASAP so that the senator could have the room cleaned and some normalcy returned to his life.

Not suspicious in itself. But Trace appreciated the fact that the captain had held tough, saying it was up to the detectives to determine when they'd finished processing the murder scene.

As soon as he got the call from the captain, Trace had asked the crime scene guys to go out again, looking for salt. They'd hit the jackpot, finding small amounts of it close to the inside edge of the wall. One of the techs had even scribbled a note next to the report. *Appears to be ground into carpet. Not noticeable to the naked eye.* That meant it took some time. Someone with access, someone who couldn't afford to hurry—not if they expected to survive the demon they were summoning.

Christ. They'd kick him off the force or send him to the shrink if they knew what he was thinking—that he actually believed a demon had killed Vorhaus.

But there was no way around it. His beliefs had altered forever the instant he'd admitted to himself just how much he loved and needed Aislinn. Now there was no going back. Not that he wanted to. He wouldn't go back to the way he was, not if it meant giving up his wife.

"We'll need a list of frequent visitors and hired help," Trace said. "Anyone who could have been in the house while both you and your husband were out."

"Certainly. Perhaps we could do that now." She made a show of checking her watch.

Trace cut a look to his partner and Dylan pulled his notebook out of his pocket. One of the charms that Seraphine had given Trace tumbled to the floor.

"What the hell?" Dylan said, but it was the senator's wife's reaction that had Trace's heart rate shooting upward. She stepped back quickly, a barely audible hiss escaping.

Dylan scooped up the charm, shooting a questioning look at Trace before pocketing it and turning his attention to the senator's wife. Her face was composed by then, though there was a tightness around her mouth and a hardness in her eyes that hadn't been there earlier.

Trace smiled inwardly. *Yeah, now we're getting somewhere. Maybe we need to look into what you do in your spare time — besides charity events. And maybe we need to double-check, just to make sure your husband wasn't fucking his aide. Maybe this was your little warning to him that the next time he was unfaithful, it could be him. And maybe that's the reason the techs only found small traces of salt, maybe you ran a vacuum around the wall when you got back home.*

As Dylan wrote down the names of frequent visitors, Trace turned his attention to the area on either side of the door. The carpet was pale peach. He worked through it with his fingers, but couldn't see a way of hiding a symbol like the ones Seraphine had drawn. Too intricate. Too noticeable. Or at least he hoped so. Was it possible that the symbols had been on the floor and the first cops on the scene had shuffled through them, so focused on the headless body that they hadn't noticed? Possible, maybe. Likely — no, he didn't think so.

His gaze moved to the walls and he almost smiled. White with a trim around the door that matched the carpet. White that if you squinted and looked at it just a certain way, and used a little imagination, you could almost see symbols traced on it, a salt-water solution that left the marks — almost without a trace. He pulled out his cell and punched in the number for the crime scene unit. "Send one of your techs back out to the senator's house."

Chapter Twelve

ॐ

"You must be Storm," Ilsa Fontaine said as she opened her door and stepped out on the porch. "I feel as though I know you through Aislinn and Sophie."

Storm smiled, immediately at ease. "I feel the same way."

"I understand that you're here in your official capacity, and we need to leave, but I'm curious about the necklace Aislinn designed for you. May I see it?"

"Sure," Storm said, hesitating only long enough to note that she didn't feel the same reluctance to show it to Madame Fontaine as she'd felt in Severn Damek's presence.

As soon as Storm pulled the necklace out from underneath her shirt, a smile spread across Ilsa's features and she teased, "Ah, I see you've found someone special, or should I say two such individuals? Only one with a pure heart could have managed such a feat."

Storm shifted uncomfortably, her hand unconsciously enclosing the faeries and their crystal as she wondered exactly what Madame Fontaine saw. Ilsa touched her hand to Storm's hand and for a second, Storm would have sworn that the crystal warmed. Madame Fontaine said, "Please don't take offense, but I'd regret not telling you this while I can. When it comes to your two men, you need only the magic in your heart to hold them."

Storm gave a brief nod before retreating to the car, praying that Brady wouldn't notice the heat in her face. God! Just how much of her night with Tristan and Pierce had Madame Fontaine "seen"—because how else would the psychic have known that two men were involved and not one? She hadn't told anyone, not even her cousin—and why hadn't Sophie or Aislinn ever mentioned that mind reading was one of Ilsa's skills? Storm grimaced. Not that she would have believed them, not completely, but still...

Her moment of embarrassment gave way to amusement as Brady hastened to open the back door of the unmarked police unit for Madame Fontaine. She'd enjoy teasing him about it the next time he called her Kid. And damned if he didn't sit up straight instead of slouching behind the wheel when he slid back into the car. And what had happened to the food wrappers that always seemed to swirl around his feet? Where had they gone? Storm hid a laugh with a small choking sound and a hasty glance out the window as the car pulled away from the curb.

The VanDenbergh butler greeted Storm and Brady for a second time in one day and once again ushered them to VanDenbergh's artifact room before departing—without commenting on anything, including Madame Fontaine's presence.

Ilsa looked around. "There are certainly more treasures than the last time I was here."

Storm held back a smile when Brady did a double-take and flushed, probably trying to imagine the psychic here in the same capacity as VanDenbergh's other female guests. Not that Ilsa wasn't attractive, she was, but she was probably Brady's age and far from a brainless bimbo.

Since her partner didn't seem inclined to hustle Ilsa over to the display case containing the knives, Storm didn't rush her either, though she once again had to hold back a laugh when Ilsa moved to the display case holding the figurines and Brady's flush deepened as the psychic examined the sexually explicit statuettes.

"This one's quite lovely. Isn't it, Storm?" Madame Fontaine said.

Embarrassment flooded Storm as Ilsa hovered over the two faerie men and the blonde mortal between them. The very image that she was sure Ilsa had already picked from her mind, though the figurines in her thoughts had taken on the very real likenesses of Tristan and Pierce, and herself.

"Yes, it's beautiful."

"Does the family plan to auction these items?"

Storm shrugged. "Probably."

"Lovely," Ilsa said once again. "So many lovely things, and yet they didn't fill the empty place inside him."

Brady shifted from one foot to the other and straightened both his coat and tie before calling attention to himself. "How well did you know VanDenbergh Senior?"

Ilsa looked at him and Storm felt her mouth gape slightly when Brady stiffened his spine and sucked in his coffee-and-donuts gut. "Not well. He sought me out for a consultation once." She smiled when Brady looked disbelieving. "Not that type of consultation, though he would have benefited greatly from a reading. He'd just acquired an ancient rune set and wanted me to give my opinion on whether or not it had special qualities."

Storm frowned. She hadn't noticed a rune set. Had that been stolen, too? "Was it on display in here?"

Madame Fontaine shook her head. "Not on the day I visited. But he gave me a tour of this room." She began moving around the displays then and Storm held her breath when Ilsa stopped in front of the case containing the daggers and knives. The psychic shuddered. "Yes, there was another knife in this arrangement. A black-handled athame with a darkened blade. The Sigil of Baphomet was carved in silver on the hilt. Small rubies were inset for the eyes."

Storm's stomach turned over. Devil worship. And now there was a link to Trace and Dylan's case.

"Sigil of Baphomet?" Brady asked, the look on his face saying he might not know what it was, but he already knew it was bad news.

"The reversed pentacle with a goat's head in the center," Storm said.

It took Brady a heartbeat to react. He reached into the pocket of his jacket and extracted a peppermint candy. "Shit, Kid. Tell me we're not talking devil worship here."

With the flick of her eye, Storm tossed the question to Ilsa, adding, "Do you remember if there was anything significant about the athame? Something that would make it particularly valuable to someone practicing devil worship." Now it was Storm's turn to shudder.

Ilsa shook her head. "I'm sorry. I didn't ask about the athame." Her eyebrows drew together with concern. "The sight of it greatly disturbed me and left me feeling uneasy even after I returned home."

There was a movement in the doorway and they turned as VanDenbergh III came in, a blustery, challenging expression on his face. "Warren informed me that you were back." A muscle jumped in his cheek. "This time with a local psychic. Obviously we want to cooperate with the police, but this is unacceptable. The newspapers are already turning the murder of my grandfather into a circus!"

"Want to tell us about what's missing?" Brady asked.

Got you, Storm thought as VanDenbergh III's eyes showed a tiny flash of alarm before he said, "What do you mean by that? What's missing? All of the cases are and were locked. The only thing the murderer could have stolen was the chalice. And I'm sure I don't have to remind you, it's valued at five million dollars."

Storm tapped her finger on the glass directly over the spot where she thought the athame had been. "There's a knife missing from here. We can get a warrant, but since I'm sure you're as anxious as we are to find out who killed your grandfather, it'd be a lot faster if you could pull up a listing of what was in this case. I'm sure your grandfather had files detailing what was in his collection and where the various artifacts were positioned. By all accounts, he was a man who enjoyed showing off his treasures. He'd want to be sure of his facts if any of his visitors had questions."

"You're probably right," VanDenbergh III said, and despite the comfortable temperature in the room, Storm thought she saw a sheen of moisture on his forehead. "But since I didn't share my grandfather's interest in this stuff, I don't know where his records are or how he's got them organized. This is a large house with a great number of private rooms that I've never been allowed to enter."

Storm's eyebrows lifted. "What about a computer?"

"Not that I'm aware of."

Brady shifted. "The butler seems to have a good handle on what happens around here. Let's pull him in and ask him."

"I'm sorry, he just left. He had some personal business to attend to. He won't be back until tomorrow evening or possibly the day after."

Brady scowled. "That's pretty convenient. I guess you're also going to say he doesn't have a cell phone and you don't have any way of reaching him."

VanDenbergh III puffed himself up and went on the offensive. "If the best you can do to find my grandfather's murderer is to involve a psychic and imply that I'm somehow standing in your way, then I think you should turn the investigation over to a more experienced team of detectives. If we're finished here, then I have a few phone calls to make. One of which will be to your captain. If there's a leak and I read in the newspaper about your bringing Madame Fontaine, then I'm going to demand that you both be removed from the case. Now if you don't mind, I have things to do. I'll escort you out."

They left, waiting until they'd reached the car and pulled out of the driveway before speaking. "The butler must have a real memory for faces," Storm said, turning in her seat so she could look at Madame Fontaine. "VanDenbergh III knew who you were, but I'm assuming he hasn't been to see you, and I know you don't advertise your services. Was the butler present when VanDenbergh Senior consulted you about his rune purchase?"

"Yes, in fact it was Warren who picked me up and then took me back home."

"What's your take on him?" Brady asked.

"Warren, or the grandson?"

Brady grunted. "Both."

Ilsa leaned forward, amazement rushing through Storm when she saw the way both Madame Fontaine and Brady flushed with color and looked away quickly when their eyes met in the rearview mirror. She had to look away herself to keep from laughing or smiling. Oh this was good. First Trace falling for a psychic, now Brady!

"It'd just be guesswork about the grandson," Ilsa said. "But I've studied people over my entire life." She gave a soft chuckle. "Those who claim that psychics are frauds generally say that we take guesses, that we read our client's body language and look for clues in what they say, and therefore it's our skills at observation and not true psychic ability that lead us to the correct answer. They're right on one count. We do read our clients, just as a good psychologist or a skilled physician looks for all the pieces of the puzzle, not just the obvious ones. So, with respect to the grandson, my impression is that he's hiding something, and he's frightened." Ilsa pursed her lips. "His belligerent attitude hides a deeper fear—at his core he's afraid that he's a failure, that what he touches turns not to gold as it always did for his grandfather, but to ash as it has done for his father."

Brady nodded. "Sounds about right. What about the butler, Warren?"

"A good man in a difficult situation. An honorable man with a strong sense of duty."

Brady grunted. "I don't see him beating a path to the station to tell us what he knows."

A small smile played over Madame Fontaine's lips. "Perhaps he has only just realized what he knows that might be of interest to you."

Storm's eyebrows went up. She risked being razzed by Brady later, but still, she asked, "Is that a premonition?"

Madame Fontaine chuckled. "No, just a guess."

They dropped the psychic off at her house, Brady waiting until she'd opened her front door before pulling away from the curb. Storm hid a smile when he asked a minute later, "What do you know about her?" His color heightened. "I mean, you think she's the real thing?"

"Let me see your badge."

"What?"

"Let me see your shield." Storm bit down on her bottom lip to keep a straight face. "Or not. It's your choice, Brady, and it's not something I'm dying to do in front of a cop, anyway. But sometimes I get little mini-visions when I concentrate on something shiny, more like little flashes, nothing fancy. That's why I thought something was missing from the knife case in VanDenbergh's treasure room. I got a little spark of something while I was staring at one of the blades. So if you want me to see if anything comes to me about Madame Fontaine, then I need to scry using your badge since you're the one who asked the question."

Brady hesitated for a long moment then fished around in his pocket and pulled out the tattered and scratched holder that contained his badge. Storm flipped it open, heart smiling when she saw that despite Brady's disreputable suits and cluttered car, he kept his badge shined.

She took a deep breath and tried to think of some nonsense words to intone, but her mind went blank so she had to settle for off-key humming, feeling like a complete idiot for a couple of seconds before she pulled her eyebrows together and peered into the shiny detective's shield.

"She lives alone," Storm said. "Right now she's thinking about the trip to VanDenbergh's house. Oh shit," Storm whispered, then went silent.

"What! What?" Brady asked.

"She's pulling out her runes. She's flustered, worried about something." Storm leaned closer to the badge. "Her lips are moving, she's asking a question."

The car slowed to a crawl along the beach frontage road. "Can you make out what she's asking?"

"Barely. Oh, I see, she's repeating the question. Maybe she's got to say it three times. Yeah, here it comes again." Storm jerked away from the badge and Brady slammed on the brakes in reaction.

"What'd she ask?"

"If the handsome detective was going to be brave enough to ask her out for a date."

Brady flinched as though he'd been hit by a bullet. "Give me that," he growled, snagging his badge case and shoving it into his pocket, his hand coming out with a peppermint. "Very funny, Kid. Very funny."

Storm grinned. "So are you going to ask her out?"

Brady crunched on the peppermint. "In case it's escaped your attention, we're busy trying to solve a crime here."

Storm turned toward the window. "Yeah, I can see how that rules out relationships. Too bad, Brady. I feel bad for Ilsa. Always on the outside looking in. A woman all alone in her house by the beach. I bet the only guys she meets are clients coming to cry on her shoulder and get a fix on their love lives."

Brady devoured three more peppermints and was pulling to a stop in the police parking lot before he asked, "You know for a fact she's single, or were you just guessing?"

Gotcha. "Know for a fact. She's friends with Aislinn, and my cousin Sophie goes to see her."

Brady grunted and got out of the car, changing the topic as they strode in to the police station. "Time to start playing hardball. Let's talk to the captain about getting a warrant to scare up a list of what was in VanDenbergh's treasure room."

"Sounds like a plan," Storm said, altering her course when the male cop manning the reception area and talking on the phone motioned with a hand for them to stop.

"Got something for you guys," he said as soon as he hung up the phone. "Came about an hour ago, but I didn't have a chance to send it up to you. This place has been a zoo today." He handed Storm a manila envelope. She opened it on the spot and started grinning as soon as she saw what it contained.

"Looks like we can put a hold on that warrant." She flipped the picture of the athame Madame Fontaine had described over and found a name. Lucifer's Blade. "Captain's going to love this," she said, handing the picture to Brady.

"Christ." He looked at the cop on reception area duty. "You remember what the guy who delivered this looked like?"

"Sure. Mercury Bike Messenger. Hard to miss a six-foot guy with tight shorts and shaved legs."

Brady looked at the envelope. No return address, no nothing to say where it came from. But his cop nerves jangled remembering what Ilsa—Madame Fontaine—said about Warren. He could guess who was behind this special delivery.

Storm grinned. "Come on, Brady, say it. Here's your chance to utter the sacred words all detectives dream of saying. *The butler did it.*"

Brady's lips twitched. "You're full of it today, Kid. What happened? You get laid last night?"

Heat rushed to Storm's face—a flare of delicious memory rather than embarrassment, though the difference wasn't noticeable to the two men. The cop behind the desk laughed. "She's got you by the short hairs now, Brady. All she has to do is file a complaint or repeat what you said in front of someone from personnel and you'll get to see your favorite diversity and sensitivity trainers again." He winked at Storm. "I'm starting to think Brady must have a thing for one of them, as many times as he's had to go to class."

143

"Ha, ha. You going to buzz us through, or you going to make us keep standing out here. We got important work to do."

The cop laughed again and hit the button to unlock the door separating the reception area from the rest of the building.

Chapter Thirteen

80

Pierce was too restless to enjoy a round of cards — even though the gold coins gleamed brightly against the green felt of the gaming tables and the dragons present in Drake's Lair were hardly a challenge.

Captured. By a mortal!

He'd returned Storm to her apartment only a short while ago and already his chest ached as though she was the oxygen he needed in order to live. His body felt tight and his cock pulsed — his thoughts returning again and again to Storm.

His partner, Tielo, looked up from his cards and smirked. "Your fire rages, Pierce. If you were one of us I would urge you to hike among rock or go to the beach lest you lose control and burn the club down."

Pierce shifted in his chair, recklessly increasing his bet, then standing a minute later when the dealer flipped over the last card and Tielo raked in the pot. A movement in the doorway caught Pierce's attention and the flame inside him immediately dampened at the sight of the woman standing there.

Morgana. The queen's current favorite and Tristan's intended bed partner — or so Queen Otthilde would have it.

Tielo stiffened, his eyes narrowing in reaction to the lady's presence. "This is an unwelcome development, one Severn will not enjoy hearing about. He loathes your queen for failing to return the Dragon's Cup when she had it in her possession, and Morgana for her haughty attitude with regard to our kind. Morgana's presence here can only mean Otthilde has heard of the chalice's reappearance."

"Perhaps," Pierce agreed before moving to where Morgana was standing, her superior smile grating on his nerves. "What brings you here?" he asked, meeting her eyes, letting her see the flame in his even as she let him see the extinguishing icy water in hers.

She looked him over, pursing her lips as her nostrils flared. "Your aura is tainted, mingled and dulled by contact with mortals."

His eyebrows lifted. "You have come all the way from Faerie to judge my aura? I didn't think you enjoyed visiting this world—especially now, when your kelpie form has been banned and you can no longer amuse yourself by luring humans to a drowning death."

Her eyes narrowed. "I thought to visit Tristan and it seemed likely that he might be with you."

Pierce snorted. "As though either of us would welcome you. You know he's not interested in sharing your bed."

"Still interfering in your cousin's business, Pierce?" Her nostrils became pinched—the knowledge in her face that she hadn't forgotten or forgiven Pierce for warning Tristan of the queen's intention to order him to couple with her and perhaps get her with a much-coveted child.

Pierce shrugged. "We have always been close. I look out for him as he does for me."

"He is a Sidhe lord and he has obligations to the court. As do you, though no true lady would consider you a prize. Who wants to couple with a fire lord?" Her eyes gleamed and her smile turned vicious. "Though I can see how mortals would appeal to one who is not comfortable at court—a dusting of glamour and we are gods among the humans."

"You sneer at them, and yet they are here and we are cast out of what was once ours."

She waved her hand as if it didn't matter, though her face tightened. "They breed like animals while we are more selective. They overwhelmed us by their sheer numbers and by their savagery. But eventually they will destroy themselves and we will return."

Pierce's eyes narrowed and he studied Morgana. There were ancient compacts governing what could and couldn't be done in this realm—surely even Queen Otthilde wasn't so vain as to try and hasten the demise of the mortals. No, it was more likely that Tielo was right and she had heard rumors that the Chalice of Enos had resurfaced. There were those among the court who claimed that if only the wizard's incantations could be divined, the cup could be used to enhance the fertility of not just the dragons but the fey as well.

Yes, that would be reason enough for Morgana to come here. To get her hands on the cup—and Tristan. Pierce's body tensed. Morgana's presence changed everything. To find out that her prey was already claimed by another—by a mortal woman…

He had better warn his cousin. Pierce didn't trust Morgana. Where some with ties to the water were warm and gentle, soothing like a spring rain, Morgana had always been as cold as the Artic currents.

Perhaps he and Tristan should hasten the moment when they revealed their true nature to Storm, so that she could draw upon the fire and air and water to protect herself.

* * * * *

"Want to tell me where the hell this came from?" Dylan asked, scowling at the charm that had fallen out of his notebook but now rested in his hand. His voice letting Trace know that his partner had already figured the answer out but was looking for a fight—mainly in response to the woody that Dylan now sported from thinking about the visit to Seraphine.

Trace grinned and maneuvered the unmarked police car out of the senator's driveway, leaving the crime scene guy behind to document the circle of salt and probably goat's blood that they'd located around the house itself. "Will it make you feel better to know that I've got one, too?" Trace countered, snagging the tiny silver links of a chain and fishing the charm out from underneath his shirt to show his partner.

Christ. Not that long ago he'd have gone apeshit if someone suggested he wear a charm to protect himself against demons and dark magic. But as soon as Aislinn had seen the charm Seraphine had given him—a duplicate of which he'd hidden in Dylan's notebook before passing it back to this partner—she'd insisted that he let her put it on a chain, and then place it around his neck. Trace's grin widened and his cock went from resting to standing at full attention with the memory of just how Aislinn had convinced him to wear the necklace.

Son of a bitch, he loved her. She was his world and some days it was like an ache in the gut to be away from her. Especially now—when he had to worry about some newspaper reporter snooping around, hounding her, scaring her. He'd even gone so far as to try and convince her to go to Italy for a while, where Moki—the gypsy woman who was the mother of Aislinn's heart—was traveling. Fuck, like that wouldn't kill him, to come home to an empty house and bed.

She'd refused. And part of him felt ashamed and guilty for being happy that she wouldn't leave. Pathetic. Yeah, Dylan had it right. *How low would The Pro go?* Pretty damn low—except strangely enough, it felt like he was pretty damn high. High on life. High on love. High on Aislinn. Christ, she was his drug and he was completely hooked.

A small snicker escaped. Oh yeah, another thing Dylan was right about, the kind of misery he was in just loved company. He was going to enjoy seeing his partner fall and fall hard for Seraphine.

"I'm not laughing over here," Dylan growled. "You want to share the joke?"

"Just thinking about Lamaze classes and potty training."

"Fuck."

"Yeah. That too. Lots of that. Can't have too much practice in the 'fucking' department before you take the plunge and start working on making babies."

Dylan shook his head. Pathetic. Hard to stay irritated at a partner and best friend who'd hit rock bottom, whose mind never strayed very far from his wife's pussy. "Want to tell me where the hell this thing came from?" he asked again.

"The witch. Not that you haven't already figured out that's where it came from. More interesting is the way the senator's wife reacted to it. You catch that?"

"Yeah. I did. I also picked up on the fact that she didn't seem real choked up about the senator's aide being murdered. Made all the right sounds and facial expressions, but underneath…"

"Something about it made her giddy, smug."

Dylan fingered the charm. "Yeah…those are the right words. Not happy about Vorhaus being dead exactly, it was more like a kid that's pulled off a big prank."

Trace frowned, concentrating on the scene with the senator's wife, not sure about Dylan's read, about the wife getting off on the deed itself instead of the death—but then again, she'd rubbed him the wrong way from the start. "Maybe," he conceded. "Definitely worth looking into. Maybe we better revisit the affair angle."

"We can do it, just for the record. But I think it's going to be a dead end. According to Vorhaus' coworkers, she had a boyfriend, one they'd all met."

"Damn, I wish we could justify a search warrant and toss the senator's house."

"You really think the sword's hidden in there?"

"We've got two circles and the symbols next to the door, just like Seraphine predicted. So yeah, X marks the spot. I think the sword never left that house."

"At least not with the murderer. But if the senator or his wife is behind this, then they've had plenty of time to get rid of it."

Trace snorted. "You're forgetting something. What was your impression of the senator?"

"Pure politician. Smooth on the outside, conceited prick on the inside."

"In other words, a guy who's going to think he's a lot smarter than a couple of lowly homicide dicks." Trace's eyes narrowed as he remembered what Seraphine had said. *Whoever called this demon will be both confident and intelligent.* Yeah, the senator and his wife definitely deserved a much closer look.

Trace pulled into a space in the police parking lot and parked. "I didn't ask Seraphine for a lot of detail about the charm. One of us needs to contact her, find out what it means when someone like the senator's wife reacts to seeing it the way she did. Maybe Seraphine can ask around, see if the senator or his wife play in occult circles."

Fire ripped through Dylan's cock at the prospect of interrogating the witch. Fantasies of handcuffing her and having her at his mercy followed. Fuck. His gut roiled. He didn't want her involved in this. Still, he said, "I'll follow up on it."

Brady looked up as Dylan and Trace walked into the Homicide bullpen. "Good to see you guys strolling in. By the lateness of the hour, can we assume that you're hot on the trail of our murderer?"

Trace sat down on the edge of Storm's desk. Dylan pulled a chair over and said, "Our murderer?"

Storm turned away from her computer screen and picked up the photo, dropping it in front of Trace and Dylan. "Lucifer's Blade. It's missing from VanDenbergh's treasure room—not that the lawyer or the family volunteered that information."

Trace glanced at the photograph and closed his eyes briefly. "Fuck."

"Son of a bitch. Not more of this shit," Dylan growled.

Storm grinned. "I prefer to think of it as a lucky break. Now we have a link between the two cases." She reached over and retrieved several pieces of paper from where they lay on the printer. "There's not a whole lot of information on the Internet about the blade, but what there is looks good for tying it to your perp. Anyone who owns the knife is supposed to be able to use it to summon and command high-ranking demon lords."

"Christ," Trace said, picking up the papers, his scowl deepening as he read them, then passed them on to Dylan.

Brady leaned back in his chair, enjoying the moment. "While you two were out, probably sitting down at the Starbucks with your coffee and croissants, The Kid and I have been working our asses off on both cases. Another little lead has come to our attention. There's a very good chance that the senator's missing sword might not be as valuable as the insurance company thinks it is."

Trace's eyes narrowed. "Where'd that come from?"

Brady grinned and made a show of looking down at this notes. "None other than Severn Damek. Who said, quote, *I'm suggesting that its value is questionable, though I'm sure its worth is well documented.* So did you two find out who insured the senator's missing sword yet?"

Dylan reached for his notebook. "Yeah. McKeller and Sons, Underwriters and Insurers."

"Bingo," Brady said, grinning. "Imagine that. The Chalice of Eros just happens to be insured by the same company. Got an agent name?"

Dylan shook his head. "No. The senator said he didn't know it offhand. He claimed that he dealt with several insurance companies and several agents and his policies were all in a bank safety deposit box."

Storm opened her mouth to suggest that they hunt down Miles Terry, the representative who'd insured the Dragon's Cup, but before she could get the words out, Captain Ellis was standing in the doorway and looking grim.

"Sinclair, O'Malley, you'd better have a damn good reason for dragging a psychic over to the VanDenbergh place."

Storm grimaced, not surprised that VanDenbergh III had made good on his promise. Damn, they should have headed for the captain's office first thing, but they'd gotten sidetracked with the photo of the stolen blade. Dylan surprised her by intoning, "We're on this like flies on shit. We're lifting every stone no matter what scum is underneath. We're…"

The captain's eyebrows drew together at hearing his own words repeated, but Storm thought she saw just the slightest hint of amusement lurking in his eyes before she stepped in and answered the question, filling him in on what she and Brady had come up with so far, his nod of approval and "Good work" making her chest fill with pride.

"What about you two?" Ellis asked, shooting a look at Dylan and Trace, the frown deepening as they revealed the direction their questioning was heading. "You sure about the wife's reaction and the vibes you were picking up?" he asked after they'd stopped talking.

"Yeah," Trace said.

"I don't need to tell you to tread carefully. The senator's got a lot of connections. He's a big fish around here. Any whiff that we think he or his wife might be suspects, or might actually be involved in devil worship or demon summoning or whatever the hell it is, and we're all going to be busted down to writing tickets for parking violations—that's if we don't get chased out of town. So be careful. All of you. And for god's sake, keep me posted! My ass and ears are still blistered from the mayor's phone call about Brady and Storm dragging the psychic to old man VanDenbergh's place." He pushed away from the doorway and disappeared down the hallway.

Dylan gave a heartfelt sigh and stood. "Guess I need to pay a visit to a witch—or at least a woman who thinks she's one." He motioned toward the picture of Lucifer's Blade. "You got copies of this photo?"

"Take that one," Storm said. She looked at Brady. "Time to pay a visit to the lawyer and try to scare some answers out of him?"

"Yeah. And since you're the hotshot detective with the connections to the psychic community and to Severn Damek, why don't you see what you can shake loose about the blade. Considering how our thief—assuming the blade disappeared at the same time VanDenbergh Senior bit the bullet, so to speak—went to great pains to make it look like only the chalice got stolen, it makes me wonder if the real purpose all along wasn't to get the knife. Somehow I can see some psycho believing that he needed to kill someone in order to get the full benefit of Lucifer's Blade." Brady grimaced. "Ties in with the shit that the media has been laying on about objects of power needing to be recharged with blood sacrifices."

Dylan groaned. "Fuck, Brady, not you too. You're not buying into this shit are you?"

"I'm trying to think like the perp, and the perp buys into it."

Trace eased off the desk. "I think I'll see if the good senator can spare some time to pay a visit to his bank safety deposit box so we can see exactly which agent he was dealing with when he insured his sword."

They scattered, with Storm calling Tristan first, only to learn that he was in a faculty meeting. She thought about calling Severn Damek directly, even went so far as to pull out the dragon-embossed card he'd given her, but then thought better of it. A man like Damek didn't do favors for free. He wanted the Dragon's Cup and he was using her to get it. She could live with that, as long as everything was aboveboard, legal.

She decided to drop by Drake's Lair. Her body burning with need the closer she got to the exclusive club—to Pierce.

* * * * *

Storm parked and got out of the car—her own since Brady had the police-issue sedan. Almost immediately, uneasiness prickled along the back of her neck and spine. Out of habit she looked around. There were some fishermen at the end of a nearby wharf. Too far away to see clearly. A grandfather and his grandson. Two other men sitting in short beach chairs. Cuban maybe, talking and laughing. Another pair of men, standing and leaning against the tall railing, facing her, and yet apparently looking down the coastline with their fishing poles propped against the railing. Cops? Storm grimaced. Damn, maybe she should have mentioned she was heading over here to the captain. The last thing she needed was to get hauled in during a vice raid.

Beyond the pier, clouds were gathering and the wind was picking up, the air getting heavier. They were edging closer to the season when sudden, furious rain, along with a show of thunder and lightning, would be an almost daily occurrence.

She glanced again at the fishermen, this time catching one of the two men leaning against the railing looking at her. Her heart jumping when he hastily looked away. Yeah. A cop most likely, a green one or he wouldn't have been so quick to avert his gaze.

Storm thought about getting back in her car and driving away. But she'd come this far... And now that she was here, she felt a prickly heat, a discomfort, an edginess, almost like her skin was shrinking or else she was expanding so it no longer comfortably contained her. She needed to see Pierce before she left, and she felt like it would kill her to get back in the car without doing it.

That thought put a frown on her face and kept her motionless. She'd never experienced anything like this before — not even when she was suffering the drama-inducing effects of teenage hormones.

She hadn't noticed it so much when she'd been busy working the case, but as soon as she'd pulled her car out of the police department lot... The need had broadsided her, as elemental as the need to breathe, to seek shelter and build a fire. Her breasts. Her clit. Her cunt. "Get a grip here," she muttered. "How many johns and prostitutes have you busted who claimed they were sex addicts? So you had *the* night of all nights last night, that doesn't mean you can't wait until later to even *think* about getting more of the same."

A twinge of anxiety moved through Storm as she remembered how she'd felt after that first date with Tristan. How she'd woken up in her own bed the next morning, her breasts rapidly becoming flushed and heavy, her nipples tightening to hard points and aching so badly that she'd squeezed and tugged on them before moving to her clit, finding no relief until she'd concentrated on Tristan—and then finding only enough to tide her over until she could see him again.

This was worse. Much worse than that. A firestorm compared to a hot, hard breeze. One that only Tristan or Pierce could put out.

She caught herself clasping the faerie necklace and laughed self-consciously. Men. A source of amazing pleasure and absolute misery.

Storm turned and resolutely made her way toward the entrance of Drake's Lair just as the first rumble of thunder sounded far away, miles from shore, but promising to draw closer.

A woman was standing in the shadows near the front door, catching Storm's attention and holding it, making her think of places in the ocean where even the sunshine couldn't penetrate the deep, cold water. The prickling uneasiness returned with the woman's narrowed eyes and the frown that marred her translucent beauty. Storm moved past the still staring woman and into the elegant foyer of the club.

A dark-suited maître d' stepped forward immediately. "May I help you?"

His tie caught Storm's attention and her eyebrows lifted at the sight of the dragon embroidered on the dark material. Gold and red, with a hint of green. The pose similar to the one she'd seen on Severn Damek's chest, but the colors different. "Is Pierce here?"

"And you are?" Arrogance rang in his voice. But underneath was loyalty and protectiveness.

Storm smiled when she normally would have rolled her eyes or felt irritated. It warmed her to know that Pierce was respected, cared for by those in his employ. "Storm O'Malley."

"If you'll wait here..." The maître d' stepped to a polished, elegant wooden podium and picked up a telephone. Within seconds of him announcing her presence, Pierce was strolling in, making the breath catch in Storm's throat as she took in his stunning looks and heated, hungry eyes.

He didn't pause to greet her, but pulled her against his body, against the erection that burned through his clothing and hers, making her ache for the feel of his cock deep inside her. His tongue stroked into her mouth, claiming her, breathing fire into every cell so that for several long moments, Storm forgot where she was, and why she'd come there in the first place.

Pierce pulled away, satisfaction and lust obvious on his face. "I was thinking about you, and here you are."

"I wanted to ask you some questions," Storm managed, though for the life of her, she couldn't focus on them.

Pierce let his fingers trail down her arm, then took her hand in his as he looked at the maître d'. "Henri, should any ask, this woman belongs to my cousin Tristan—and to me."

The maître d' nodded. "Very good, Pierce, I'll let any who express an interest know."

Storm's heart filled with laughter and warmth, with pleasure and a touch of mortification at Pierce's open claim, but she didn't say anything as Pierce led her through the club, skirting a room full of men who reminded her of Severn Damek, before finally unlocking a door and ushering her into a cozy apartment. "This woman belongs to my cousin Tristan—and to me."

Pierce's fingers went to the buttons of her shirt, brushing over her nipples and in the process sending a flame of lust straight to her clit. "Do you deny the claim?"

"No, but—"

He stopped her words with a searing kiss. "There are men who frequent the club who would consider it a challenge to try and acquire you."

Storm shivered as her shirt parted and Pierce made short work of opening her bra so that her breasts tumbled out. She knew she should stop him. She knew…and yet she ached for him. Burned.

"I'm on duty…" she protested, aware of how breathless she sounded.

"And now you're on personal time," he said against her aroused flesh before his mouth latched onto a nipple and she cried out, her fingers tunneling through Pierce's hair and holding him against her breast for a moment before trying to push him away. He growled against her flesh, making her think of a roaring forest fire, and her cunt quivered at the sound, at the ruthless way he zeroed in on her pants, opening and pushing them down so that she was standing in her thong, trapped by his arms and the shackle of her pants around her ankles. "Pierce…" she tried again, unable to continue when his teeth tightened on her nipple, sending a rush of arousal into her saturated panties, the overflow moving to coat her inner thighs.

This was crazy. Insane. She couldn't do this. She had duties. Responsibilities.

She was a cop for god's sake. "No."

"Yes." His fingers tightened on her nipple almost painfully.

God, she couldn't believe how wonderful his touch felt. How much it turned her on when usually she hated it when a man went right to her breasts, as though the rest of her didn't matter.

But not with Pierce. She savored the knowledge that her breasts inflamed him, that he couldn't wait to see them, to touch them.

And she knew it was just the beginning. That by the time he was finished, no place on her body would be untouched, no place in her heart and soul would remain unplundered.

His hands dragged her thong down and almost immediately Pierce was on his knees before her, his mouth on her mound, his tongue thrusting deep and purposefully into her gushing cunt.

There was no resisting him. No denying him.

Pierce groaned against her wet, heated flesh. The taste of her was beyond compare, her cries more beautiful than the music created by the most skilled elves. Her body was pressed into him, her pussy pulsing and grinding against him, making it impossible to think about anything but claiming her, fucking her, giving more of his essence to her.

His forever wife. Nothing else could explain what had happened to him from the first moment she touched him.

He thrust his tongue deeper into her channel, then pulled back, circling her clit, rasping over it again and again with his tongue, reveling in the way she both fought and embraced the pleasure he was giving her.

He took everything she offered and demanded more. Pulling her downward so that she was on the floor, thrashing wildly, helpless against his onslaught, his hunger, the out of control fire that raged through him, demanding that she burn like he burned.

Over and over again she screamed, her body convulsing, writhing in orgasm, until she was weak. Compliant. Stretched out with her legs spread and her thighs glistening, and even then the wildness in his eyes wasn't dampened.

"Touch your breasts," he ordered, rising onto his knees and circling his cock with his own hand.

Storm's cunt spasmed at the sight and she had no thought to disobey him. She took her nipples between her fingers, turned on by the way he was watching her, by the way his hand was moving up and down on his penis, the sight of his huge erection and heavy balls making her feel like a primitive ancestor in the presence of a male in his prime.

She widened her legs, letting him see the arousal escaping from her swollen folds, not embarrassed to display herself, to show him what he did to her. And at the same time, she wanted to see her effect on him, to revel in her feminine power. She licked across her own nipple and watched his body jerk in response, watched as a drop of his arousal escaped, winking at her from the tip of this penis.

Her tongue stroked across her nipple again, slowly, and Pierce's hand tightened on his cock as his lips pulled back in a feral snarl. He pounced before she could do it again. Positioning her on her hands and knees, forcing her chest to the floor before mounting her, fucking into her so hard and fast that one scream seemed to merge into the next until she was hoarse, sated, left boneless by his absolute possession.

"Have you ever heard of something called Lucifer's Blade?" Storm asked a while later, her front curled against Pierce's warm chest as she trailed her fingers along his sweat-slick spine.

He tensed, uneasiness replacing the languidness in his body and Storm couldn't help but think about his reaction, and Tristan's, when she'd shown them the picture of the circle and symbols from Trace and Dylan's murder scene.

"Why do you ask?"

She hesitated, part of her still uncomfortable with mixing her private life with her professional one. And yet…despite what had happened between them, despite the fact that his cock was still lodged inside her from their second fuck…she really had come here in order to consult with him.

"We think it was stolen from VanDenbergh's place at the same time the chalice was."

Pierce hugged her to him, his fingers tangling in her necklace and pulling it around so that he could take possession of the winged faeries and their multi-hued crystal. "Such a powerful artifact should never have been created. If you come across it, promise me that you'll take care."

Tension and concern vibrated from his body to hers. She moved so that she could look into his face. "Are you saying that you believe someone can actually use it to summon demon lords?"

He tightened his grip on the necklace. "You doubt it?"

She frowned. Did she? Did she really? She didn't know. In a way she didn't want to know.

Storm grimaced, muttering, "Just call me Trace, or Dylan."

Pierce laughed. "I think not. I have never hungered for a man. Never burned for any other woman as I do for you."

Storm brushed her lips against his, his words and the look in his eyes filling her in a way that left no room for doubt.

Somewhere in the tangle of clothing next to them, Storm's cell phone began ringing and heat rushed to her cheeks despite the fact that no one could see her. She rolled out of Pierce's arms and retrieved the phone.

Brady. "We got a break on the case. How soon can you get back to the station?"

"Half hour, less if I put the siren on."

"Hit it then. I just got a judge to sign off on a warrant to search the insurance guy's place."

Chapter Fourteen

🔊

"What gives?" Storm asked as she slid into the unmarked sedan and closed the door.

"Cornered the butler and finally got something we could use," Brady said, pulling out of the police parking lot. "Turns out that the insurance guy, Miles Terry, brokered the deal for the chalice. And since we know it was stolen property, Judge Cabot signed off on a warrant to search Terry's place. Turns out that Terry works from his home, so Cabot okayed the entire house."

Storm grinned. Damn, this was every bit as exciting as a car chase—and a hell of a lot less nerve-racking. "Good work, Brady."

"When you got it, you got it, Kid."

"What about Lucifer's Blade? The butler come up with anything on that?"

Brady grunted. "I got him to admit that he was the one who had the picture delivered to the station. Seeing Ilsa—Madame Fontaine—set off an alarm bell in his head and he realized it had gone missing. The day she visited VanDenbergh Senior, he noticed how uneasy the thing made her. But there's no connection to Miles Terry, or McKeller and Sons. Old man VanDenbergh got the knife about twenty-five years ago and insured it with another company."

"Anything from Dylan or Trace?"

"Nada. Zilch. They were still out in the field when I popped in to update the captain and get the okay for the warrant."

They pulled to a stop in front of Terry's beachfront house. "I'd say the insurance business pays well," Storm said.

Brady looked out over the ocean, zeroing in on a boat with radar perched on the top for tracking fish. "Yeah."

They moved to the front door, knowing as soon as they got there, that they were probably too late. Terry's office was to the left of the door with a big window so he could take in the view. The room had been ransacked.

"Damn. Whoever did this is probably long gone." Still, Brady pulled his gun before he reached for the doorknob.

The house was unlocked. Storm had her gun out and ready as they both went inside.

They searched first, noticing immediately that whoever had tossed Terry's office had not done equal damage to the rest of the house, and hadn't been after the usual items. The TV, sound system, and collectables were all undisturbed. For a fleeting second, Storm wondered if Severn Damek was behind the search, but her gut told her that if he'd ordered it, the place would look like it had never been touched.

"Found a gun," she yelled to Brady a few minutes later. "On the nightstand next to the bed. Same caliber as the one that killed VanDenbergh." Excitement gave way to speculation. Was Terry running scared? Why else would anyone keep a loaded gun out in plain sight?

Once again, the image of Severn rose in Storm's mind. Deep auburn hair and the dragon raging across his chest. *I don't generally deal pleasantly with those who think to cheat or play with me.*

Stupidity, arrogance, fear on Terry's part—time would tell once they ran the gun. Storm bagged it for ballistics testing then joined Brady as they concentrated on the office.

It was Brady who got the first hit when he found a file containing ten or fifteen photographs of the Medici Chalice of Eros. "Wonder how many times our boy has sold and stolen this thing back?"

Brady passed the stack of photos to Storm. She studied the top one for a second, confirming Brady's initial impression. The picture was identical to the one Severn had given to her. Halfway through the stack the photographs changed to the "chalice on display" version, the same one they'd originally gotten from Terry. "As far as we know, no one else has been murdered over it. The last time the thing was reported stolen was a hundred years ago."

"As far as we know, Kid, that's the key phrase here. We don't really know squat about where the thing has been, except that Terry didn't have it a hundred years ago—unless buying and selling it was the family business—and if the thing's worth five mil, what's he still doing in the business?"

"Good question."

"The photos are enough to get an all-points-bulletin out on him as a person of interest."

"And this," Storm said, adrenaline surging as she placed an open folder on the desk.

Brady looked down and actually smiled. "Yeah, that's the ticket. Lucifer's Blade nestled safe and sound in VanDenbergh's display case. I'm betting Terry used a cell phone to snag this shot."

"Maybe if we could find the phone, we could find out if he sent the photo to a potential buyer."

"Good thinking, Kid. That's why they've got you riding with me, so you could learn from the best."

Storm snickered. "Right, Pops."

* * * * *

Frustration raged through Dylan. *Fuck, where the hell was she?* He'd been outside the witch's house longer than he'd intended to be, waiting for her to show up even though she wasn't expecting him and hadn't returned his call telling her that he was on his way over and had some follow-up questions for her.

Christ. He had a hard-on that wouldn't quit. Had gotten it as soon as he heard her voice telling him that she wasn't available and to leave a message.

It pissed him off.

He didn't believe in spells, but she'd done something to him. Fire crawled up Dylan's neck and into his face.

Son of a bitch, it had taken all his concentration to fuck the woman he'd gone home with last night—and even then, he'd had to picture Seraphine to do it, and once was all he could manage before he'd escaped, claiming he'd been paged in to work.

He shifted restlessly then picked up his cell phone and punched in a number, the green stone in the ring Aislinn had made for him glowing in the sunlight as Seraphine's husky voice said, "Hi, I'm not available right now. But your call is important to me, so please leave a message."

Dylan ended the call, his gut going hot and anxious when he looked down and found that he was gripping his cock at the sound of her voice.

* * * * *

Excitement gave way to uneasiness by the time Brady and Storm made it to Ballistics. "You picking up on something strange going on around here?" Brady finally asked.

"Like stares, stopped conversations, then whispering?"

He patted a couple of pockets and retrieved a lone peppermint candy. "Yeah. That."

"No, I haven't noticed a thing."

"Smartass."

Storm pushed the door to the crime lab open and they moved through it. "We've got a gun for you to look at Skinner," she said. "It might be the murder weapon in the VanDenbergh case."

Skinner grinned. "What are you bringing it to me for? Take it to the psychic." Long-boned fingers moved through the air, hovering as he intoned, "Come closer. Let me see the weapon. Yes, yes, it's speaking to me. It says…"

"Ha ha," Brady growled. "Very funny. The city pay you to sit on your pale scrawny ass while evidence cools off?"

Skinner's eyebrows swept upward. "Didn't they cover the inappropriateness of making comments about a person's various body parts in diversity and sensitivity training, Brady? And for the record, scrawny is in the eye of the beholder. My wife happens to love my ass. Can't keep her hands off it as a matter of fact, especially when we're…"

Storm held up her hand, dangling the bag containing the gun in front of Skinner's face. "That's way too much information about your ass, Skinner. Way more than I want to picture."

Skinner snickered and took the gun. "I'll process this ASAP. In the meantime, maybe I can get your autographs. You two made the news."

Storm grimaced, almost sure she knew where this was heading. "Want to tell us about it?"

"Does the name Madame Fontaine ring any bells? Or how about this—" Skinner positioned his hands as though he was framing a shot. "Detectives stumped in the VanDenbergh murder case and call in a psychic for help. Family of murder victim outraged!"

"Shit," Storm said.

"The captain know about it?" Brady asked.

"He and the chief are down at the mayor's office as we speak. If I were you two, I'd hightail it out of here."

They handed over the folders containing the photographs of the chalice and Lucifer's Blade then left, intending to tough it out and return to the Homicide bullpen. But halfway there, Brady said, "Maybe we ought to swing by Ilsa—Madame Fontaine's place, and make sure she's not being hounded. Some of those news guys can get overzealous."

Storm bit her lip to keep from saying, *That's why we've got phones, Brady.* "Sounds good to me."

He squinted at her. "What? No other comment from the peanut gallery?"

"Just backing you up, partner. And if you're still running scared about asking her out…"

The corner of Brady's mouth moved upward just a hint. "Keep it up, Kid, you'll be sitting in class with me. Calling me scared might damage my self-esteem and make me a target of ridicule among my peers."

Storm grinned. "Like the clothes don't already do that."

On cue Brady looked down at the rumpled suit and multi-stained tie. "What's wrong with this outfit? Brown's a good color."

"Black would be better."

"Black? Geez, then people would mistake me for an undertaker like my old man."

"Your old man's an undertaker?"

"Yeah. Old man. Uncles. Brothers. Even a couple of female cousins. Sinclair Mortuaries. That's the family business."

Storm's eyebrows went up. Sinclair Mortuaries was a big outfit if the number of funeral homes up and down the coast was any indication. "So what happened to you, Brady? You decide to work the supply side of the business? You shoot 'em, they box 'em?"

Brady raised his face to the sky. "Why me, God? What'd I ever do to deserve this? Especially if you're willing to overlook that little incident behind the church. Why'd it have to be me that got stuck with a rookie homicide cop who thinks she's a comedienne?"

Storm snickered and ducked into the unmarked police car. "Incident behind the church, huh. I can hardly wait to hear about that."

The thunder sounded like it was almost on top of them by the time they got to the ocean frontage road and Madame Fontaine's house. The sedan crawled past on the first go round.

"No sign of trouble," Brady said, easing the car around first one corner and then another so that they were traveling on a street parallel to Ilsa's.

"Don't tell me we're going to settle for a drive-by," Storm said, amusement warring with a rush of softer emotions as she looked at Brady and read acute nervousness in his rigid posture. "Hey, for all we know, she's inside, traumatized by the news coverage or threats of a lawsuit by the VanDenberghs. No way of telling how bad it's been since we haven't heard the news reports ourselves. Nothing strange about us dropping in on her. It's in the line of duty since we involved her in this case to begin with."

Some of the tension left Brady. "Yeah, you're right, Kid. Nobody'll ever say that Brady Sinclair shirked his duty." Two more corners and a couple of blocks and he parked the unmarked car in front of Ilsa's home, though he was much slower to get out of it than Storm was.

Ilsa's front door opened, but rather than wait for them to come to her, she rushed down the walkway. Brady surprised Storm by moving around the car in a hurry, intercepting Madame Fontaine just as the first drops of rain began falling.

"Thank God you got here in time!" Ilsa said a second before the wind shifted, bringing with it the sound of a woman's panicked screaming—"Bryce! Bryce! Someone help! Please! Bryce! Bryce!"

Storm and Brady both turned and saw a woman running back and forth along the edge of the surf, her focus on a flailing child several hundred yards out. Storm hesitated only long enough to take off her jacket and shove her gun underneath the seat of the sedan. Brady did the same, locking the car and handing off his keys to Ilsa before racing after Storm.

She hit the water first, glad it was warm instead of frigid like the Alaska-chilled ocean water on the west coast. Overhead the thunder cracked, loud and ominous, completely obliterating the sound of the woman's screaming as lightning splintered like a hundred tongues darting downward in an attempt to taste the earth.

Storm could hear Brady behind her, but losing ground against her stronger, steadier strokes. She didn't get to the beach much anymore, but she'd grown up addicted to sun and surf and had worked as a lifeguard from the time she was sixteen until she joined the force.

Hang on, just hang on, she chanted internally, seeing the raw terror on the thrashing, flailing child's face as she got closer.

Almost there…almost there — and then with a suddenness that sent terror racing through Storm — the boy disappeared, jerked under the water with a force that made her heart lurch and her mind scream *Shark! Shit, there's a shark out here!*

She dived, forcing her eyes open in the stinging saltwater, then propelling herself forward blindly when she spotted the panicked boy struggling to get to the surface in water that was free of both blood and sharks.

Blindly Storm swam, hearing the boy and aiming toward him, her hand striking flesh and immediately pushing both him and her toward the surface. They broke in a heavy downpour that washed the salt from Storm's face, though her eyes still burned and stung. "You're safe now," she managed, trying to fight off the boy's hands and arms and get him in a safe hold so that he couldn't drown them both.

A cold swirl of rapidly moving water curled around Storm, momentarily freezing the breath in her chest, and she lost her grip on the kid, only to have him plaster himself to her back and grab her neck, choking her as his legs wrapped around her, forcing the air from her lungs and allowing the water to rush in. She tried to stay calm, but as they sank underneath the surface of the water, his hold tightened and she began to fight in earnest as blackness threatened around the edges of her consciousness.

And then as quickly as the boy had latched on to her, he was pulled off. She shot to the surface, choking and coughing, gagging as water rushed out of her mouth and air tried to rush in.

Brady surfaced a few feet away, the kid held tightly, his back to Brady's chest, his arms pinned to his sides by one of Brady's, the secure position calming the previously terrified boy. "You okay, Kid?" Brady said.

"Yeah, nice save there."

He grinned. "Stick with me, Kid. This old dog still knows a few tricks."

Storm laughed, relief and joy making her almost giddy. "What, go fetch? Ilsa will be thrilled. It's right up there with housebreaking when it comes to a potential husband."

"God save me from comedienne cops. See you back on shore, Kid."

Storm stayed where she was for a minute, giving herself a little more time to catch her breath and let the frantic beat of her heart slow. *Shit. She'd almost died.* And the worst part of it was that she still couldn't get her mind around what had happened. The way the kid had been jerked under, the cold blast of water that had allowed the boy to escape her grip and climb on her back, nearly drowning them both.

Something glittered underneath the surface of the water. The necklace.

Storm's heart did a quick jump at the sight of it. The necklace must have gotten pulled out from underneath her shirt while she was struggling with the kid. Thank god it hadn't gotten lost in the ocean.

She started swimming then, moving closer to Brady with every stroke. At least the kid was still calm. At least they'd been able to save him.

Shit. How had he gotten so far from shore? How had he managed to stay alive as long as he did if he couldn't swim — and why hadn't the mother come in? Unless maybe she didn't know how to swim either. Storm's stomach tightened. That was probably it. Crazy. Crazy to live near the ocean and not know how to swim. Hell. It was crazy not to know how to swim. Period. At least in her opinion. And to bring a kid here, one who couldn't be more than four or five years old. It was almost asking for a disaster. Shells. Fish. Sand crabs. Warm water. They were just a few of the things that could distract a parent or lure a kid into danger.

Storm kicked a little harder, wanting to catch up with Brady, but before she'd managed three strokes, her legs and arms and chest went numb as a swirl of freezing water engulfed her, pulling her under before she could make a sound.

She fought her own body, trying to move limbs that felt like dead weights. Managing to inch upwards, only to be pulled down by an icy hand that had no form. Panic set in. Raw terror that translated into intense cramping as her arms and legs tried to respond to demands to kick and claw to the surface — only to have her body rolled and tumbled so that she no longer knew which way was up.

Her lungs burned while the rest of her froze. And once again blackness threatened at the edge of Storm's consciousness. She fought to hold on, forcing herself to open her eyes and suffer the sting of the saltwater to get her bearings.

The necklace caught her attention and images of Tristan and Pierce moved through her mind — and with them heat. Blessed heat, almost painfully warm as it moved down her arms and legs, chasing the cold away.

As quickly as the freezing water had engulfed her, it dissipated and Storm was surrounded by warm water pushing her to the surface and then to shore.

"'Bout time you showed up," Brady said, then squinted, his face slowly turning red. "Jesus Christ, Kid. Put that thing away before someone else sees it."

Storm glanced down, transfixed by the brightness of the necklace, the wash of colors reflected in the crystal — all shades of red and blue—the anatomically correct faeries reminding her of Pierce and Tristan and the strangeness of what had happened in the water.

She tucked the necklace back in her shirt. The boy's voice distracting her as she caught him saying over and over, "But I saw a horse in the water! I was riding a horse and then it stopped carrying me and went away!"

Storm shivered, remembering the fey stories about Kelpies that she had in her collection, stories about Scottish water faeries that took the form of young horses and lured humans into the water, only to drown them. And then a chill of a different kind went through Storm as she looked behind where the child and his mother stood and spotted the same woman she'd seen in the shadows outside Drake's Lair. Just like then, the woman's narrowed eyes were focused on her, and just like earlier in the day, the woman's translucent beauty made Storm think of the places in the ocean where even the sunshine couldn't penetrate the deep, cold water.

The woman turned and walked away, but Storm's uneasiness remained. Unconsciously her hand moved to where the necklace rested underneath her shirt and as soon as she noticed what she'd done, Aislinn's words rang clear in Storm's mind.

Freely given, freely accepted, let the wearer see both the beauty and peril of the hidden realms.

Storm glanced toward the ocean where she'd nearly died and decided to visit Aislinn and share what had happened. She couldn't pretend anymore that the crystal was ordinary and the necklace just a beautiful piece of jewelry.

Chapter Fifteen

ಐ

Pierce paced restlessly around Tristan's kitchen. His chest ached with emotion, as though the hollow space left by Storm's calling of his fire had filled with an ice-cold fear that threatened to expand and consume all his heat.

"She is okay," Tristan said yet again. "She is not our wife, but she holds enough of our essence so that we would know if some harm had come to her."

Pierce stilled only long enough to look out the window and view the flowers in Tristan's yard, his body going tight as memories of taking Storm on the hot tub cover rushed through his mind and enflamed his cock. "You will claim her tonight?"

"Yes."

* * * * *

The rain had ended and the storm had moved on, lightning flickering and thunder booming in the distance by the time Storm went home, showered, changed into dry clothes and then drove to Inner Magick. She parked in front and turned the engine off, hesitating as she looked at Aislinn's shop.

"I'm going crazy," she muttered, feeling ridiculous and uncertain now that the adrenaline had faded and she was by herself. "But at least Aislinn won't think so. Right? I mean, she really *believes* in supernatural stuff, including crystals."

Storm fished the necklace out from underneath her shirt and looked at it. *Okay. Not so crazy. All these colors weren't there before. I know that for certain. And there's no sunshine hitting it now. There's no logical explanation why it's not all blues and reds, like it was on the beach.*

She got out of the car, hesitating again, aware of the gun underneath her jacket. She was officially off duty, and yet... Storm grimaced, acknowledging to herself that the events at the beach had spooked her. Not that a gun would do any good. But it was a measure of just how rattled she was that she didn't want to take it off and stash it in the trunk of her car like she normally would.

Storm sighed and locked the car door before closing it. What she needed was to talk to Aislinn, then go to Tristan's house. A night of mind-blowing sex would fix her right up.

She snickered and grinned, some inner tension giving way as she headed for the front door of Inner Magick. The relief lasted until the moment she got close enough to see the shattered display case and the crystals scattered on the carpet.

Her cop instincts kicked in, compounded by fear for Aislinn. "You!" she said, pointing her finger at a middle-aged man who was standing with his wife and window-shopping at a quaint country store several yards and an alley away from Inner Magick. "I'm a cop. Call 911!" She pulled her gun, only barely noting the fear that flashed across the man's face at the sight of it, before she turned and tried to open the front door.

Locked.

Storm's fear escalated and she didn't hesitate. She jammed the butt of the gun against the glass, smashing through so she could reach in and unlock the door. The sound of shattering glass meant there was no hope of catching anyone off-guard. Storm pushed the door open and ran for the far wall, stopping next to the curtained doorway.

She thought she heard a whimper behind it before she grabbed the edge of the fabric, yanking it back and taking in the nightmare scene — Aislinn bound and gagged, bloody, beaten, nearly naked — even as she barked, "Hands up! Hands up! Now!" Rage swirling through her so that she wished the man struggling with his pants would make a move toward the workbench where a gun lay — black and deadly, with a silencer attached to it.

"On the ground, arms out, hands flat," Storm ordered, tense, ready to fire if the man in front of her made even the slightest movement toward the gun. He dropped to his knees and she moved around him, heading for the workbench but making sure she stayed a safe distance. "All the way. Now!"

He dropped the rest of the way but Storm didn't relax, didn't give in to the desperate need to tend to Aislinn, though she carefully shifted out of her jacket and draped it over Aislinn's body. "Hang on, Aislinn. I can hear the sirens now."

It seemed like a lifetime passed before she heard movement in the front of the store. "Back here," she yelled. "O'Malley, Homicide. I've got a gun on the perp."

"Christ!" the first uniform through the door said, moving in with his gun drawn.

"Take care of this piece of shit," Storm said, only holstering her own gun when a second uniformed officer, one she recognized from her days as a beat cop, joined the first, putting his gun up and pulling out his restraints.

Storm removed Aislinn's gag first. Hating the wounded look in Aislinn's eyes, hating the sight of her bruised, swollen face—hating the need to ask her if she'd been raped. "Hold on, let me get your hands free. Then we'll get you out of here."

Aislinn was shivering so hard that it made the task of freeing her more difficult. "Hang on," Storm murmured, working at the knots and wishing she had a knife with her, but not wanting to leave Aislinn, even for a minute.

She got the last knot free just as Trace stormed in, fear and rage and absolute agony written on his face, beyond words, though the hint of tears spoke as he scooped Aislinn up and held her tight, his expression lost in her pale blonde hair. For several long minutes they stood there, clutching each other, deep in a private, silent conversation, aware of only each other. And then Trace shuddered and lowered Aislinn to her feet, helping her into Storm's jacket before shifting, encircling her in his arms and sheltering her against his body as he finally lifted his head and met Storm's gaze. "You got here in time," he said, his arms tightening on Aislinn.

Relief surged through Storm. "Get her out of here, Trace. We can handle this slimeball."

Bennett, the cop Storm recognized, jerked the handcuffed man to his feet, his own anger evident in the rough handling. Hatred burned in Trace's eyes at the sight of the perp's fly, still open, his jeans hanging off his hips.

The other uniformed policeman jerked the zipper up, then patted the man down, pulling out a switchblade before retrieving a wallet from the guy's pocket and opening it. "Dwight Vaughn. Miami address, if the license is legit." The cop's expression hardened. "Let's get him processed." He separated a piece of paper from the wallet. "I think Dwight here is looking at ra—" he glanced at Trace, "at conspiracy to commit murder for starters."

Storm stepped closer, gut going hollow and cold when she saw what the man had in his wallet. Addresses—for Aislinn's home and Inner Magick—along with a description of her car and a license plate number.

"Get him out of here, Bennett," she said, eyes going to the gun with the silencer attachment. "I can get her statement and secure the area."

"Sure thing."

They left with the perp and his weapons. Storm moved closer to Aislinn, feeling suddenly awkward. "We can do this after Trace takes you to the hospital."

Aislinn's arms tightened around Trace. "No. No hospital."

"Aislinn…"

Trace interrupted. "No. It's okay. You got here in time. I'll take her home. Let's just get this over with." His voice was curt, angry. His face tense, jaw clenched. But Storm saw the slight tremor in his hands as he rubbed them up and down Aislinn's back.

Aislinn shivered for a minute longer, then pushed back against his hands, forcing enough room so that she could turn and face Storm, though Trace immediately pulled her back to his front and settled his arms around her waist, everything about him screaming protectiveness. "I was rearranging one of the display cases when he came in." Her hands settled on Trace's arms and she squeezed. "I know I should have had the door locked, but it was still light out, people were back on the streets again, window-shopping, and Storm was on her way over." She shuddered. "He locked the door when he came in. His gun was already out and he was so close. I tried to get away. I threw the crystals I was rearranging at him and he swung the gun. He missed the first time and broke the case, but then he got me with his fist. There was only time to scream once."

She licked her lips and tears formed at the corner of her eyes. "Then he was hitting me and dragging me into the back room. I fought him."

"It's okay, baby," Trace whispered, rubbing his cheek against her hair. "I know you did. I called it in as soon as I knew you were in trouble. I got here as quick as I could."

Storm's eyes widened at Trace's pain-filled admission. At the confirmation that he and Aislinn were connected telepathically. His gaze met hers but she didn't call him on it. Instead she gently finished questioning Aislinn so that Trace could take her home. Afterward Storm stayed just long enough to sweep up and cover the broken glass in the door with cardboard before setting the alarm and leaving.

* * * * *

Tristan's house welcomed her, or at least that's the way it felt when Storm finally got there. Warm and sweet-smelling, like comforting arms and the smell of home. God, she needed it. She felt like she'd been off to war and was only back on leave.

"Hard day?" Tristan asked, coming out of his library, wearing only jeans for a change, his body looking tense to Storm though his voice sounded as it always did.

"More than hard." Now that she was with him, she didn't want to think about it, didn't want to talk about it. But she couldn't stop herself. "I wanted to talk to Aislinn and she stayed late at Inner Magick, waiting for me to get there. If I'd been minute later…if I'd hesitated at all…she would have been raped." Storm started shaking and Tristan was there, wrapping her in his arms and pulling her against his body, stroking along her back.

"But she wasn't violated," Tristan murmured. "You got there. You prevented it."

The guilt that Storm hadn't allowed herself earlier tried to crush her. "But I'm the reason she was there."

"Bad things happen to good people, Storm. The same thing could have happened another night, in another place."

She knew it was the truth. Knew that the guy could just as easily have killed Aislinn. The silencer, the paper in his wallet with both the Inner Magick and Aislinn's addresses, the car description and license plate number—were all evidence of his intention to kill her. Storm knew it and yet it was hard to shed the images, the guilt. "He hit her. He gagged her and tied her up. He cut her clothing. Her eyes were so wounded, so hurt…"

Tristan's voice was tender. "Don't worry about her tonight, Storm, let your concern go. She has a heartmate, he'll see to her needs. He'll heal her with the truth of his love."

Storm pulled back and looked into Tristan's face, surprised by his words, by his use of the term heartmate. "You know Aislinn and Trace?"

"Of them."

Confusion washed over her. A prickling along her spine. "How do you know about the heartmate thing?"

He chuckled and brushed his lips against hers. "I forget that the cop and the woman I've fallen in love with share the same skin."

Her heart jumped at his words. She trailed a finger down his smooth chest, wanting to believe his words, and yet... "We haven't known each other that long. How can you say..."

"That I love you? Easily. You're funny and loyal, tough and serious, smart and challenging..." He kissed her. "Beautiful. Generous. Caring. And more, so much more, Storm—you're everything I want so that all I need is to be with you, to make love with you, to share in your pleasure."

"And Pierce?"

He laughed. "You'll have to coax Pierce's feelings out on your own. But until later tonight, it's just the two of us. He has business to attend to at Drake's Lair—business that I'm sure my beautiful cop doesn't want to learn about."

My beautiful cop. It warmed her. Made her smile and laugh inwardly. "So that makes you *my gorgeous professor*—which then begs the question, so what are you going to teach me?"

"Hmmm, what subject would you like to study?" he asked before sealing his mouth to hers, teasing along the seam of her lips with his tongue until she opened and let him fill her with warmth and heat and desire.

By the time he lifted his mouth from hers, she was wet, swollen, her nipples tight points against her shirt. "I'm starting to get an idea..." she whispered, looking into blue eyes that made her think of a warm summer sky.

His hand moved down her spine, smoothing over her buttocks. "Tell me one of your fantasies."

Unbidden—perhaps her subconscious way of dealing with the fear and horror from earlier in the day—she thought about what it would be like to handcuff a man—him—to her bed and tease him until he was helpless with lust.

If she believed in vampires, then she would have claimed it was hidden compulsion that made her answer, because even as the words were drawn from her, her face flamed with embarrassment.

Tristan's eyes darkened, a storm of lust whirling within them that had her heart racing and her body tightening. "If you command it, I will let you bind me, I will let you have all that I am," he whispered, his voice stroking over her erect clit, so elemental and raw, so much like Pierce in that moment that she had to reassure herself the eyes were blue and not green.

Storm licked her lips, suddenly nervous, surrounded by undercurrents and deeper meanings that she had no way of interpreting, and yet…warmth moved over her, a breeze coming in through the windows and swirling lazily down the hallway, toward the bedroom, the air heavy with the fragrant scent of flowers, with the promise of peace and pleasure. "I want to take a shower first," she found herself saying, laughing when he immediately swept her into his arms and carried her to the master bathroom, the laughter quickly giving way to murmurs and sighs as hands stroked over flesh, baring it, caressing it, arousing it.

"You're beautiful, inside and outside," Tristan whispered, his hands cupping her breasts, his thumbs stroking over her nipples, his face taut. "I want to pour myself into you, to fill you completely with everything I am. To tie myself to you in the most elemental way."

"I want you the same way," she found herself saying, lost in his eyes, lost in him. Opening parts of her heart she'd never given to any man before, letting Tristan fill them as the potent fragrance of flowers filled his house. "Make love to me," she whispered, unable to stand another moment without feeling him inside her.

He lifted her easily, settling her on his cock, filling her with a sense of rightness, completeness. Of being home. Safe, secure. The ugliness of the world that her job required her to face, a separate existence.

Her legs went around his waist. Her lips found his and her eyes closed.

One slow stroke followed another as the water cascaded over them.

By The Goddess and The Fates alike, he felt as though his heart would explode with the intensity of his feelings for Storm. He'd thought to lay her down on a bed of rose petals, to worship her, to declare his love and only then open himself completely, joining his body to hers and making her his wife in truth, irrevocably binding his life to hers through his kiss and seed.

But her distress had waylaid his plans. Then her teasing and whispered fantasy had destroyed his resolve. And now he felt the openness of her heart. He couldn't resist. He held her tighter, deepening the kiss, the movement of his hips quickening, sheer joy racing through him at her answering moans, at the way her legs clamped around him, her body answering his silent call, shuddering, meeting his thrusts until she was crying out in release, begging him to join her in ecstasy. But he held back. Wanting it to last, wanting the moment to be worthy of the occasion.

Somehow they managed to dry off and get to bed. And then he was on her again. Stroking, coaxing, driving her higher with his words, his hands, his lips, his cock.

It felt as though they were in the midst of a howling storm, a violent swirl of emotion and sensation that left them defenseless, helpless against a force so elemental that there was no denying it, no controlling it, no fighting it. They clung together, breaths mingling, bodies slick, so tightly joined that two became one. So entwined that the death of one was the death of the other.

It was like nothing he'd ever experienced, and yet it was everything that was important to him. He wanted it to last forever, even as he knew that something so fierce couldn't be sustained for long.

Sweat washed across Tristan's face and body like raindrops rushing to earth. His mouth covered hers. His body thrust in and out of hers, the touch of her flesh becoming more necessary with each stroke, as the storm that surrounded them found a center, a balance between mortal and immortal, earth and air and water.

And only then did he cry out, his release echoed by hers as she took his seed, as her body welcomed everything that he was. As they both became something other than what they had always been.

For a shimmering instant Storm felt as though she had no distinct form, as though she and Tristan were free of their bodies, one joined entity as vast and endless as the sky, as fluid and deep as the ocean.

Distantly she could hear her heart thundering in her chest, the primal beat of a mystical drum giving her power over wind and rain and sea, before calling her back to her body, leaving her breathless, yet strangely exhilarated. Leaving her wondering what had just happened.

"That was incredible," she said, her arms tightening involuntarily around Tristan. He laughed in response. A husky sound of masculine satisfaction as his lips teased her ear and then pressed against hers in a quick kiss before he pushed himself off her.

Storm would have been satisfied to cuddle under the covers but a laugh escaped and her body surged back to life when Tristan disappeared, only to return with a pair of padded handcuffs. "Hmmm, so the good Professor Plum is into kink."

"Only for Miss Scarlet," he said, dropping to the bed next to her, laughing, enjoying the play. "Though I'll admit, it was Colonel Mustard who showed up with these earlier in the day." He leaned in and kissed her, intoning in his best professor voice, "A warning, my dear, the colonel is up to no good."

Storm laughed, threading her fingers through Tristan's hair. "So you think he intends something wicked?"

"Very, very wicked if I'm any judge of the colonel, but I'm sure Miss Scarlet can handle him."

"Like I can handle you?"

Tristan's eyelids lowered, but didn't cover the sudden heat in his eyes. "Do your worst."

Storm rose to her knees, taking the handcuffs from him before he rolled to his back and positioned his arms so that she could secure his wrists to the bed frame. Heat pooled in her cunt lips—a hot rush that parted them. And when she looked down her body, at her tight nipples, her clit—erect, swollen, the skin pulled back from its tiny head—she almost faltered.

Fuck! Was there something wrong with her that she was this turned on by the idea of restraining him?

"Storm," he murmured, his voice making her look at his face and meet his eyes—his gaze sultry and heated, encouraging. "Use the cuffs or I will."

She used them. Securing him to the bed before lowering her body onto his, taking his lips first, and then the rest of him. Her mouth and tongue relentless as they tortured his tiny male nipples before moving lower, driving him mad as she sucked and licked and let him feel the sting of her teeth on his cock.

He begged for release. Threatened retribution. Shivered and shook and enjoyed her assault, once again giving her everything he was, entrusting her with his life. Savoring the moment when she released him and let him roll her underneath him, pounding in and out of her body with the violence of fast-flowing rapids, his cries echoing hers on a shore of pure ecstasy.

They climbed underneath the covers, lying together, entwined, content. Tristan felt her smile against his chest and smiled in response, her happiness as important to him as the air and sea from which his ancient ancestors had first formed.

"That was good," she murmured. "But next time we'll allow Professor Plum the upper hand."

A jolt went through Tristan, not just because of the promise of sexual pleasure, but at the words not spoken—the trust implicit in her comment. He rubbed his cheek against her blonde hair, the color so similar to his own and Pierce's that it was easy for anyone looking at them to believe that the three of them belonged together.

"I spoke to Pierce earlier. He said you had reason to believe that Lucifer's Blade was stolen from VanDenbergh's collection."

Storm sighed. "Just when you think it can't get worse…"

She filled him in on her day—or most of it, hesitating only briefly before remembering the collection of books she'd seen in Tristan's office and plunging in, leaving out the part about the necklace but telling him about the boy being jerked under, the ice-cold current in the ocean, the phantom hand that had wrapped around her ankle, the little boy's insistence that he'd been riding on a horse. The woman that she'd seen both on the beach and at Drake's Lair.

Her body was tense by the time she finished, her heart racing, wondering if he was going to think she was nuts. Hell, saying it out loud made *her* wonder if she was nuts.

But then she realized that his body was just as tense as hers, his arms like iron bands around her, his heart racing as fast as hers. She pushed back far enough so that she could look into his face. "You don't think I'm crazy or suffering from some kind of fatigue syndrome, do you?"

Tristan forced his body to relax, forced a smile onto his face. He and Pierce would deal with Morgana.

"No, I don't think you're crazy, Storm. Far from it. You see more than most." He shifted so that she was underneath him, her legs opening automatically, her pelvis tilting and her channel welcoming his penis as he pushed into her—chasing thoughts of kelpies and worries about sanity away as he made love with her. Offering his heart. His body. His soul.

Chapter Sixteen

‮‬ ಬ

"Storm sees much, Cousin. Part of her already guesses what we are," Pierce said, weaving a small ball of fire through his fingers as he sprawled in his usual manner, watching Tristan pace restlessly along the bookcases in his den. "And now you tell me that the reason I felt her pull on my fire was because Morgana was in the water with her. It's fortunate that Storm possessed some of our essence and somehow managed to use it or she would have drowned."

Tristan sank heavily into his own chair. "True. And she is no longer merely mortal. She is my wife. The elements will protect her where they can, but..."

"She is still vulnerable in this realm. As you are now." Pierce extinguished the ball of flame in his hand. "As I will be soon."

Despite his worry, Tristan managed a small smile. "So you have come to believe in the faerie tale of the forever wife?"

"I have come to believe that I will never find such a treasure as Storm," Pierce countered. "If you'd told me about her encounter with Morgana when I joined the two of you in bed early this morning, I would have acted then. Making Storm my wife will help ensure her safety."

Tristan laughed, not surprised by his cousin's refusal to acknowledge a belief in faerie tales. In the end it didn't matter, and Tristan didn't doubt the depth of Pierce's feelings for Storm. "Perhaps if either of us enjoyed Faerie, we would be tempted to lure her there, where she'd be safe—but this world suits both of us and I doubt Storm would enjoy a life under Queen Otthilde's rule. To take her to the fey realm is to sentence her to eternity among the shallow and pompous, to a life with nothing but political intrigue and frivolous pursuits."

Pierce snorted. "Our kind look down upon the mortals, but most of the fey have forgotten what we were once like, that we rose from the purest of the elements in order to see to the world around us—not to see to our own pleasure or abase ourselves for the pleasure of the kings and queens that rule us. Storm would wither in our realm. She would see it as a prison instead of a paradise." He grinned, "And there is still plenty of treasure to search for here, our own as well as that belonging to the dragons and the mortals."

Tristan laughed. "True on all accounts."

Pierce allowed fire to form on his fingertips, drawing it out and stretching it to form a continuous looped thread of flame, then manipulating it to create first a tea cup and then a complex bridge in the same manner as a children's string game. "I would make her my wife before we reveal what we are. But soon after we must do it. We can't risk that she'll break the compacts by accidentally using air and fire or water in a way that will stand out in this world."

Tristan nodded. "And in the meantime, I need to return to Faerie so that the queen will see that I am no longer free to order into the bed of her current favorite—and to remind her that mortal wives are protected by the same laws as govern the fey. No doubt Morgana will escape punishment this time, given the queen's favoritism and the fact that Storm was not yet my wife, though I'm sure Morgana saw both you and me in Storm's aura."

Pierce closed his hands around his fiery toy, making it disappear. "I'll go in your place. It's too risky for both you and Storm. It would serve Morgana and the queen should Storm be killed while you're in Faerie. Storm's mortality is yours now while you're in this world. Her death would trap you in Faerie forever." Pierce grimaced. "A fate almost worse than death itself."

Tristan looked at his cousin for several long moments, knowing how much Pierce hated to return to the court of Queen Otthilde. But also knowing that Pierce was right. To leave now was risky. The queen wouldn't like it—neither would the ladies of the court, especially Tristan's own mother—but any looking at Pierce and seeing some of Storm's aura contained within his would know that he had the right to speak and to announce both his own intent of taking a mortal wife and Tristan's already consummated marriage. If necessary, he could even call upon Morgana to confirm what she had seen when she encountered Storm outside Drake's Lair.

"I appreciate your offer and sacrifice," Tristan finally said. "I will stay here and guard Storm from a distance while you make the relationship known to those at court."

Pierce rose from his chair. "I'll see you later then." He grinned. "Much, much later—after I have returned and claimed my bride."

* * * * *

The Homicide bullpen was quiet when Storm walked in, the atmosphere tense. She handed off a cup of Starbucks to Brady and took her seat. "What gives?" she asked, voice low.

"Trace is in with the captain. That piece of shit you took down at Inner Magick last night plea-bargained and turned over the name of the guy who arranged the hit on Trace's wife. The captain took it to the chief and the chief made some calls. Some of Miami's finest are trying to find the asshole."

"The captain wants Trace to go on leave?"

"More likely he's trying to figure out whether or not it's safe to leave Trace armed."

The phone on Dylan's desk rang and he picked it up, getting to his feet within seconds. "On our way." He dropped the receiver back in its cradle and looked over at Storm and Brady. "The senator's wife found his body in their house. There are already some uniforms on the scene."

They swung by the captain's office and Storm could see that Trace was skating a thin, dangerous edge. His eyes practically glittered with the fierce need to eliminate any threat to his wife. The captain shot him a hard look. "Keep it under control or I'll put you on a desk, Trace."

Trace nodded briskly and they left. By the time they got to the senator's house, the media had arrived, too. Brady, Storm and Dylan stepped in front of Trace, blocking the mass of reporters that descended, microphones thrusting forward.

"No comment. No comment. I'm sure there'll be a press conference as soon as we've processed the scene. Get out of the way. Let us do our job," they repeated as they pushed through the reporters and finally got inside the house.

"In his office," a uniformed cop said and by the expression on his face, Storm knew it was going to be bad.

"Where's the wife?" Trace asked.

"Upstairs in her bedroom. She had her personal physician come by and shoot her up with a sedative—first cop on the scene said she was practically hysterical. Can't say that I blame her."

Trace paused for an instant, thinking about his last encounter with the senator's wife, finding it hard to picture her in hysterics, but then he didn't know how bad it was yet. He nodded and moved down the hallway, knowing that he needed to force himself to push thoughts of Aislinn from his mind. She was safe and she wasn't alone. She and Sophie were at the house. Alarm system on and guarded. Not by cops. Not that he didn't trust cops. But she was too important, and he didn't want the captain or the chief calling the shots. He wanted answers and anyone coming after Aislinn would beg to tell everything they knew by the time Xanthus got done with them. Uneasiness moved through Trace at calling in the old favor. There'd always been rumors that Xanthus traveled in the same circle as Severn Damek.

Trace shrugged the uneasiness off. Nothing was more important to him than Aislinn. Nothing.

He'd been plunged into hell last night. Driving like a maniac and knowing that he'd never get to her in time to save her from rape…death.

And then he'd found heaven. Her need as desperate as his own by the time he got her home. Despite her injuries, despite almost being raped, she'd welcomed him into her body, clung to him, let him chase the fear away first in the shower and then in their bed.

He hadn't wanted to leave her. Had half expected the captain to send him back home.

Son of a bitch. The only big case he was working right now was this one—and it was tied to the VanDenbergh case. There had to be a connection to the attack on Aislinn, nothing else made sense.

He pushed into the senator's study with Dylan, Brady and Storm right behind him, and came to a halt just inside the door. "Fuck." His guts roiled despite how often he'd looked on a murder scene.

The senator was leaned up against the wall next to a display case full of knives, internal organs spilling out, his intestines twisted around his neck as though he'd been strangled with them, eyes open, face frozen in horror. "Shit," Dylan said.

Brady grunted. "That the missing sword in his hand?"

Trace's attention shifted away from the senator's face. "Not in his hand, through his hand."

"Jesus," Brady weighed in.

There was movement behind them and they stepped aside, letting Skinner and his crime scene technicians in, signaling that it was time to get down to business. Trace turned his face toward Dylan, the movement sending a burning pain through his chest.

His stomach went hard and tight when he realized that the charm Seraphine had given him felt like a hot coal against his skin. To Storm and Brady he said, "Dylan and I can take the wife. You two want to start in here?"

"Sure." Storm moved toward the senator's desk.

"You talk to Seraphine about the charm?" Trace asked as soon as he and Dylan were in the hallway.

A muscle jerked in Dylan's face. "Not to her face. I never caught up with her. But she finally returned my call."

Despite everything that had happened, Trace felt a flash of amusement. "What'd she say?"

"Fuck, Trace, you don't want to know most of it. Makes my gut hot just thinking about it."

Trace rubbed his chest, noticing that the charm felt cool on his skin now. He wanted to believe that he'd imagined the burn of metal against flesh. Maybe before Aislinn came into his life, he would have—then again, before she came into his life, he wouldn't have been caught dead wearing the charm. "Might as well tell me what she said. First. Anything connecting the senator and his wife to dark magic?"

"Not yet. She's asking around. And she said that the wife's reaction meant she knew what the charm stood for."

"And that is?"

A sour expression settled on Dylan's face. "It's a ward against demons, devils and spells meant to do harm. Christ. She really believes in that stuff. What a fucking waste—worse than finding out a gorgeous babe with suck-dick lips is a lesbian."

Trace couldn't suppress a grin. "Personnel department hears that kind of talk and you're going to end up in class with Brady. Seraphine say anything else?"

"Yeah. The thing is supposed to flare up, burn you if you're in the presence of a demon or anything else nasty." He pulled the charm out of his pocket along with a few coins and a casino chip from the Luxor. "Imagine that. Feels the same as everything else."

Trace shook his head, but didn't say anything. Dylan was going to have to find out the hard way, the same way he'd found out, by falling and falling hard for a woman unlike any he'd ever been with before. Yeah. It was going to be a hell of a show—if they survived this one. Christ. What did it mean that the charm had practically scorched a hole in his chest when he'd been in the senator's office?

An image of the senator with his intestines looped around his neck rose in Trace's mind as Seraphine's words rang clear in his memory. *A demon would have more strength than an ordinary human... Most demons, by their very nature, don't like being used by ones they consider inferior. Torment is often a demon's appetizer, the main dish being death by whatever means the demon chooses.*

Yeah, having a sword driven through your hand, then being gutted and strangled with your own intestines would qualify as torment. Son of a bitch, this case couldn't be closed soon enough to suit him.

"Same perp that killed Vorhaus?" Dylan asked, interrupting Trace's thoughts. "The sword being some kind of message? But to who? The wife?"

They stopped in front of a door with a uniformed policewoman outside. "She alone?" Trace asked.

"No. Got her personal assistant in there with her."

Trace nodded and knocked, but pushed in without waiting for a response. The senator's wife was sitting in a chair, splotchy-faced though he saw the same dislike in her eyes that he'd seen on his last visit.

"I've already given my statement to one of the other officers."

"I still need to hear it from you," Trace said, feeling the same sandpaper over raw skin sensation as he had before, something about her just rubbing him the wrong way.

"Is this really necessary?" the assistant asked, coming to stand next to the wife's chair, her features young and harsh. "Mrs. Harper has had a horrible shock. She's under sedation."

"It's necessary." Trace stared at the senator's wife.

Mrs. Harper stared back, nothing in her eyes making Trace think there were drugs in her system—though she was subdued. "It's all right, Camille, there's not much to tell and the sooner it's done, the sooner these detectives can look for the senator's killer…and Anita's." Her hand tightened on a tissue. "I left yesterday evening for a meeting in Atlanta. I spoke to the senator briefly from my hotel room at about eleven p.m. I stayed overnight. Had breakfast with some acquaintances of mine, then took a flight back. I tried reaching my husband several times, but got voicemail—which is not unusual. I was a little concerned when I saw that his car was still in the garage, but thought perhaps he'd had a late-night strategy session and then overslept, or had decided to work at home for several hours. I checked his office and…that's when I found him."

There was a light tap on the door and Storm appeared. "Trace, you got a minute?" He nodded and stepped out into the hallway. She opened a folder with latex-covered fingers and showed him a photograph. "We found this in the senator's desk. Brady and I found one just like it at the insurance guy's place. It's a shot of Lucifer's Blade in VanDenbergh's display case."

"What's the agent's name?"

"Miles Terry. We've got an APB out on him."

Trace smiled. "Interesting coincidence. That's the guy who wrote up the policies insuring some of the senator's most recent acquisitions. Let's see what Mrs. Harper has to say about it."

They stepped back into the bedroom and Trace moved over to where the senator's wife was sitting. At a nod from Trace, Storm opened the file. Trace said, "Does this knife look familiar?"

There was the barest tightening around Mrs. Harper's eyes. "I'm not sure, Detective. I don't…I didn't share my husband's interest in knives and swords."

"This photograph was in the senator's desk. A similar one was found in the office of a man wanted in connection with the VanDenbergh murder. We believe that the knife was stolen at the same time as the murder."

She straightened, ice and steel. "Are you implying that my husband had something to do with Carl VanDenbergh's murder?"

Trace shrugged. "The senator collected knives and had dealings with a man we want to question. We'll want to look through the senator's records."

"When you can show me a warrant, Detective. My husband's records are sensitive and confidential." Disdain dripped from each word.

Trace waved a hand over the picture of the athame but didn't take his eyes off Mrs. Harper's. "This thing is called Lucifer's Blade. True believers think it can be used to call high-ranking demon lords. It can't be a coincidence that the senator's aide was killed in a manner that suggests contact with a devil worshipper. The manner of the senator's death suggests the same. To your knowledge, did he have anything to do with black magic?"

She stood, nostrils flaring. "Get out. I won't tolerate you saying those things about my husband. Under normal circumstances I'd overlook your insensitivity given the recent assault on your wife, but I can't find it in my heart to forgive or overlook. Your captain is going to hear about this, as is the chief, and the mayor. You don't deserve to wear a uniform."

Rage whipped through Trace, and suspicion. His hands clenched at his sides. "And how do you know about the assault on my wife?"

Her eyes widened slightly, as though realizing her mistake, but she didn't hesitate to answer. "The news. Now leave. From this moment forward, any contact between you and I will go through my lawyer."

He left the room with Dylan and Storm behind him. All three of them returning to the senator's office. The charm flaring to life as soon as Trace stepped into the room.

His gut roiled. Fuck. What did it mean? That there was a demon hanging around? A spell?

"She knows more than she's saying," Dylan said.

"Yeah, she does. Let's get done and get out of here."

They finished searching everything they could legitimately search, then stood by as the crime techs processed the scene.

It bothered Trace that there were no pentagrams, no symbols, no salt, not even that much blood. Shit, the senator's stomach had been opened up and a sword shoved through his hand, shouldn't there be more blood? He moved over to where Skinner was standing. "He was killed somewhere else, right? This is the dump site."

The head of the crime lab smiled, a baring of teeth. "You missed your calling, Trace. Transfer to my department and we'll put your skills to better use."

"Christ."

"He may know everything, but I doubt he's going to respond. I, on the other hand, am happy to answer your question. In all likelihood, the senator met his grisly death elsewhere. You ready to have the body hauled out?"

"Yeah."

They left behind the crime scene guys, fighting their way through a thick crowd of reporters, only to get a call from the captain when they got to their car. "The feds are making noises about taking this case over," he said. "Get back here. Now."

They returned to the station, though Trace paused next to the car. "I need to make a couple of phone calls, then I'll be up."

Dylan shrugged. "See you in a few—probably in the captain's office."

Trace nodded and punched in a phone number. Aislinn first. Needing to hear her voice even though he knew she was okay. Seraphine second. He got a machine and left a question.

* * * * *

The throne room glittered, a thousand shades of blue against a backdrop of icy white. Pierce dropped to one knee and lowered his head slightly in front of Queen Otthilde, banking his fire enough to avoid being called disrespectful but not so much as to be truly respectful.

Twitters and whispered words of snide amusement filled the air, the muted background music of the court. On the steps leading to the throne sat the queen's ladies, his mother and Tristan's included, but he acknowledged neither of them, nor Morgana who was also among the women flocking around the queen like peacocks.

"So it's true," the Queen said, her voice as cold as an arctic stream, the silver flashes in her dark blue eyes hinting at the icebergs lurking in their depths. "You have spent so much time among the mortals that your aura has been sullied by them."

"Is that the tale Morgana has brought back to the court? Did she also beseech you to overlook her breaking of the covenant by trying to drown the mortal that Tristan and I have found pleasure with?"

The queen waved her hand through the air in a gesture of dismissal, sending a cold breeze over Pierce as she did so. "Human children often see us in our elemental forms when we are in their lands. It has always been so. Just as it has always been so that their guardians rarely think of the tales told by the children as anything other than stories created by wild imagination. No harm was done. No covenant was broken."

Pierce let the comment slide by him, knowing that little would be gained by arguing the matter with the queen. He wanted only to ensure that there wouldn't be further attacks on Storm, and then leave. "I am here on behalf of my cousin and your nephew, Tristan, who has asked that I share the news of his marriage with you."

A hiss greeted his announcement and he spared a glance at Tristan's mother, Otthilde's youngest sister—though by a different father—then returned his attention to the queen as she stood, air and moisture gathering around her like the beginnings of a violent storm. "He has taken a human as a wife?" Her hand flung outward, a gust of frigid wind whipping past Pierce and knocking some of the lesser fey over, leaving them prostrate before her anger.

"Yes. He has shared all of his essence with her so that now she is tied to the air and water while he is tied to her mortality."

"Then why has he sent you instead of bringing this human to our realm and presenting her to the throne himself?"

Pierce's gaze moved to the jewel-rich goblet that rested on the right arm of the queen's throne. A sip from the Chalice of the Throne and a mortal became faerie—radiant and beautiful, equal in glamour to all but the queen, a full member of Faerie in every regard save one—once in their lands, a human was trapped forever. To leave Faerie was to die, to age in the span of seconds and become as dust on the wind, as a drop of water in an endless ocean.

A flame of temptation flared in Pierce's heart and burned through him like wildfire, a question that perhaps his cousin, with all his ancient tomes, would know the answer to, *What would happen should Storm drink from the queen's chalice while in the mortal realm?*

He pushed the question aside lest the air somehow carry his hidden thoughts to the queen. "Tristan is not yet ready to leave the mortal world," Pierce said.

Queen Otthilde's face tightened in rage at having her plans for Morgana and Tristan thwarted, in distaste at the idea of a faerie lord taking a mortal as a mate. The pale ice of her skin was just a hint of how cold she could be. How ruthless and deadly.

Though none spoke of it openly, many wondered what had become of her husband, a weak and overly arrogant king who had made her queen after his first wife was killed by a dragon's hot flame. A king who warred against the other fey kingdoms in the time before their numbers were decimated and they all fled from the world now held by the mortals.

It was Morgana who broke the silence, her voice chilly and disdainful. "Even to get with child, I would not lie with a Sidhe lord who has debased himself so—not only by taking a human wife but by sharing her with one such as Pierce. I have no interest in taking the leavings of some human female. She is welcome to both of them."

Pierce's eyes met hers. "That is good. The dragons were excited by news that a kelpie had been sighted."

Her nostrils flared, reminiscent of a horse's. "You disgrace yourself by associating with beings that are little more than exalted reptiles. Perhaps that explains why you sully yourself with the aura of a mortal woman. It is said that the humans also evolved from such beginnings, reptiles who climbed out of the water and are still as primitive as they have always been though they have taken our shape."

"Or we have taken theirs," Pierce said, knowing how offensive the words were to the court and hiding his smile when Otthilde reacted, her anger gusting over him in an ice-cold wave that carried him through the doors of the throne room and out of her sight.

Chapter Seventeen

ജ

"Can't stay out of the news, huh?" the uniformed cop manning the reception area said to Storm as she and Brady paused to wait for the buzzer. He shook his head and grinned at Brady. "'Course, you're not setting a very good example, Brady. Want to read my palm?" He snickered and pressed the button releasing the door lock.

"Funny," Brady grumbled. "Everybody around me thinks they're a comedian."

Storm laughed, despite the sense of foreboding that was starting to churn in her stomach. What had the uniform meant by his crack?

Dylan caught up to them as they were walking into the bullpen. "You hear from the captain?"

"No," Storm said.

"The Feds are making noises about taking over both of our cases."

Brady dropped into his seat. "Figures. Chance at glory and some publicity and the Feds come buzzing in like flies on shit."

His comment triggered a thought. Storm directed her attention at Dylan and said, "Speaking of publicity, did you catch what the senator's wife said? She knew about the assault on Aislinn. Then when Trace called her on it, she said she'd heard about it on the news. Anybody hear anything on it? See anything? I didn't have time to look at the paper this morning." A shimmer of heat raced through Storm as she remembered the reason why, the wonderful experience of waking to two amazing morning erections, and the subsequent scramble to get to work after satisfactorily dealing with said hard-ons.

Dylan sat on the corner of Storm's desk. "Do a search. Channel 6 has gone high-tech. They run their website in real time, or close to it. See what's there."

Storm found the page and the churning in her stomach turned into a dead weight. Shit. The guys on the fishing pier near Drake's Lair hadn't been cops, they'd been reporters, freelancers probably or this would have hit earlier.

"Geez, Kid," Brady said as they took in the photograph of her standing in front of Drake's Lair with Pierce, his hand on her hip, their faces only inches apart—the glaring headline over it screaming, *VanDenbergh Family Outraged by Police Handling of Murder Investigation and Theft of Chalice Insured for Five Million Dollars!*

The article went on to not only mention the Medici Chalice of Eros by name, but rehashed the story of a psychic being called in to assist on the case, and then "exposed" a connection between Detective Storm O'Malley and Severn Damek—a man of questionable background who was known to be after the chalice himself.

"Christ, Kid," Brady repeated. "You think you could boil the water any hotter?"

Storm couldn't think of anything to say. She'd screwed up. Hadn't even been thinking about being seen when she let Pierce walk her to the car after the mind-blowing sex in his apartment. Fuck. Yeah, she could blame the fuck...her stomach tightened and she wondered if Channel 6 was saving pictures of the goodbye kiss for the evening news.

There was nothing she could do about it. She scrolled down and found what they'd been looking for to begin with, under *Breaking News*. It was the first blurb down, right above the news that the senator's body had been discovered in his house. *Aislinn Dilessio, wife of Detective Trace Dilessio, the lead detective in the murder investigation involving Senator Harper's aide was assaulted...* Even as they watched, the screen refreshed and a new blurb moved into the first position, pushing the Senator's murder into the third position and the story about Aislinn into second.

"The way I see it, the senator's wife called the story about Aislinn in as soon as we cleared the room," Storm said. "If Channel 6 had it earlier, it would be lower down in the list, *after* the story about the senator's murder, if it even showed up at all."

"We won't get shit from them on who their source was," Dylan said, pushing off from the desk in disgust.

Storm closed the computer window and stood. If the captain didn't already know about her being at Drake's Lair, he would soon. She'd rather have him hear about it directly from her.

Her chest tightened and her stomach knotted. She'd probably get booted out of Homicide. She was new and the captain didn't need the headache of having a detective on his squad who had connections that were guaranteed to draw media attention.

A couple of days ago, she could have dealt with that…might have even welcomed it. But now…damn, she liked this work. Liked the puzzle of it, the variety, the challenge. The guys. Especially Brady.

"You going to see the captain?" he asked.

"Yeah, figured I'd better."

"You want backup?" His phone rang before she could answer. He picked it up and motioned that she should stay put. "On it," he said, dropping the receiver and standing. "They just found Miles Terry's car. His body's in it. They've got a crew out there now, pulling the car out of the water."

* * * * *

Pierce looked up as Tielo walked into his office and dropped into the seat across from his desk. "You should find your cousin's wife and stay by her side," his partner said. "The word is out about the Dragon's Cup." Tielo frowned. "Severn is not pleased."

Pierce lowered the ancient manuscript to his desk, thoughts of hunting treasure immediately leaving his mind. "What do you mean the word is out?"

Tielo waved toward the computer monitor. "The family of the murdered man gave a press conference, railing against the police and your cousin's wife in particular. They mentioned the chalice — by its mortal name — but plenty will know it all the same. The dragon princes will focus on the police, especially Detective Storm O'Malley. They will watch her actions and see if she leads them to the cup. Many still remember the old days, when Queen Otthilde held what was ours and refused to return it to us. The loss of a mortal wife to one of the fey would be an acceptable price to pay for securing the Chalice of Enos."

"A mortal wife not to one fey, but two," Pierce growled and Tielo's eyebrows lifted.

"Her aura mingles with yours, but not completely. You intend to bind yourself to her as well?"

Pierce stood. "Yes."

"You risk much. Unless one of the fey kings or queens grants her a sip from their Chalice of the Throne, Storm's mortality becomes yours while you are in this realm."

Pierce grinned. "When have I ever avoided a risk in the pursuit of a priceless treasure?"

Tielo laughed. "True. Then I will put the word out. You have always been a friend to our kind, regardless of lair. We would not reciprocate by killing your wife." He grinned. "But we are dragons and none will fight their nature to collect and hoard should you steal a fey treasure and bring it to this realm — or should your wife find the Dragon's Cup."

Pierce laughed as he stood. "So be it. I have been warned."

* * * * *

"Who found the car?" Storm asked one of the uniformed cops standing several feet away from where Brady had pushed in among the evidence techs, light bouncing off the silver car as flashes went off, capturing the scene before the corpse was removed. Not far away people were already gathering, tourists, snapping their own shots and Storm could imagine them sitting around the dinner table with their coffee, saying, *And here's a picture of the dead body that your Uncle Sal…*

"Couple of college kids." The uniformed cop shook his head. "Drunk and high. Said they saw some little alligators taking in the sun. Before you know it, they've dared each other to catch a gator, thinking their stories'll impress the girls and get them laid."

"At least they called it in."

The cop snorted. "Passing motorist called it in. Thought the kids were possessed or tripping on bad acid the way they were screaming and jumping around. Motorist was scared to get out of her car. Kept on driving but used her cell."

Storm looked around. "Where are the kids?"

"Had the paramedics haul them off to the hospital. A uniform's going to meet them there and stay put until you guys talk to the kids and clear them to go."

Brady stepped away from Terry's car and joined Storm. "Found a cell phone jammed between the seats. Throwaway job, but the techs think they might be able to salvage enough information so we can find out who Terry's been talking to. Also found another gun. Same make as the one beside his bed." Brady grinned. "Only strangely enough, this one's wrapped in plastic. They're ready to pull Terry out. You want a look first?" The expression on his face said she'd be better off saying no.

She said yes, and knew almost immediately that Terry had been in the warm water for a while—probably not more than twenty-four hours, thirty-six at most. Long enough to become a source of food. And she also knew that he hadn't been a victim of a car accident. The knife wound in his chest testified to that fact.

Storm stepped back out of the way so they could pull the body out. Another one of the techs working downstream yelled that he'd found something. Storm and Brady moved in that direction. Storm's heart jumping with excitement as soon as she saw the square black case nestled among the vegetation. A couple of photographs and the tech opened it with latex-covered gloves.

Blue velvet and an indentation where the Dragon's Cup had once rested.

Brady grunted. "Looks like the same case that was in that picture Damek gave you."

They expanded the search. Staying 'til dusk, staying past the time when Terry's car and body were hauled away, but ending up empty-handed all the same.

"Might have already sold it again," Brady said. "Or maybe whoever killed him has it. Not our job to find it. Insurance company wants it badly enough, they can hire a PI."

"Yeah, but we've got a body. The count's getting higher." Storm felt tired. Worried. Her stomach was churning and not just from lack of food. She wondered if Severn Damek now had the chalice and knew in her gut that they'd never catch him if he did.

Thoughts of Damek led to Pierce and the goodbye kiss in front of Drake's Lair. It was past dinnertime and the evening news. She still had to face the captain.

They got some drive-thru burgers and swung by the hospital. The kids who'd found the car didn't know anything useful. Brady cut them loose with a warning about driving impaired, saying afterward, "Dumb fucks, you look in their eyes and see it's a waste of breath to tell them to clean up their acts. Time to call it a day, Kid. Give Skinner and his techs a chance to process what they found and maybe give us some good news tomorrow."

Storm stopped by the Homicide bullpen and found it cleared out. Her throat tightened thinking about cleaning out her desk and putting the uniform back on—not that she'd heard the word from the captain. He was gone for the day.

She rubbed the back of her neck, knowing that she was tired and that it made her emotional. Storm grimaced. Good thing none of the guys were here to see it.

Maybe she was blowing the whole thing out of proportion. Hell, Trace had stashed Aislinn in his house and thoroughly fucked her while he was investigating the Dean murder!

Storm's hand curled around the necklace and as soon as she touched it, warmth flowed through her, the smooth feel of the crystal and the naked faeries making her smile. Brady's red face and voice echoing through her mind. *Jesus Christ, Kid. Put that thing away before someone else sees it.*

She grinned, thinking about Rebecca, the female cop manning Reception giving her the thumbs-up and saying "You go, girl. That's a hunk of a man" before buzzing Storm through.

Time to get home—to Tristan's beautiful Victorian. It was hard to think of her apartment as home, even filled with her books on faeries.

Her cousin called. "Where are you?" Sophie asked.

"Just left the station. What about you?"

"Just leaving Trace and Aislinn's place."

Storm's heart dipped. Images of Aislinn's wounded eyes and battered face bringing the guilt back in a rush. "How is she?"

"Okay. She's okay. Trace on the other hand…" Sophie gave a soft sigh. "They're so perfect for each other. I wish…" Silence. "One day…" This time she gave a self-conscious laugh. "Aislinn looked at the heartmate necklace she made for me and said, 'Soon'. Speaking of which—you've been holding out on me. Who is the hunk? Is that the professor? Because if it is, I'm going to go sign up for college classes and see if there are any more like him!"

Storm almost said *There are—but they're both mine.* She avoided answering the question by saying, "I didn't catch the TV news. How bad was it?"

Sophie snickered. "How about well-endowed *Playboy* centerfold candidate in a torrid lip-lock with Mr. Romance-Book-Cover."

"I was afraid of that. What about the sound bites from the VanDenbergh family?"

"Not too bad. Had the grandson, but it was taped earlier. The senator's murder took up a lot of airtime. Trace said you went to the scene. Bad?"

"Very. He tell you about it?"

"Are you kidding? Aislinn was there."

"What are the news reporters saying?"

"That he was found with the stolen Medici Sword of Vengeance driven through his hand. And there are rumors on the net that he was strangled with his own intestines." There was a hint of a question in her cousin's voice.

Storm shook her head. There were always leaks. Especially when a murder was sensational or involved someone with a high profile. But she knew she could trust Sophie. "That's what I saw. Anything in the news about the attack on Aislinn?"

"Yes, but not much. They hit on the Dean murder. Some of them are trying to jack up their ratings by playing with the idea that there's an ancient Medici curse on the sword and the chalice. Speaking of which, Aislinn asked Trace about the chalice. He said that your number one suspect is dead."

Storm sighed. "Yeah."

"No sign of the VanDenbergh chalice?"

"Just the empty case. Found in some weeds downstream."

"So you're pretty sure your suspect had it?"

"Almost positive. Though for all we know he'd already sold it. If he did, he didn't leave a trail at his house. Brady and I went through it pretty thoroughly."

"Aislinn called it the Dragon's Cup, and started smiling when they flashed a picture of it on the news. What gives with that?"

Ice flooded Storm's system as she realized where Sophie was heading. "You are not going to go looking for it, Sophie!"

"Of course not. I assume that your number one suspect didn't die of natural causes. Right? So the thing is still tied up in an open murder investigation."

Images of Severn Damek filled Storm's mind along with the conversation in Tristan's office. Pierce saying, *There are others who will move to take possession of the chalice—others who are far more deadly and determined to possess it than those who think it is only a legendary cup that once belonged to the Medici Family and is famed for bringing about lust-inspired orgies.*

It would be just like Sophie to chase after the Dragon's Cup, not because she wanted it for herself or for a reward, but because she would consider it "research" for use in one of her books—and because Sophie loved mysteries. "I'm serious, Sophie, don't even think about trying to find it."

Sophie sighed. "Are you off for the night?"

Storm ground her teeth together, wanting to nag at Sophie until she promised not to even think about the Dragon's Cup, but knowing by the change of subject that it was pointless. "Unless there's another murder," she tried to make it dark and ominous.

Sophie laughed. "Tiff and I are heading to a Psychic Fair You want me to ask around for you? Or better yet, you can come and talk to the psychics yourself—maybe even get a reading done to see if the professor is *the one*."

Storm shivered, remembering how Madame Fontaine had apparently read her mind, had looked at the necklace and known about Tristan and Pierce. No way did she want to be in a building housing a lot of psychics, even though she doubted that many of them were the real thing. "Don't you ever get enough of that stuff? I'm amazed you can even fit more crystals into your apartment."

"There's always room for one more. Besides, Tiffany's gotten interested in runes. That's the main reason we're going. You want to go?"

"No thanks."

Sophie laughed. "Hot date?"

Storm stopped in front of Tristan's Victorian and watched as Pierce emerged, a grin breaking out on her face when she realized that she knew both men so intimately that even without being close enough to see their eyes, she could tell one from the other just by the way their bodies moved. "Yeah. Definitely a hot date."

Chapter Eighteen

ΕΟ

Pierce's cock made its presence and desires known, pushing hungrily against his pants as he watched Storm get out of her car. Lust roared through him, flickering along his nerve endings like a fire testing its boundaries, desperate to spread.

He pulled Storm into his arms as soon as they were close enough, covering her lips with his, not waiting for an invitation to stroke his tongue over hers, to share his fire and need with her. He wanted to strip her, to take her where she stood, but he settled for embracing her.

For long moments they stood there, kissing, tasting, pressed tightly to one another, the heat they were generating so intense that only Pierce's control kept their clothing from being reduced to ash so that flesh could touch flesh.

It was Storm who pulled away first, cursing and looking around nervously, trying to calm the thundering of her heart, to distract herself from the raging need she felt for Pierce by saying, "Did you see the news tonight?"

"Yes." His cock stirred. "The pictures of the two of us kissing are not nearly as good as the real thing." When she didn't laugh or smile, he tensed. "They brought you trouble at work?"

Storm sighed. "I don't know yet. The jury's out—or more accurately the captain was by the time I got back to the station. I haven't had a chance to talk to him about it yet."

Tenderness filled Pierce. An almost foreign emotion—especially when dealing with mortals. And yet she was not just any mortal. She was his wife…or would be soon.

Pierce leaned down, brushing a soft kiss across her lips. "It will turn out okay." He would see that it did, using his fey glamour to make it so if necessary.

"Yeah, probably." She stroked a hand along his spine, finding the need to touch him, to feel the warmth of his skin almost impossible to resist. Something had changed inside her since making love with Tristan last night. She didn't know what, and even now she didn't have time to think about it, didn't want to look too closely at it. "Let's go in, no point inviting trouble by putting on a show out here."

"No, we wouldn't want to do that," he said and watched the way her nipples tightened with the promise of pleasure in his voice.

They moved into the house, the scent in the air changing as the house welcomed Storm with the fragrance she found pleasing. And as though Storm was aware of the gesture she said, "I love this house."

Pierce laughed and pulled Storm back into his arms, lifting her and holding her against the wall. She wrapped her legs around his waist as she'd done at the university and he rewarded her by rubbing at the juncture of her thighs, by sealing her lips with his, his tongue mimicking the thrusting of his cloth-covered erection until she was moaning, her breasts pressed against his chest, the hard tight nipples begging for his attention.

When they came up for air, Pierce murmured, "If we don't go to the bedroom now, I'll take you here, in the hallway."

Storm's eyes darkened and he instantly regretted his choice of words—he'd prepared the bedroom earlier, but now his balls were pulled tight against his body, his cock leaking with excitement, his resolve disappearing completely when she bit his bottom lip before saying, "The hallway sounds good to me."

Pierce groaned, using his lower body to keep her pinned to the wall as his hands moved to the front of her shirt, hastily stripping it from her body and discarding her bra so that he could feast on her breasts. She arched her back, her own hands coming around to cup them in an offering that had his seed threatening to erupt.

"Storm," he growled, unable to keep himself from lifting her higher so that he could take possession of her nipples, biting and sucking, wanting to pull them down to his very soul. By The Goddess she enchanted him, enslaved him, made him burn for her and her alone. He'd never thought to look for, much less find a woman like Storm. A woman full of honor. A woman who embraced his heat, took him, burned for him without the play of court politics or fey glamour or the lure of treasure, without anything else but honest desire. A woman he could share with his cousin, the combination of air and fire so intense that it was worth any price to experience it over and over again.

"Storm," he groaned again, his mouth immediately returning to her nipple.

"Please," she whispered in response, her hands moving through his hair, over his shoulders. "I've got to touch you. I've got to feel you inside me, Pierce."

He lowered her to the floor. Never taking his mouth off her breasts as he pushed her pants down and opened his own, only raising his head again when he plunged into the heated, wet fist of her cunt and gasped at the exquisite shards of ecstasy that shot through his cock and up his spine.

"Whenever I'm with you, I feel like I'm burning up," Storm said, her fingers spearing through his hair, torn between the desire to pull his mouth to hers or pull it back down to her nipples.

He decided for her, covering her lips with his, plunging his tongue into her mouth as he slammed his penis in and out of her slit, driving them both higher and higher until she was thrashing mindlessly against him, crying out in release as his seed scalded her and his body settled heavily on top of hers.

"I take it that Tristan isn't here," she said later, still too lethargic to insist that they get off the hall floor—a part of her surprised at how comfortable the wood was, how warm and pliable, almost as though there was a thin cushion of warm air between her and it.

"He's got evening classes, then a meeting with a colleague where they'll argue over some moldy manuscript until the wee hours of the morning." Pierce's hand stroked her breast, finally settling over her swollen, tender nipple, the pained pleasure of the touch going directly to her clit and making it stand erect. "He agreed to stay away—for a while—only because I told him that I needed this time alone with you."

Pierce rolled off her and got to his feet, stripping his clothing all the way off and then doing the same to hers before lifting her into his arms with no effort. Storm laughed, her face flushed with soft color. Until Tristan and Pierce had come along, no man had ever carried her—not that she was overly heavy, but she was a far cry from Aislinn's petite size and delicate beauty.

He tossed her on the bed, immediately coming down on top of her, restraining her wrists with one of his hands, pinning her. "Tristan told me what he allowed you to do to him," Pierce murmured, eyes and voice full of dark promise as he reached above them and grasped one of the padded cuffs, bringing it to her hand, making her aware of it.

"I am not so easily enslaved as my cousin. He was content to flow into your heart and fill it like a warm storm, but I intend to make you plead for me to consume you, to fill you so that your heart burns as ruthlessly as mine does." He put the restraint around her wrist, giving her plenty of opportunity to pull away or deny him, but Storm licked her lips, her heart thundering against his chest, her cunt swelling.

When she didn't resist, he rose to his knees and bound her other wrist then trailed his fingers down her arms, moving slowly, his gaze locked with hers, both of them anticipating the moment when he would touch her breasts.

"Beautiful," he said when he reached his destination and she gasped at the exquisite feel of his hands cupping her, measuring the weight of her breasts, his eyes moving lower to feast on them while his cock stood full and proud, pressed against his abdomen, the sight of it making Storm feel powerful even though she was the one in restraints.

Her stomach quivered, her labia was swollen and flushed, coated with arousal. She couldn't keep a small pant of need from escaping. He made her feel like a goddess, made her want to stay naked in his sight just so that she could see his admiration and appreciation of her body.

"Put your mouth on me," she whispered, hoping that he wasn't going to make her beg as she'd made Tristan beg. She already felt as though she was burning up. As if a howling wind was rushing through her.

Pierce's laugh was husky, full of masculine satisfaction. But he didn't obey her command.

He leaned down, whispering kisses across her mouth, making her plead for his kiss to deepen just as his fingers on her nipples had her arching upward, whimpering, his touch so erotically painful that her entire world became one of desperate need.

When her body gleamed and shimmered in the muted light coming through the window, he trailed kisses down her neck and over her breasts, teasing, tormenting before finally sucking, biting, driving her to orgasm with only his mouth on her nipples.

Her inner thighs were coated with her own arousal, the scent of it a heavy musk that drew Pierce to her cunt. He moved lower, burying his face between her legs and spearing his tongue into her channel.

By The Fates, *he* was on fire. Enflamed by her, by the way she offered everything she was to him. Opening her body and her heart.

He lapped at her, fucked her with his tongue and sucked her lower lips, her clit, reveling in the sound of her begging, pleading, the way her beautiful body was his to pleasure and take pleasure from.

His cock threatened to erupt and spew hot seed across his stomach, and only his own hand stayed it. But when she came again, crying out his name, burning him with her release, he couldn't stay separate from her any longer.

He crawled up her body like fire, taking only enough time to release her wrists before plunging into her. Pumping furiously as she wrapped her arms and legs around him, as his mouth covered hers.

It was like being caught in a firestorm of crashing timber and howling winds, a primitive violent place where earth and air and fire battled for supremacy, where the lines between immortal and mortal blurred. The two of them burning brightly, a solitary flame, consuming one another with the fierceness of their desire.

Pain and ecstasy blended in a heat so intense that it melted barriers and changed the compositions of the entities it touched, making them other than what they'd been only moments earlier.

Both of them cried out as Pierce gave her his fire and his seed, his heart and his soul, his life, as he took into himself what she gained from Tristan along with the dust and ash of her mortality.

And underneath him, Storm burned, trapped in an instant just as intense as the one she'd experienced the previous night with Tristan. Feeling as though her soul was separate from her body, completely entwined with Pierce's, the two of them commanding the fire around them, their heartbeats a howling roar beating at the center of a powerful force of nature.

Long afterward Storm lay snuggled against Pierce, thinking about the intensity of what she'd shared with him, and with Tristan, the glow from the moon striking the crystal so that it looked like flames danced inside it. Strange how the thing never got tangled in her hair, even during wild sex or when she slept. She'd taken it off the first night, but not since then, it was almost as though it had become a part of her.

She frowned, shifting only to have the feel of Pierce's cock against her backside chase the frown away. Pierce's face nuzzled against her neck, his hand smoothing over her abdomen before cupping her breasts, his palms settling over the nipples, his touch warm, comforting, so pleasurable that she put her hand over his, holding it to her body.

"Have you always had a breast fetish?" she teased, womb fluttering, unexpected joy moving through her like a slow tide with the knowledge that she was glad that part of her body gave him so much pleasure.

His husky laugh was like a stroke between her legs. "I have a fetish for storms—especially the one that has taken your form and rages through me, turning my own fire back against me so that my cock burns with lust and my heart pounds furiously." His hand moved lower, taking hers with it, settling over her cunt, his fingers teasing along her slit, gathering her arousal and preparing her back entrance with it. "I need to fill you again, Storm. As does Tristan. He will join us in a few minutes."

She stilled, not hearing a sound, yet somehow knowing that Tristan was in the house—and then he was there, moving through the starlit bedroom, leaving a trail of clothing as he went. He greeted Storm with a kiss, his cock hard and ready, his chest pressed to hers, the fires of lust blazing hot between the three of them. A tempest of need that had her rolling on top of him, her hand guiding his cock into her desperately needy channel as Pierce worked his way into her anus.

There was no thought. No words. Only sensation. Love. A joining that felt so right that it left Storm shivering in their arms, face wet with emotion, heart open to whatever the future might bring.

They were still touching hours later, gently caressing, defying the dawn to arrive and end their time together as they told each other about the previous day.

Pierce eased Storm's mind even as he made her frown by saying, "Severn Damek doesn't have the Dragon's Cup. And he didn't kill your suspect—even if it was your suspect who was foolish enough to use Severn to drive the price of the chalice up. If Severn killed him, or had him killed, there would be nothing left of the body but a pile of ash. It is far more likely that whoever now has Lucifer's Blade killed the thief. You said he was stabbed in the heart?"

"Yes."

"And you think the blade was stolen at the same time as the Chalice of Enos?"

"Yes. I'm almost positive." She hesitated for only a second before adding, "We found a photograph of the blade at Terry's house. The athame was shown in VanDenbergh's display case."

Tristan rubbed his thumb over Storm's bottom lip. "Promise us that you'll take care if you come across Lucifer's Blade."

A cold tendril of fear snaked up Storm's spine. "You believe like Pierce does? You think the blade is for real—not just hype and mumbo jumbo."

"Oh yes, it's real," Tristan said and there was no hint of teasing in his voice or expression. "You saw what was done to the senator."

She shuddered. "Yes."

"You've seen death. Was his death mask like any you've ever seen before, Storm, a face frozen in absolute terror?"

Her heart jerked in her chest. "How do you know that?"

"Because I have heard how he was found and it sounds like the work of a demon lord." Tristan's blue eyes held a wealth of emotion as he added, "The athame should never have been created. Take it as evidence—if you must—but don't allow it to be handled more than is necessary, and be careful not to let its blade touch your skin. A mere touch and it will cut, forming a link with the flow of blood. If it was used recently, given power by the killing of your suspect, then it will be even more dangerous to handle." His thumb stroked over her bottom lip again, and he leaned in. "Promise you'll be careful, Storm. You hold our lives within you. If you die, we die also."

His words chilled her. "I promise," she said.

Tristan's mouth covered hers, the kiss a gentle breeze that flowed into her and chased the chill of their conversation away. When he lifted his lips from hers, she smiled, a suspicion working its way into her consciousness. "Pierce said you were meeting with a friend tonight, arguing over some moldy manuscript—you were researching demons and Lucifer's Blade for me, weren't you?"

"Yes." He kissed her. "But not just for you, for the three of us. We are bound together now."

Chapter Nineteen

ഔ

Storm swung by Trace's house on the way in to work, feeling relieved when she saw Sophie's car, but not Trace's. She could talk freely about the necklace in front of her cousin.

Storm grimaced and got out of the car. There'd be a price to pay for openly admitting that she wasn't so skeptical about crystals anymore. Sophie would tease her later, and probably drag her to a few psychic fairs and shops when she went looking for more crystals to add to her collection—but Storm could deal with that.

She rang the doorbell. It opened almost immediately and a jolt of shock went through Storm when she saw the long-haired blond standing there. Shit! She almost reached for her gun. "What are you doing here?" she asked, suspicion in her voice at seeing the man who'd been at Severn Damek's house.

"Trace asked me to guard his wife."

His voice was a smooth rumble, different than it had been at Severn's house. Deeper. But then again, she'd been overwhelmed by the sights around her, the heat of Pierce, the worry over meeting Damek and hadn't paid much attention to the blond—hadn't even noticed how his irises were so dark that they were almost black. Damn, did Trace have any idea about this guy's tie to Severn?

Sophie emerged from the kitchen and smiled when she saw Storm. "Hey, we're in here. I swung by and picked up Marika. She's got some really cool runes that a friend of hers makes. Come and look at them. Aislinn's thinking they might need a display case all their own."

Storm gave up on the idea of talking to Aislinn about the necklace—not with her assistant and the hunk from Severn's house there—but felt some of the knots in her stomach loosen with the thought that Aislinn must really be okay if she was thinking about new displays for her shop.

Still, there was a moment of awkwardness, lingering guilt when Storm stepped into the kitchen and saw the bruises on Aislinn's face. "I'm sorry…"

Aislinn shook her head and held up her hand, not letting Storm finish. "It's not your fault. Please don't blame yourself. I've stayed at the shop late a thousand times and never feared for my safety."

"But…"

"No. You didn't ask me to stay. You even said you'd be happy to come over to my house or meet me at Sophie's. Please, it makes it worse for me to have you blaming yourself."

"And she's got enough to worry about with Trace doing his caveman impersonation," Sophie teased, making Marika laugh and Aislinn blush, coaxing even a smile out of Storm.

"There is that," Storm said, letting her guilt go.

"So look at the runes already," Sophie ordered. "You want some coffee or are you holding out for a mocha on the way in to the station?"

She checked her watch. "I'll have a cup here."

Sophie said, "Oh and did Xanthus introduce himself, or did he give you the silent, menacing treatment?" She waved between Storm and the blond. "Xanthus, Storm—my cousin. Storm, Xanthus—Aislinn's bodyguard."

Storm suppressed the urge to say they'd already met, sort of. Instead she admired the runes, drinking from the mug Sophie handed her while the conversation about the symbols and their various meanings went over her head—her own thoughts alternating between the faerie-held crystal that burned warm against her chest and the almost feral look on Xanthus' face as his dark eyes seemed to devour Aislinn's assistant.

By the end of the second cup of coffee, Storm's companions had moved from admiring the runes to teasing her about the hot kiss that the photographer had captured in the parking lot of Drake's Lair — though she didn't correct their assumption that it was with Tristan instead of Pierce.

Xanthus knew though. His eyes glittered with amusement.

Storm escaped to the police station, the worry about the captain's reaction to the bad press and the VanDenbergh complaints trying to return, but she was too happy to let it. Aislinn really did seem okay. And then there was the conversation with Tristan and Pierce as she'd been dressing for work, her body sated and well loved.

Her heart turned over, treasuring Tristan's words in the morning light about being bound together, his comment about moving her things into the Victorian. Pierce's cupping of her breasts as he said he'd be moving in too so that he could spend each night lost in her body. Crazy. Impulsive. But right. It felt so right.

Trace was the only one in the Homicide bullpen. He looked up when she walked in. Storm said, "I just came from your house. Marika and Sophie were there. I saw Xanthus." He tensed at the mention of the name and Storm tried to figure out whether he knew about the connection to Severn or not, and whether she should mention it. "Did he call you or did you call him?"

"I called him. He owed me a favor from way back."

"I saw him the day I went to Severn Damek's house."

A muscle jerked in Trace's cheek. "Either the VanDenbergh case or the case involving the now late senator got too close for comfort to one of the perps. I'm not going to risk Aislinn getting hurt over it. I'd throw in with the devil to keep her safe."

"I'm not going to mention Xanthus to anyone, Trace. I just wanted to make sure you knew."

"Yeah, well, I owe you one."

"No you don't. She's my friend too, and Sophie's best friend." He gave a slight nod, acknowledging her statement.

Storm's gaze dropped to his balled fist, her attention drawn to the ring that had once belonged to Aislinn's father, his wedding band and now Trace's. The lavender stones were the same color as Aislinn's eyes, glowing just as softly as the haze she'd seen around Aislinn the other night.

Storm blinked, but the haze remained for seconds longer, then dimmed. When she looked up, Trace was scowling, but there was a wary alertness in his eyes. It startled her and then her cop-instincts rushed in.

The scene at Inner Magick played out. Aislinn's tears as she'd said, *Then he was hitting me and dragging me into the back room. I fought him.*

Trace rubbing his cheek against his wife's hair, his whispered, *It's okay baby, I know you did. I called it in as soon as I knew you were in trouble. I got here as quick as I could.*

Storm had never said anything to Trace about what happened the night he saved Aislinn from a serial killer, but now she did. "You can talk to her telepathically. You called the attack in before anyone else got on the scene. Probably figured that if anyone checked the transcripts and noticed, you'd say that you'd been worried about her and set up a system where she checked in at intervals and if she didn't, it meant she was in trouble — but that's not how it really was."

He tried to bluff his way out of it, saying, "Bullshit, Storm. You've been reading too many of Sophie's stories."

She sat on the edge of his desk. *Okay, if that's the way you want to play it, Trace, I'll be the one with balls big enough to get this out into the open.* "What would you say if I told you that I think a demon killed Senator Harper?"

Trace was good, but then he'd been a cop longer than her. There was the slightest flinch, the slightest widening of his eyes. "Christ."

"You want me to continue?"

"Why not?"

She grinned at his attitude, not surprised that Trace wasn't yet willing to openly talk about "supernatural shit" with another cop.

"Here's how I think it happened. Miles Terry sold the Medici Chalice to VanDenbergh, probably planning all along to steal it back. He also insured some of the senator's knives and swords. Somewhere along the line, Terry mentioned Lucifer's Blade to the senator. Maybe the senator had bought stolen items from Terry before, or maybe something the senator said made Terry think that the blade would be worth big money from the senator. There's nothing in Terry's house to suggest he was involved in anything supernatural. So no connection there."

Storm paused. Wrapping her mind around the theory she'd been working on as she drove from Trace's house to the station. "However it happened, Terry decided to take the blade the same day that he took the chalice. Why he killed VanDenbergh Senior is still open and we don't know if we have the murder weapon yet. But Terry gets in touch with the senator, who leaps at the opportunity to own the blade. For all we know, that's why his aide was killed, for the insurance money on the sword. Terry's spooked. He's keeping a gun on his nightstand, but there's no way he can run without drawing suspicion to himself. Still, he wants to get rid of the chalice and the blade as soon as he can. He meets the senator somewhere and the senator pays him back by killing him with the knife. Then later, the senator can't resist playing with his new toy—only something goes wrong—and he ends up dead in a way that practically screams *demon*."

"And the wife, how do you see her playing into this?" Trace's serious voice and frown were a silent acknowledgement that he accepted what Storm was saying.

"I'm guessing she knew what he was up to." She shrugged. "But I don't have a feel for her beyond seeing her the one time."

Silence settled over them and Storm didn't fill it. Trace finally said, "I talked to Skinner this morning. He confirmed what we'd both already guessed—the senator wasn't killed where he was found. Time of death was probably a little after midnight. No prints on the sword other than the senator's. Got a confirmation on the wife's alibi. We can dig into it, but I think we're going to find she was in Atlanta when the senator died. Neighbors didn't hear anything or see anything. But if the senator was into black-magic shit, I can't see him doing it out in public, and I can't see him being murdered in front of witnesses who'd be left to walk away, much less bring the body back to his house and set it up for us to find."

"So you're thinking he was killed somewhere in the house and the wife came home and moved the body?"

"No blood trace anywhere else. Besides that, he'd have screamed. No way was that much damage done in silence." Trace hesitated, then pulled the chain out from underneath his shirt and showed Storm the charm. "Ever see one of these?"

She leaned closer. "I've seen ones like it, but not the same. It's some kind of protection charm. Against demons?"

"Among other things. Aislinn sent Dylan and me to see a witch, Seraphine. She gave me two of the charms — one for me, one for Dylan. Dylan's dropped out in front of the senator's wife and got a reaction. He looked over at me and it was obvious that he didn't know where it came from or what it meant. Then the next night Aislinn got attacked."

"The senator's wife worried about you being on the case and obviously knowing something about supernatural stuff?"

Trace shrugged. "Or the senator — who isn't going to be answering any questions in this realm."

The word triggered a cascade of memories. Tristan and Pierce moving back slightly as she placed the photograph of the pentacle and symbols from the Vorhaus murder scene on Tristan's desk. Tristan saying, *I'm afraid this is not something from our realm*…catching himself, then adding…*of knowledge*. Aislinn's words as the faerie-held crystal had swung between the two of them. *Freely given, freely accepted, let the wearer see both the beauty and peril of the hidden realms. And if The Fates so choose, let the wearer hold something of the fey with her heart.* Aislinn knowing how enchanted Storm was with faeries — with fey creatures.

221

Pierce grasping the necklace, his voice rough and raw, *You've caught us both. Now what do you intend to do with us?* Tristan's hand sliding down the chain until Pierce yielded the faerie-held crystal, *You've caught us both. What can we do to serve you?*

The sex that had seemed like so much more than sex. So different than anything she'd ever experienced before. The feeling of being completely merged with them, formless, vast, part of the sky and sea, of being filled and surrounded by fire. The red and blue of the crystal. Fire and air and water. The way her body felt different now, almost too small for the sensations swirling around inside her.

The words from last night suddenly having new meaning, sending fear through her. *Promise you'll be careful, Storm. You hold our lives within you. If you die, we die also.*

Storm stood abruptly and walked to the window. God, she needed to talk to Aislinn. Needed to know what was real and what wasn't before she ended up in a padded room wearing psych-ward issue clothing.

Trace was saying something, touching her shoulder, voice concerned. "Hey, you okay? If you think you're going to faint, you'd better tell me now and I'll start digging around in the trash can for those smelling salts."

Storm took a deep breath. *Hang tough. Yeah. Hang tough. Use it. Use what you know.* She forced herself to look at the charm that was still visible outside Trace's shirt. Nothing special. It could just as easily have been a Saint Christopher's medallion.

Trace caught the direction of her gaze and tucked it inside his shirt. "It burned like a sonofabitch when I was in the senator's office yesterday with the body. I've got a call in to Seraphine asking her if that meant the...demon...was still there, but she hasn't gotten back to me yet."

Trace's expression at having to say the word demon restored some of Storm's humor. "So we're back to the original question. Where was the senator actually killed?"

"Yeah."

Storm forced her mind back to the murder scene. She'd only been in the senator's study twice, once when he was alive, once when he was dead. The second time she'd been okay— yeah, the scene was straight out of a horror movie, but she hadn't gone black and fuzzy around the edges like she had the night of the Vorhaus murder. She relived it, seeing the senator sitting behind his desk, framed by darkness, like he was sitting in a doorway, an old-fashioned letter opener in his hands, a glimmer of condescension in his eyes. On a hunch, Storm said, "Try Seraphine again. See if the charm would burn if it was near Lucifer's Blade—especially if the blade had been used recently."

Trace shrugged and pulled out his cell rather than using one of the department phones. "You must be psychic," Seraphine said and he could imagine the small smile that somehow managed to convey a wealth of sharp amusement. "I was just getting ready to call you."

"I've got a new question for you." He ran Storm's question by her.

"Yes. That would explain what happened. The demon would have returned to its own realm as soon as it finished with the senator." She made a soft clucking sound. "The senator was a fool. He should never have touched the blade, much less used it. He was barely more than an acolyte."

Trace's heart jumped. "You found a connection between Senator Harper and this stuff?"

"Yes. A master who once taught the senator's master…or more appropriately, his mistress."

"You're not talking D/s or extramarital affair. You're talking about his teacher, the one with the power." Trace hesitated only a second. "His wife."

"Good guess."

"Will the guy you talked to testify?"

"He won't need to. Find Lucifer's Blade and invoke the name of Gressil. That will be enough for the senator's wife to confess to taking part in the murders."

"Gressil is the guy who taught her?"

"No, it's the name of the demon lord who first answers when Lucifer's Blade is used in a ceremony."

"Shit. Why would saying the name suddenly make her talk?"

"It'll only work if you find the blade—and only because she's seen the charm. She'll think you're capable of using the blade and calling Gressil who would have it in his power to release a demon bearing a grudge against her."

"Christ! Anything else?"

"Be careful if you find the athame. Be careful not to let its blade touch anyone's skin, a mere touch and it will cut. Even a drop of blood is enough to form a link to the dark realms."

"Fuck."

Trace closed his cellular and relayed the conversation to Storm. She said, "Hear me out before you say I've been reading too many of Sophie's books. Okay?"

He gave a slight nod. "I'm listening."

"If it's both the senator and his wife, then it makes sense that they practice at home and have a special place in the house to do it. I don't know a lot about this kind of thing, except that there's usually blood involved—maybe always—and I'd guess that sometimes there's a lot of it. Even if they never sacrificed anything larger than a goat, there'd be plenty of blood to deal with. They'd need a way to clean up, to dispose of it without dragging buckets and mops through the house. So I'm thinking a floor with a drain. They'd also need some kind an altar. They've got money so they're going to want something nice. Fancy. Something that makes them feel important and powerful."

Trace shook his head and interrupted. "Christ, Storm. I want to nail her as badly as anyone—worse because of what happened to Aislinn. But we've gone through the place over and over again."

"But you weren't looking for a hidden room. One that's near the study. She couldn't have dragged him very far from where he was killed, not without leaving way too much trace evidence." Dylan came strolling in just as Storm added, "What have you got to lose by humoring me? Laugh's on me if we don't find anything. And you'd be going there anyway to take a shot at Mrs. Harper with Seraphine's tip."

"The witch called you?" Dylan said, joining them at the window, his bad mood at hearing Seraphine's name arriving before he did and making Storm wonder what was going on with him. She let it pass when Trace started talking, updating his partner, conveying the most important facts without getting into anything supernatural.

It worried Storm, especially when Dylan rolled his eyes over the warning about Lucifer's Blade. She didn't want to see anything happen to him, but she couldn't fault Trace for staying away from the subject of demons and dark realms. No way was Dylan ready to hear it—especially if just brushing against a witch was enough to set him off.

"You heading there now?" Dylan asked when Trace got finished talking.

"Yeah. Might as well."

Trace turned to Storm. "You riding with us or taking your own car?"

"Better take my own in case I need to hook up with Brady."

She left a note on her partner's desk, wondering where he was—smiling at the thought that maybe he'd gone out on a date with Madame Fontaine and then stayed over at her place. Storm's heart did a little flutter, remembering Ilsa's words. *Ah, I see you've met someone special, or should I say two such individuals? When it comes to your two men, you need only the magic in your heart to hold them.* She shivered, anxious to get the workday over with so she could find Tristan and Pierce…and then what? Ask them if they were a couple of faeries?

225

A small laugh escaped. Yeah—she could see the shape of the padded room that was waiting for her right now.

Mrs. Harper's personal aide opened the door, frowning when she saw Trace. "I believe Mrs. Harper indicated that all communication with her was to be done through her lawyer."

Trace shrugged. "Fine. But this is still a crime scene and we have access." He pushed in, forcing the woman to back up, then headed for the study.

Anxiety moved through Storm. Doubt. Now that she was here, it seemed so far-fetched...and yet...why wouldn't they want to practice their craft here? Other than the fact that it was insane to invite a demon into your home.

She hesitated at the doorway as she had that night they'd been called out for the Vorhaus murder. Nothing. No black, fuzzy edges. She looked at Trace who was rubbing the front of his shirt, surreptitiously getting the charm away from his skin as though it was hot again. Her eyes met his and he nodded slightly before moving to the desk and beginning to search. Her hand curled around her own necklace. She felt silly doing it, but she concentrated, using the words Aislinn had said, chanting silently, *let the wearer see both the beauty and peril of the hidden realms.*

Even separated by a layer of clothing, she felt the difference in the crystal immediately—the touch against her palm making her think of a flame flickering in the breeze. Her gaze moved over the room, coming to rest on the old-fashioned letter opener on the senator's desk, its outline hazy and dark.

He'd been holding it in his hands that night. Playing with it as Trace and Dylan questioned him.

She moved to the desk and picked it up, noting the strange symbols engraved on the hilt. Like the room where Anita Vorhaus had been killed, there were plenty weapons on display in the senator's study. Storm looked around, her eyes widening as they settled on a small, velvet-lined box in the open display case that had been built into the wall. There was just a trace of a dark aura around it and Storm almost grinned. Clever. The senator's body had been found against the wall right next to the case—a ready explanation for any blood-trace found there.

She walked over to the case and put the letter opener in the velvet-lined box, heart jumping when she heard a soft click. "Son of a bitch!" Trace said, he and Dylan joining her. "Push in," Storm guessed, letting Trace and Dylan do the honors.

"Fuck," Dylan said when the case yielded, revealing a small room with an altar—the rubies in Lucifer's Blade glittering like wicked temptation from where the blade sat at the altar's center in the now sunlight-filled room. "I don't believe this."

"Might be a good time to locate Mrs. Harper," Storm said, "and see what she has to say."

Dylan said, "I'll stay here and call this in to Skinner. For some reason this shit fascinates him. He'll probably come out with the evidence techs himself."

Trace and Storm left, but didn't have far to go. The senator's wife was coming down the staircase, hard-eyed with her aide in tow. Trace got off the first shot. "You want to tell us about the hidden ceremony room and Lucifer's Blade, or would you rather tell it to Gressil?"

Mrs. Harper staggered at the sound of the name, grasping the banister and stopping for a second, swaying. Her aide grabbing her to steady her, saying, "You don't have to talk to them. I'll call…"

"No. I'll talk to the detective."

"You'll confess to committing, taking part in, or arranging for the murders of Anita Vorhaus, Miles Terry, and your husband?"

"Yes."

Trace's eyes narrowed. His face hardened. "You'll confess to being behind the attack on my wife?"

"Yes."

Storm spoke up. "What about the murder of Carl VanDenbergh Senior and the theft of the Medici Chalice of Eros?"

Mrs. Harper's gaze skittered to hers, then back to Trace. She licked her lips nervously and shook her head. "Not VanDenbergh's death. I don't know who killed him. I don't know anything about the whereabouts of the missing chalice."

Chapter Twenty

ॐ

Storm's cell buzzed as Trace was reading the senator's wife her rights. Brady said, "I was with Skinner when Dylan's call came in. If you're finished playing ball for the other team, then maybe we can go pick up our suspect in the VanDenbergh murder."

"VanDenbergh III?"

"Good guess, Kid. But wrong—even though I liked him for a suspect, too. The gun we found wrapped in plastic in Terry's car came back as the murder weapon, and it had only one set of prints on it. Old man VanDenbergh's lawyer. Forget the hype about magical artifacts, Kid, and follow the money. I bet we're going to find that the lawyer's been embezzling from VanDenbergh and his trust funds."

Storm took a second to tell Trace she was leaving, then headed out to her car. "So the lawyer took the chalice and the blade and handed them off to Miles Terry for a cut of the proceeds?"

"We'll have to ask him, but more likely it was just bad luck that Terry showed up with the idea of stealing the blade and the chalice and caught the lawyer in the act of killing VanDenbergh, then somehow managed to walk away with what he came for along with the murder weapon."

"You got an address for the lawyer?"

"Yeah. Already had a patrol car go by and check out his house. Wife says he should be in his office. We've got a uniform keeping her from calling and warning him that we're looking for him. Skinner's got a financial guy heading over to start going through the lawyer's paperwork."

Brady gave her the office address. But it didn't take two of them to make the arrest. VanDenbergh's lawyer rose to his feet when they walked in, then sunk heavily when Brady started reading him his rights. Storm stayed around until after a team from Skinner's department got there and collected the records they needed in order to look for embezzlement.

"He lawyered-up," Brady said as soon as Storm got back to the Homicide bullpen. "No surprise there. But I still think we've got him."

"The captain knows?"

"Yeah, got a press conference scheduled in a couple of hours. In the lobby if the squall that's moving in hasn't come and gone by them. Wants all of us there—you, me, Dylan and Trace."

Storm nodded. "What about the chalice?"

Brady shrugged. "Not our problem. Read the sign on the door, Kid. *Homicide.*" He grinned. "And we didn't do too badly working our first case together."

"Not bad at all, Pops."

Brady snorted and went back to his paperwork. Storm's thoughts went to Tristan and Pierce. "Did the captain say he wants to see me first? About the photo?"

"No. Captain was all smiles and so was the chief when I saw them in the hallway."

"Good. Then I'm going to take an hour or so of personal time before the media dog and pony show."

"You do that," Brady said, then stopped her at the door by asking, "You going to swing by Starbucks on your way back in?"

"You want something?"

"Yeah, get me one of those frozen drinks."

She grinned. "Still trying to cool off from your hot date last night?" When color edged over the collar of his shirt and up into his face, her jaw almost dropped. "You asked—"

He cut her off with a hand gesture. "Geez, Kid, can you keep it down? There are guys in here trying to work in case you haven't noticed."

She snickered and left. Brady and Ilsa Fontaine. That was going to be good.

* * * * *

Storm hesitated at the Victorian's beautiful wooden door, noticing the scenes carved into it, stories that she'd never stopped long enough to see before. Scenes of unity followed by battles fought between magical creatures. Scenes of heartbreak and hope and exodus. Scenes not so different from those in human history.

She put her hand on the crystal doorknob and felt only welcome as she entered the house, the scent of flowers following her in. She'd managed to catch both Tristan and Pierce and ask them to meet her here. They both stepped out of Tristan's den— the sight of them filling her with lust and love—making her want to forget her questions and lead them to the bedroom for the short period of time she had before she needed to return to the station.

There was no way she could deny herself at least a kiss. She joined them, slipping her arms around their waists, kissing Tristan first, then Pierce—wanting to keep going.

Pierce laughed, his hand moving instantly to her breast and sending exquisite heat throbbing through her nipple and into her clit. "I'm glad you summoned us home."

Tristan's laugh was equally husky as his mouth found the delicate shell of her ear, his tongue teasing. For a long moment Storm disappeared in their touch, soaking it in, savoring it, letting it wash over her like a cleansing flame.

But when they pulled away, intent on leading her to the bedroom themselves, she said, "I've got to get back to the station soon."

They halted, curious expressions on their faces. Tristan was the first to speak, a question in his voice, "You asked that we meet you here."

Shit. She could feel the heat rising to her face — confusion, fear of making a complete and total fool of herself. But if demons existed and Trace could talk to Aislinn telepathically, was it really so hard to believe that faeries existed? Was it really so hard to believe what her own body was telling her, her own mind?

Tristan's face grew concerned. "What is it?"

"You're faeries."

Her color heightened even further when Pierce's eyebrows went up and he joked, "I think we've more than demonstrated an interest in women."

"No," Tristan murmured, studying her intently. "That's not what she means." Her eyes locked with his and he suddenly grinned. "Our wife is both beautiful and clever. Very mortal, but still worthy of two Sidhe lords who find more pleasure in this realm than their own."

Disbelief washed through Storm for a second — shock — even though it was her own theory that was being proven correct. She blurted out the first thing on her mind. "Show me what you really look like."

Tristan laughed, reaching for the buttons of her shirt and making her nipples ache for his touch, his mouth, for Pierce's as well. "Don't distract me," she said.

Pierce's hands joined Tristan's and there was no fighting them. But as her shirt parted, it was the necklace that Tristan grasped even as Pierce opened her bra and caressed her tight nipples.

"Pierce," she warned, trying to sound stern even as her nipples begged for more of his attention and her breasts grew swollen in anticipation of his admiration.

He smiled and his eyes danced with masculine appreciation. "Look at the crystal, wife."

She looked, heart jerking at his calling her his wife—at both of them calling her wife—and then at the sight of crystal. It was blue in Tristan's hand, with just a hint of red and a starburst pattern of black originating in its center. Storm's stomach tightened at the sight of the starburst, instinctively knowing that it reflected her own mortality, now theirs as well.

Pierce reached for the necklace and in his palm the crystal was fiery red, with just a hint of blue, and the same starburst pattern of black starting in its center. "Aislinn gave this to you?"

"Yes."

"What did she say when she did so?" Tristan asked.

"Freely given, freely accepted, let the wearer see both the beauty and peril of the hidden realms. And if The Fates so choose, let the wearer hold something of the fey with her heart."

Pierce and Tristan both laughed, though it was Tristan who said, "Caught by The Fates and Elven crystal."

Storm frowned and pulled away, out of their arms, a fear that she'd been harboring at the back of her mind surfacing. Her throat tightened and her heart skipped in her chest. "So the crystal is responsible..."

Neither man let her finish the thought. Tristan's fingers stilled her lips as they both moved in, pressing their bodies to hers so that she could feel their heat, their need.

Tristan's smile was soft, the amusement in his eyes gentle. "A forever wife is caught and held by the heart with the blessing of The Goddess and The Fates, Storm, not made so by Elven magic. The necklace protected you in the beginning from the effects of our glamour so that your feelings were your own and the love you offered to us was real."

She wanted to believe, wanted desperately to believe. "That first night when the three of us were together, you held the crystal and said, 'You've caught us both. What can we do to serve you?' Pierce did the same, only he said, 'You've caught us both. Now what do you intend to do with us?'"

Pierce rubbed his cheek against her hair. "We're going to have to be very careful what we say from now on, Cousin, there are hazards to being bound to a detective."

Tristan took Storm's hand and brushed a quick kiss across her knuckles. "In part, we were playing, Storm, though it's true that the crystal captured some of our essence when you brought us to pleasure for the first time—me on the beach, Pierce in the hallway. But the crystal captured only what we willingly gave, and was meant to serve as a focal point so that you could call upon the elements that are a part of us should you need to do so. Aislinn's gift also let you see a hint of what most humans can no longer see."

"The halos around some of VanDenbergh's artifacts," Storm said, remembering the effect that she'd attributed to inventive lighting.

Pierce laughed and his hand moved over her bare abdomen, traveling upward until it was cupping her breast, his fingers tugging and playing with her nipple. "Describe some of these artifacts," he said, his voice making her smile, making her heart fill with laughter.

"And then end up having to arrest you for stealing them?"

"You could put me under house arrest and confine me to the bedroom."

She laughed, her body growing needy, her cunt swelling with images of tethering him to the bed as she'd done to Tristan. She licked her lips. "Let me see what you really look like."

Tristan shook his head. "This is how we will always appear to you, Storm. You are our wife. The one who holds our life in hers while we live in this realm. There's no place for glamour between us, no need for its lure or its camouflage. Even without the necklace, you would still see us as you do now, you'd still be able to command the elements as we do." He smiled slightly. "With a little practice, of course. And there are ancient covenants, rules that we must teach you so that you don't violate them in the presence of those who don't know of the other realms." His expression grew worried, uncertain, and he brushed his lips across hers. "I hope the lack of wings doesn't disappoint you. The lack of glamour."

She kissed him, answering with her heart, and then her voice. "Nothing about either of you could ever disappoint me."

Storm turned toward Pierce, kissing him also, not resisting when they both moved in, when their hands finished undressing her.

There were so many questions she wanted to ask, so many ideas she had to get used to—including being a wife to two Sidhe lords—but they could wait. They had to wait because right now she needed this more, needed to feel them inside her.

"Just a quickie now," she managed. "The captain's got a press conference scheduled."

"A quickie," Pierce agreed, "and then a long night of exquisite pleasure."

Tristan swung her into his arms and moved toward the bedroom. "Followed by a lifetime of the same."

Enjoy An Excerpt From:
SARAEL'S READING

Book 1 in the Carnival Tarot Series

Copyright © JORY STRONG, 2005.

Sarael took a deep breath and tried to see into the darkness that swallowed everything up beyond the exit.

Come.

Stronger this time. Sending tendrils of sensation through her belly, her breasts.

She took a few more steps before grabbing the metal fencing used to form chutes for the crowds to line up in. The exit just on the other side of the carousel.

Her delay nearly cost Matteo his control. He was no closer to Sarael than he had been earlier, and yet now there was no one else around. No one to prevent him from closing the distance between them, from striding over and taking her in his arms, stilling any protest she might make by sealing her lips with his. Thwarting any attempt at escape with a show of strength.

His nostrils flared as a breeze brought her scent to him. His heart sped up, matching the rapid dance of hers. Two sides of a single coin. Prey and predator.

The urge to close the distance, to rush in, was nearly impossible to resist. His gums ached where sharp fangs fought to descend. His cock leaked, unwilling to accept the restraint he forced on the rest of his body.

Come. The command lashed out and she jerked in reaction to it. The deep night, the absence of others around them making it easier to press his will on her. He'd held back earlier, but now he intended to begin as he meant to continue. To eliminate any resistance. Any thought to escape.

She had not been raised properly, trained, prepared. So now she must suffer the consequences of her mother's choice to run. Rather than moving easily and willingly — happily — into the life of a kadine, she would enter abruptly, her fate suddenly in a stranger's hand. One who would expect obedience. One who intended to own her, body and soul. And yet one who offered everything she could ever desire in return.

Frustration, impatience, made him command her again, this time with a hint of menace. The night was leaking away more rapidly than he wanted. They should be in the limo even now.

Sarael caught a glimpse of the man standing past the carnival entrance, his aura dark, his sudden burst of anger making it easier for her to fight the need to go to him. The way it struck at her reminding her of the slaps her mother had delivered more than once, the blows given over the then-hated wristband. The words that came with it as sharp as the sting from her mother's hand. *If you're found, your life won't be your own.*

An ominous warning left with nothing to put it into context, with no understanding of what it meant. Until now.

The Moon. On Helki's deck it rose, framed by ancient pillars. Both full and crescent. Beautiful. Alluring. Shining over a land of magic where souls could be trapped — or freed.

Soon you will be joined with the one you were meant to be with, living in his world with him.

A small sound escaped, a whimper, and Sarael tightened her grip on the metal railing, refusing to take another step despite the way her body fought to do so.

Come to me. Softer this time, though no less insistent as the man detached himself from the darkness, moving into the moonlight with flowing grace.

Sarael's heart sped up, her stomach fluttered at the sight of his handsome features.

"Come to me, Sarael," he said, his voice like pure honey, swirling around her, sweet and thick, trapping her so that in the end she stood in front of him, her breathing fast, her body slick with sweat, her face upturned, her thoughts in chaos.

He reached out, taking her hand and holding it against his heart while the other cupped her cheek, his thumb brushing over her lips. "I am Matteo Cabrelli."

She shivered, fighting to hold a part of herself separate as he forced her to meet his gaze. Their eyes locking, causing heat to move through her so that her body felt as though it wanted to meld, to blend, to become entwined with his. So that her nipples beaded, her vulva grew swollen, making her acutely aware of the place between her legs.

For long moments they stared into each others' eyes and her thoughts were scattered, lost. But finally she pushed a word through lips that were wet, parted, as though waiting for a kiss instead of an explanation.

"How?" she whispered.

"Because you are mine, *carissima*. From the moment of your conception you were destined for me." He brushed his thumb across her mouth again. "Over time you will understand, but now we must leave."

"No." It was barely more than a puff of air as she tried to step back. But his hold was too tight and her own body too uncooperative.

He leaned down and some instinct warned her against jerking away. Her breath caught in her throat but she was frozen in place, a whimper escaping when his mouth touched her neck, a gentle kiss followed by the feel of his tongue, then his teeth, lightly gripping her skin as the hand which had been cupping her cheek moved to stroke along her spine before pulling her against his body.

Instantly she was lost under wave after wave of sensation. Swimming through thick, unfamiliar desire. Barely able to think or breathe. To protest when he swung her into his arms and began walking.

Matteo cursed himself even as he stretched her out on the limo seat and forced his mouth away from her neck, her throbbing pulse leading him into a temptation he didn't dare yield to. And yet it was too late to keep from sampling what was his.

He'd thought to overwhelm her senses so that he could get her to the car, but once he'd touched her... Lust raced through him, a flame burning him with the need to claim her. He covered her lips with his, spearing his tongue into her mouth, dominating hers, thrusting in and out, a warning of what was to come. An imitation of what his cock would soon do as he mated with her.

She moved restlessly underneath him, her hands going to his sides, his hips. He pressed more of his weight down on her, reveling in the way her body was soft under his, already so submissive.

He lifted his lips from hers, meeting her eyes in the dim interior light of the car, reading them. They were dazed, feverish—leaving him dissatisfied and angry with himself. He'd moved too fast with her. Swamping her senses and enthralling her, treating her as though she was a female to be used without thought or conscience—not as his future kadine should be treated.

Matteo levered off Sarael, moving to the end of the seat and creating a distance between them. If she'd been raised properly then she would already possess enough of his blood that this wouldn't have happened. They would already know each other, be comfortable in each other's presence so that the first joining would be a much anticipated event. A mutual seduction entered into by both parties instead of a taking, an enthrallment better suited to dealing with prey.

Enjoy the following excerpts from:

Ellora's Cavemen:
Dreams of the Oasis I

Featuring:

Myla Jackson, Liddy Midnight, Nicole Austin, Allyson James, Paige Cuccaro, Jory Strong

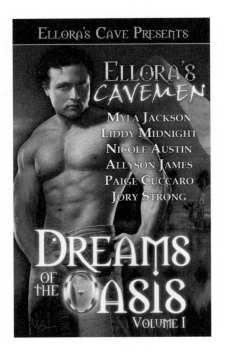

*A special edition anthology of six sizzling stories
from Ellora's Cave's Mistresses of Romantica.
Edited by Raelene Gorlinsky*

THE AMBASSADOR'S WIDOW

"Okay, give me everything you've got." Andre settled in his seat on the small Lear jet blasting through the sky en route to Padel. Having showered at the hangar, he wore sweats and a T-shirt, preferring to make the transformation in clothing that didn't bind and had a little give.

Sean O'Banion leaned over Andre and pressed a button on the panel above him. A computer screen dropped down and blinked to life. "Here's all the footage we could muster on the man and we provided notes from one of our operatives on the inside."

"What about DNA?"

Melody handed him a jacket with several brown hairs scattered across the shoulders. "Try this. It was the jacket they found on him when he died."

Andre turned the jacket over. Armani. The guy had taste.

"No one saw him croak but our operative. We think we got him out in time, the press didn't get wind."

Andre knew how the agency worked. The less the press knew, the more easily a Chameleon blended in.

"For now." Melody sat in the leather seat next to Andre and crossed one leg over the other. "But we can only hold them off so long. When the ambassador doesn't show up for the meeting tomorrow morning, the media will be all over it."

"So how much time does that really buy us?" Andre's gaze remained on the screen.

"Since only our operatives know he's dead, we have until he doesn't show up in his room tonight."

"Why should that matter?"

"His wife will worry."

"Wait a minute. You guys didn't say anything about a wife." Andre leaned back in his chair and held up his hands.

Melody laid a hand on his arm. "Keep your shirt on, big guy. They're somewhat estranged."

"Somewhat?" Andre's eyebrows rose. "Define 'somewhat'."

"Insiders say they sleep in separate rooms and as far as anyone knows, they haven't made love in months."

Muscles knotting in his belly, Andre had a sudden feeling of being trapped. "You know how I feel about widows. I don't do widows. You can turn this plane around right now. I'm not doing it."

CALL ME BARBARIAN
Copyright © LIDDY MIDNIGHT, 2006.

"Oh, look! The gladiators are up next! You should hear the buzz among the women, about the two brothers from Sudania. They are quite the swordsmen, if you know what I mean." Her arch expression made me look at her a little more closely.

"Really?"

Before I could pursue this line of inquiry, fighters entered the arena and I became distracted, too busy admiring their oiled muscles and strutting bodies to start up a gossip session. As a rule, I understand, gladiators are a vain and rutting lot, but oh, are they gorgeous!

The southern brothers led the second round. From the moment they stepped forward, they dominated the arena. They moved with confidence and a charismatic quality that kept all eyes on them. Their peers and opponents paled in comparison. My pulse quickened and I could not tear my attention away, even when Tilda touched my elbow.

I could understand the excitement generated by their bouts in the ring, for they were in truly excellent shape. Not overdeveloped, as some bodies in the arena appear, but balanced and fluid in their movements. I admired their tanned skin and what looked to be strong profiles, although their faces were mostly hidden by their half-helmets.

Dark hair flowed down their backs, worn longer than is customary in the ring—especially as they favored trident and net as weapons. Those permit the wielder to capture his opponent's weapon and render it useless, then move in to grapple hand to hand. Close fighting can be dangerous with long hair, as it gives an opponent something to grip. Flexible as eels, the brothers eluded every attempt to hold them and won the ensuing wrestling matches in short order.

Flowers and coins showered into the arena as the crowd awarded them the victories. They had mastered what I call the "winning strut", the victory lap that every winner takes around the arena, to cheers and catcalls.

When they turned to acknowledge the Emperor and removed their helmets, my breath caught in my chest.

SPONTANEOUS COMBUSTION

Copyright © NICOLE AUSTIN, 2006.

"Tell me your deepest, darkest fantasies."

The words were breathed in a husky, sultry tone against Maddy's ear. Warm breath caressed her neck, raising the fine hairs at her nape and sending chills coursing down her spine.

She didn't have to turn around, knowing instantly to whom that deep sexy baritone voice belonged. How she would love to provide explicit graphic details of her most intimate fantasies for him. Or better yet, maybe they could act them out.

"Come on. Tell me, babe. What is it? Being bound to the bed, or maybe oiled up on a Slip N' Slide? Do you dream of sweet lovemaking, or hard fucking? One lover or several?"

Icy shivers prickled along her skin. Just the sound of his voice, his erotic words, had her nipples puckered and pressing against the bodice of her little black dress. She had worn it in hopes of catching his eye. Not that he would ever notice Maddy as a woman. His buddy, sure. A woman, never. His words were all in jest as usual, right?

"How much have you had to drink tonight, Jake?" she questioned, then gasped as he licked a hot wet path along the ultrasensitive skin behind her ear.

"Stop it, Jake!" Maddy squealed in protest. Of course, stopping him was the last thing she wanted to do. But giving in meant risking both heart and soul. She couldn't stand the thought of being rejected by this man, the only one who really mattered.

Jake Cruise had been her best friend and neighbor since college. They had shared everything. Well, almost everything. She couldn't share her true desires with him, could she? As if he'd ever want to have sex with her. He was such a tease.

Maddy gave herself a mental shake. What was she thinking? Of course she couldn't. It would ruin their friendship. Probably freak him out to hear her dark, forbidden passions.

DRAGONMAGIC

Arys felt his dragon body turn inside out, then there was a bright light and he was standing, naked, on two human legs inside a cozy, one-room cottage.

"Damn witch," he growled at the voluptuous woman bent over the fire. "What do you want now?"

The witch Clymenestra stood up calmly, eyeing him with her usual smugness. Arys was tall, with bronze-colored skin over hard muscle, waist-length white-blond hair, and dragon silver eyes. Clymenestra looked him over like she owned him.

The bitch knew his true name and could call him from Dragonspace anytime she liked. *Not forever, darling*, he thought. *Not forever.*

"I need dragon's blood," she said, letting her gaze rove his body.

"Always blood. What is your spell this time?"

"Never you mind." She looked at him with dark, possessive eyes. "I hold you, dragon, and you'll give me your blood." She smiled. "I'm always willing to pay for it."

He knew her thighs were wet with her cream, her opening hot, anticipating. Arys' cock was already swollen and hard, standing straight out from his body. His long hair warmed his back, but his arms prickled with cold in the night air. Human skin was too damn thin.

Clymenestra had bound him to her with the magic of his name—but one day, one day, he'd be free. He knew the secret of his freedom, she didn't.

"So you called me all the way from Dragonspace for a drop of blood?" he growled. "I was deep in important business."

"Two drops. And you were lying on your back in the snow, sunning yourself. Silver dragons are the laziest things in creation."

Arys didn't deny this. In his dragon form, he lived to eat and hoard and mate as often as possible. He also worked his own kind of magic, which was lightning fast, like a fiery needle in his brain.

He loved dragon magic. Human magic was too much like work.

FALLEN FOR YOU

Copyright © PAIGE CUCCARO, 2006.

"You think they'll try to kill me?"

"Yes." Zade wouldn't look at her. His gaze fixed on the streetlamp across from Isabel's bedroom window. The light's honey glow was a safer sight by far than the little witch drifting toward sleep behind him in the dark.

He was a Watcher, a once-mighty angel, and still this woman could bring him to his knees with a negligent sigh. Zade clenched his jaw, his hand fisting around the Roman coin he always carried in the pocket of his slacks.

Her soft, sleepy voice already had his cock as stiff as a Watcher's sword. And the scent of her sheath was only a wicked tease of how perfectly she'd fit his blade. His dick twitched at the thought, but he pushed the erotic image from his mind.

A rustle of covers, like the sound of a warm body rolling in bed, teased behind him. "Why now?" she said.

"Your skills have grown these past months. All those attuned to the ancient power will have felt your touch. You are a threat to the Oscurità as well as a temptation."

Her small snort was muffled in the pillows. "And here I was only hoping to tempt you."

Zade's nails dug into his palms, every muscle in his body coiling tight. He closed his eyes and reached soul deep for the strength to deny his need. He was here to ensure her safety and train her in the use of the ancient power—nothing more.

Isabel and her kind were the key to destroying the Oscurità, the prideful fallen angels. A mission he and his Watcher brothers had failed to achieve so long ago. For ten thousand years they'd suffered the punishment for their ill-fated complacency. Sentenced to an eternity linked in name and penalty with those they'd been sent to destroy.

She and her witch sisters were the Watcher's second chance and Zade would let nothing distract him this time.

THE JOINING

Rumors abounded of women not only being taken to brothels or sold as slaves, but of ending up on the nearby planet of Adjara, where the men formed marriages with each other, and needed a woman only long enough to produce a child for them.

Siria shivered. Little was known about Adjara. It was primarily a desert planet, harsh, unforgiving, closed to outsiders. Few in their right mind would attempt to go there, though the dream of gaining riches beyond measure by exploring the small range of mountains for rich deposits of precious stone had lured many to their deaths.

Her mother had been fascinated by Adjara, making it a game in the evenings to search though whatever news reports could be captured using their ancient computer. Telling Siria that her ability to locate water would make her a princess in such a place.

Once her mother had even found a rare picture of an Adjaran without the trademark robes and face covering they wore even when they weren't in the desert. He'd been stripped to the waist, his body bronzed by the sun, lean and fit from life on a planet where the weak didn't survive, one arm covered from shoulder to hand with exotic tattoos. Siria closed her eyes, remembering that day.

"Here's a prince to your princess," her mother teased.

"And what about the rumors of women being used to produce a child and then being disposed of?"

"I'm not so quick to believe them," her mother answered with a shrug. "Look at the rumors that abound on Qumaar!"

"You win. Of course, what makes the rumors about Qumaar so frightening is that the truth is often more horrifying!"

"True. Now admit he's handsome at least," her mother pressed, running her finger over the computer screen.

Siria knew when she was beat. "I'll admit it. He's handsome."

"And if rumor is true, he comes with a second man."

"Mother!" Siria yipped, her face flaming, only to realize by the play of expressions on her mother's face that she hadn't intended it to be a sexual comment. But once she did realize how her comment had been interpreted, her mother's laughter filled the room, contagious and fun, irresistible, and they'd both ended up in tears, holding sides that ached from their amusement.

"Still," Siria said, when they finally stopped. "No one has ever heard of a woman going to Adjara and leaving again."

Her mother shrugged. "The same could be said, except in reverse, for Qumaar. No one who leaves here is ever heard from again."

Why an electronic book?

We live in the Information Age—an exciting time in the history of human civilization, in which technology rules supreme and continues to progress in leaps and bounds every minute of every day. For a multitude of reasons, more and more avid literary fans are opting to purchase e-books instead of paper books. The question from those not yet initiated into the world of electronic reading is simply: *Why?*

1. ***Price.*** An electronic title at Ellora's Cave Publishing and Cerridwen Press runs anywhere from 40% to 75% less than the cover price of the exact same title in paperback format. Why? Basic mathematics and cost. It is less expensive to publish an e-book (no paper and printing, no warehousing and shipping) than it is to publish a paperback, so the savings are passed along to the consumer.

2. ***Space.*** Running out of room in your house for your books? That is one worry you will never have with electronic books. For a low one-time c ost, you can purchase a handheld device specifically designed for e-reading. Many e-readers have large, convenient screens for viewing. Better yet, hundreds of titles can be stored within your new library—on a single microchip. There are a variety of e-readers from different manufacturers. You can also read e-books on your PC or laptop computer. (Please note that Ellora's Cave does not endorse any specific brands. You can check our websites at www.ellorascave.com or

www.cerridwenpress.com for information we make available to new consumers.)

3. *Mobility.* Because your new e-library consists of only a microchip within a small, easily transportable e-reader, your entire cache of books can be taken with you wherever you go.

4. *Personal Viewing Preferences.* Are the words you are currently reading too small? Too large? Too... ANNOYING? Paperback books cannot be modified according to personal preferences, but e-books can.

5. *Instant Gratification.* Is it the middle of the night and all the bookstores near you are closed? Are you tired of waiting days, sometimes weeks, for bookstores to ship the novels you bought? Ellora's Cave Publishing sells instantaneous downloads twenty-four hours a day, seven days a week, every day of the year. Our webstore is never closed. Our e-book delivery system is 100% automated, meaning your order is filled as soon as you pay for it.

Those are a few of the top reasons why electronic books are replacing paperbacks for many avid readers.

As always, Ellora's Cave and Cerridwen Press welcome your questions and comments. We invite you to email us at Comments@ellorascave.com or write to us directly at Ellora's Cave Publishing Inc., 1056 Home Avenue, Akron, OH 44310-3502.

THE
✞ ELLORA'S CAVE ✞
LIBRARY

Stay up to date with Ellora's Cave Titles in
Print with our Quarterly Catalog.

TO RECIEVE A CATALOG,
SEND AN EMAIL WITH YOUR NAME
AND MAILING ADDRESS TO:

CATALOG@ELLORASCAVE.COM

OR SEND A LETTER OR POSTCARD
WITH YOUR MAILING ADDRESS TO:

CATALOG REQUEST
C/O ELLORA'S CAVE PUBLISHING, INC.
1056 HOME AVENUE
AKRON, OHIO 44310-3502

erridwen, the Celtic Goddess of wisdom, was the muse who brought inspiration to storytellers and those in the creative arts. Cerridwen Press encompasses the best and most innovative stories in all genres of today's fiction. Visit our site and discover the newest titles by talented authors who still get inspired - much like the ancient storytellers did, once upon a time.

Cerridwen Press
www.cerridwenpress.com

Discover for yourself why readers can't get enough of the multiple award-winning publisher Ellora's Cave.

Whether you prefer e-books or paperbacks,

be sure to visit EC on the web at
www.ellorascave.com

for an erotic reading experience that will leave you breathless.